Pangea's Chosen

Rise of the Element Hero

Written By Virgil A. Walker

Published by House Walker Publishing

HOUSE WALKER
PUBLISHING

Acknowledgment

Pangea's Chosen: Rise of the Element Hero was born from a spark kindled by my son, Isaiah, whose boundless imagination lit the path to this tale. A fervent lover of RPGs and medieval fantasy, he urged me to weave stories from the worlds he dreamed, heroes clashing with shadowed foes, lands alive with elemental wonder. What began as RPG tales, spun by our hearth, grew into Pangea: a realm of wind-swept plains, fire-forged crags, and faith that shines through the darkest coils. "This could be a book," I told Isaiah, and his eager nod pushed me to craft my first novel. His passion for epic adventures fueled Felix's journey, and for that, I am endlessly grateful. Thank you, Isaiah, for dreaming with me.

This saga also carries a deeper hope: to restore beauty and purpose to fantasy, as J.R.R. Tolkien and C.S. Lewis once did. Their tales of hobbits bearing burdens, lions breathing redemption wove wonder with faith, offering light in a shadowed world. Today, many fantasies lean toward secular themes, and while such tales have their place, I sought to craft a story in which the Lord's light burns unashamedly. In Pangea, crosses rise over pagan runes, and a carpenter's son wields elemental grace to mend a broken land. This is my humble offering, a debut woven from love and faith, that readers might find hope in Felix's quest as I found it in Tolkien's hills and Lewis's stars.

Pangea's Chosen: Rise of the Element Hero

Chapter 1: The Divine Summons

In the year 832 of the Creator's Renewed Light, when spring's tender breath stirred the verdant vales, there lay Eldenwold—a humble hamlet cradled beneath the rugged embrace of the Cragspire Hills. These ancient sentinels, their stony brows arcing northwest and north, guarded the village where the Cragbeck river, a silver ribbon born of the hills' eastern flanks, murmured softly along Eldenwold's eastern bounds. Perched upon the northwestern fringe of Pangea, a storied isle of jagged dales and shimmering shores kissed by the boundless Cordelia Ocean, Eldenwold stood as a hearth-fire to the Witsgarian people. These were a stalwart people, their hearts knit by oaths of kinship and devotion to the Creator's eternal light. Their timbered halls, stout and rune-graven, lined the Cragbeck's western banks, adorned with woven cloaks and crosses carved in sacred oak—emblems of a tribal honor entwined with divine redemption. Their songs, rich with tales of valor, rose like incense through the ages.

Eastward, the Windweave Plains unfurled in a mantle of emerald, stretching south and southeast across the river's flow—a sea of grass swaying under the sky's wide gaze. To the west and southwest loomed the Gildergrove, a vast and ancient wood where mighty oaks and ash stood sentinel, their shadowed glades teeming with deer whose antlers crowned the mead-hall's beams. The forest's loamy heart yielded treasures: yarrow, comfrey, and feverfew gathered by the hands of healers, among them Elara, mother to Felix, who wrought salves and teas in the Creator's name to mend the broken and soothe the fevered. In springtide, the Gildergrove sang with life, its boughs alive with the chorus of birds, its paths trodden by villagers seeking game and sacred herbs beneath the Creator's watchful gaze.

The year marked eight centuries and thirty-two since the Creator, in His boundless mercy, poured forth His Renewed Light to redeem His faithful through mortal confession and contrition, restoring Pangea's sacred harmony and purging its ancient sins. In this season of rebirth, the Witsgarians—clad in woolen tunics and cloaks clasped with iron brooches—kindled torches and lifted their voices in solemn chant for the Feast of the Creator. The church's steeple, a tower of weathered stone, stood resolute, its iron cross catching the dusk's golden fire like a beacon of faith unyielding. Yet on this night, a wind, borne from the high places, carried a hymn of urgency, and Felix Aldric, son of a carpenter, felt its divine summons stir his soul.

Felix, in his twenty-second year, was a youth of sturdy frame: broad of shoulder, lean and swift of foot. He wore a homespun tunic of earth-brown, belted with leather, and a green cloak of Witsgarian weave—its hem wrought with subtle knotwork honoring the Creator. His boots, crafted by his father Torin's skilled hands, gripped the stony path, while a carved oaken cross, gift of the same loving father, hung warm against his heart. The Cragbeck's gentle song echoed from its cradle in the hills, a faithful companion to his ascent.

For weeks, dreams had haunted his rest—visions of a golden eagle whose wings cleaved storm-tossed skies, casting a radiant cross that bathed the ancient sky-altar atop the Cragspire in holy light. These dreams, vivid and unyielding, left him restless, their meaning veiled yet urgent, driving him at last to seek answers in prayer at the sacred ruin he had beheld in slumber.

As he climbed, a memory rose unbidden—Rowan, his elder brother, bold and broad-shouldered at five-and-twenty, laughing by the Cragbeck's banks three summers past. "Swing harder, Felix, lest I best thee again!" Rowan had jested, his light brown hair agleam in the sun, dodging with a warrior's grace as they sparred beneath the mead-hall's eaves. The river had sparkled beside them, and their laughter had rung clear, heedless of the strange lights that would one day steal Rowan away. For two moons now, Rowan had been lost—vanished into the Cragspire Hills in pursuit of those eerie glows during winter's bitter grasp. Whispers spoke of unholy sorcery, but the snows had swallowed his tracks, and the village, gripped by cold, could not muster a search. Felix's throat tightened, guilt a heavy mantle for not following his brother's path. He murmured a prayer taught by Elara: "O Creator, kindle my heart anew in Thy light."

The sky altar, a ruin of weathered stone, crowned the highest peak of the Cragspire range. In elder days, it had been a place of pagan rites, its slabs witness to the offerings of those who once harried Pangea. In the third century, Crusaders, armed with the Creator's light, laid siege to the altar, casting down its idols and carving crosses over ancient runes to proclaim their triumph. Now the stones—worn by centuries, etched with faded sigils beneath victorious crosses—stood as a monument to faith's dominion over heresy. There, amidst the silent ruins, Felix sought clarity for his dreams and solace for the wound of Rowan's absence. The path grew steep, and he leaned upon his staff, its tip striking the rocky earth with a steady cadence. Below, Eldenwold dwindled, its thatched roofs and stone church nestled in the valley's embrace.

At last, Felix attained the sky altar, its weathered stones standing stark against the velvet mantle of a star-strewn firmament. Before the central slab, he paused—its ancient face marred by pagan runes, now overshadowed by a cross hewn rough yet resolute. Raising his eyes to the heavens, Felix beheld the boundless canopy of stars that arched over the Cragspire Hills, their cold fires kindling memories of his dreams golden eagle, its wings ablaze with a radiant cross, soaring above these very stones. What portent did it bear? Was it the Creator's voice, calling him to His will? Guilt and hope warred within Felix's breast, his thoughts a silent prayer for guidance, seeking to unravel the vision's truth and find his kin.

A fierce wind roared, tugging at his cloak and biting his cheeks with spring's lingering chill. The altar's central stone, etched with crosses over ancient scars, pulsed suddenly with a radiant glow. Felix's breath caught as the heavens themselves seemed to rend asunder. From the firmament descended a great eagle, its wings vast as the dawn, its feathers agleam with molten gold, wreathed in a halo of divine light. Yet, as it alighted upon the altar, its golden splendor faded gently, its plumage settling into a rich, earthy brown that shimmered with a golden aura, sparkling like embers caught in twilight's embrace. Her eyes, burning with sacred wisdom, pierced Felix's soul, and her voice—calm yet resonant as a bell- spoke within him: "Felix Aldric, son of Eldenwold, the Creator hath chosen you. The elements waver, for a fallen sorcerer, once blessed, now wields profane arts to seize the elemental crystals, seeking to corrupt Pangea's sacred peace and bind its peoples in thrall. Will you bear the Wind's holy might and rise as the Element's Champion?"

Felix stumbled back, his staff clattering upon the stone. "I am no holy warrior!" he cried, his voice trembling as the wind. "A mere villager, unworthy of such a charge!" The eagle—Titania—inclined her noble head, her gaze both stern and tender. "The Creator renews the humble who seek His mercy with true hearts. A traitor, once anointed in His light, now defies it with sorcery profane, coveting the elemental crystals to shatter Pangea's sacred balance and enslave its folk. Your faith, courage, and love mark you as His chosen."

With a sweep of her talon, Titania summoned a gem, the Wind Crystal, gleaming with airy radiance, hovering before Felix. Its warmth sang to him, whispering of tempests that might bear him aloft to lofty heights or carry him swift across the land. Yet doubt gnawed at his heart. He thought of his mother, Elara, weaving salves in the Creator's name; of his father, Torin, carving crosses with steady hands; of Rowan, lost to the strange lights that flickered in these hills, whispered to be sorcery unholy. "I cannot forsake Eldenwold," Felix murmured, his voice scarce above the wind. "My kin have need of me."

Titania's voice softened, like a breeze through summer leaves. "Behold what fate awaits should evil rise unchecked." A vision surged into his mind: villages swallowed by unholy flames, skies choked with roiling storms, and Rowan—bound in chains amidst fiery peaks—lips moving in fervent prayer for deliverance. Felix's breath caught in his throat. "Rowan lives?" he gasped, hope kindling amidst his fear.

"His fate is woven with thine," Titania answered. "Trust in the Creator's renewed light, and you shall not tread this path alone."

Felix's heart raced, torn between duty and fear. He was no hero clad in storied mail like tales of old. How could he stand against a sorcerer fallen from grace? Yet the vision of Rowan—suffering yet alive—tugged at his soul. He recalled his father's words, spoken by the hearth's glow: "Faith is not the absence of fear, but the courage to walk through it." His hand clutched the oaken cross at his chest, its warmth steadying his trembling fingers.

Titania's eyes gleamed with compassion, her golden aura shimmering softly. "The Creator chooses not the mighty, but the willing. Your faith and love for the Creator shall be your guide. The Elemental Beasts, guardians of Pangea's crystals, shall lend their strength to one who proves worthy."

Felix drew a deep breath, closing his eyes. In the silence, he prayed: "O Creator, grant me the strength to walk the path of righteousness, to shield my kin and my land." The words anchored him, though doubt lingered like a shadow. Opening his eyes, he met Titania's gaze. "I would do as you ask," he said, his voice faltering yet resolute. "But this burden is vast. How can I, a mere man, be the chosen?"

Titania tilted her head, her voice calm yet firm. "The Creator's light shines brightest in those who humble themselves before Him, not the arrogant or proud. See the crystal, it calls to you alone."

Felix gazed upon the Wind Crystal, its radiant glow steady and warm as a hearth-fire, pulsing with divine promise. His heart churned thoughts of Rowan's unknown fate, Eldenwold's fragile peace, and the shadowed trials that loomed ahead swirled like leaves in a storm. Yet within him, a spark of resolve kindled, fragile but growing, fanned by faith and love. "I will do it," he declared, his voice rising firm above the wind's murmur. "For the Creator, for Eldenwold's hearth, for all of Pangea."

The Wind Crystal drifted towards his chest, merging with a flash of celestial light. A surge of divine power coursed through him, his senses sharpened, as if the world's edges were etched in starlight; the spring breeze bent to his will, whispering secrets of the air; and the Creator's presence wrapped his heart like a shield forged of faith. Titania spoke with a voice clear as a temple bell: "As the Creator's herald, I shall guide you. Seek the Elemental Beasts, for their crystals are the keys to vanquish the fallen one. But beware his dark minions hunt you even now."

A chilling howl tore through the night, sharp as a blade against the Cragspire's ancient stone. Felix's grip tightened on his staff, the Wind Crystal's warmth pulsing at his chest, unfamiliar yet alive, like a heart not his own. Below, Eldenwold's church bell clanged, its iron toll a cry of alarm against the starlit dark. Screams rose, shrill and fervent, as Felix sprinted down the rugged trail, loose stones skittering beneath his boots. The wind swirled about him, unbidden, tugging his cloak with divine haste, as if the Creator Himself urged him forward. Cresting a ridge, he beheld a dire sight: shadowy wraiths, spawn of the fallen sorcerer, slithered through Eldenwold's streets. Their forms writhed like smoke given malice, eyes blazing with profane fire, claws of darkness scorching thatch and timber as they hissed in voices like burning pitch, "The Crystal!"

Around the church, the militia rallied, their round shields each bearing a white cross and a raven in flight, emblems of faith and vigilance forming a crescent bulwark. A spearman, his cloak singed, staggered as a wraith's claw shattered his weapon's shaft, yet he raised his shield, defiant. Beside him, Halric—grizzled, blonde beard streaked with salt—thrust his spear through a gap, grazing a wraith's smoky flank. It recoiled with a shriek like tearing cloth. A youth, face pale but jaw set, young Tobin, Felix's sparring-mate from summers past, swung a torch, its flames flaring as a wraith hissed and frayed. "Hold fast!" Halric roared, his voice a bellow over the chaos.

Felix's heart pounded, fear and faith warring within. *O Creator, renew my heart in Thy light,* he prayed, Elara's words anchoring him. The Wind Crystal flared, its power surging like a river unbound, but wild, slipping from his grasp. He leaped from the ridge, the wind catching him, guiding his descent with unsteady gusts that nearly pitched him into the dirt. Landing in the square, his cloak snapped like a banner, and he gripped his staff, Torin's lessons echoing: *Strike swift, guard low.* A wraith lunged, claws slashing for his chest. Felix sidestepped, the wind curling instinctively around him, but the Crystal's power bucked, a gust flaring wide, rattling shutters but missing the foe. The wraith's talons grazed his staff, splintering wood, and Felix stumbled, his breath sharp with panic.

"Tobin, to me!" Felix shouted, voice cracking. Tobin, torch in hand, darted to his side, thrusting flame at the wraith. It recoiled, and Felix swung his staff, willing the Crystal's power to obey. A gust roared, sharp but erratic, clipping the wraith's flank. Its form frayed, but it rallied, eyes blazing, claws arcing for his throat. Felix ducked, rolling across the dirt, the wind whispering warnings in his ears, a divine nudge he barely understood. Coming up, he thrust his staff upward, and a cyclone spun from its tip, small and wobbling, tearing at the wraith. It wailed, unraveling into ash, but the effort left Felix's arms trembling, the Crystal's power heavy as a storm in his veins.

Three more wraiths surged from the shadows, their hisses a chorus of malice. Felix's breath came fast, his militia training straining against the Crystal's wild energy. A wraith darted low, tendrils coiling for Tobin, who stumbled, his torch guttering. "Creator, guide me!" Felix cried, planting his feet. He spun his staff, summoning a gale, but it flared too wide, scattering debris and nearly knocking Halric off balance. "Steady, lad!" Halric growled, spearing a wraith's core, its form dissolving like mist. Felix focused, clutching the oaken cross at his chest, its warmth grounding him. *Faith, not strength,* he thought. The Crystal pulsed, and a precise gust lashed out, slicing a wraith in two. Its ashes scattered, but the third lunged, claws raking Halric's shield, leaving scorched trails. Halric fell to one knee, groaning.

Felix charged, the wind propelling him, but his footing faltered on uneven stone. He swung his staff, a blast of air striking the wraith like a hammer, yet it drained him, his vision swimming. It dissolved with a final wail, its ashes swirling into the night. The remaining wraiths hissed, retreating into the shadows, their fiery eyes dimming as they fled. The militia lowered their spears, their cheers rising like a hymn, ragged but triumphant. An elder approached, her cross pendant glinting in the torchlight, her eyes wide with awe and gratitude. "Felix," she said, her voice trembling with reverence, "the Creator's light shines through thee this night."

Felix leaned upon his staff, his breath coming in ragged gasps, the Wind Crystal's warmth ebbing like a tide retreating from the shore. The militia lowered their spears, their cheers rising hoarse yet hearty, a chorus of warriors after a hard-won moot. An elder drew near, her cross pendant catching the torchlight's flicker. "Servants of the fallen one," she whispered, her voice trembling with awe. "You are the Creator's anointed." Felix lifted a silent prayer: *O Creator, guide my steps to him.* He stood tall, the church's chants swelling behind him, a beacon of faith piercing the starlit silence. Villagers emerged from the sanctuary's shelter, their faces pale as moonlight, some nodding with murmurs that wove awe and fear into a tapestry of reverence, as if witnessing a moment hallowed by divine will.

Heart still pounding, Felix crossed the village square, the Cragspire Hills casting their ancient shadows over him. The church's stone walls, weathered by centuries of wind and rain, stood resolute. He pushed open the heavy oaken door, its hinges groaning, and stepped into the sanctuary's warm embrace. Candlelight danced upon crosses carved deep into the beams, their glow a soft hymn of devotion. The villagers parted, their prayers a low, resonant hum, as Felix approached the sanctuary's heart, where his parents awaited, their faith his anchor in this sacred hour.

Within the candlelit sanctuary of Eldenwold, Felix stood before Elara and Torin, their faces etched with a mingling of dread and joy, like a tapestry woven with threads of hope and fear. The sanctuary, a humble bastion of hewn stone and weathered oak, glowed with the flicker of beeswax candles, their light dancing across walls carved with spiraling runes of wind and earth, relics of the Creator's ancient covenant with Pangea's folk. Elara knelt by a wounded spearman, her healer's hands binding his gashed arm with trembling precision, her long blonde hair, woven with strands of feverfew from the Gildergrove, shimmering like spun gold in the candlelight, a beacon of healing amidst the scars of battle. Her eyes, bright as the Cragbeck's silver waters, brimmed with tears, yet held a quiet strength forged in countless nights mending Eldenwold's wounded.

Torin stood resolute beside her, his broad frame unyielding as the oaks he hewed by the Cragbeck's sacred bend, where the river's murmur sang of the Creator's enduring grace. His thick beard, dusted with sawdust and blood from the wraith fight, framed a face carved as if from Eldenwold's timber, stoic yet warm with unshakeable faith. His hammer, still gripped from felling a shadowy claw alongside his village kin, rested at his side, its handle worn smooth by years of crafting and defending. Yet beneath his steady gaze, a storm churned.

Felix paused, his heart steadying with reverence, the weight of their love anchoring him amidst the storm of his calling. He raised his right hand to sign the cross, a deliberate act to affirm his orthodoxy against the shadow of heresy. His index and middle fingers extended, parted slightly, his thumb tucked beneath to form a sacred triangle, while his ring and pinky fingers folded against his palm. With solemn grace, he touched his fingertips to his forehead, then to his chest, then to his left shoulder, and finally to his right, tracing the holy cross as the villagers' murmurs fell silent, their eyes fixed on their chosen champion. The Wind Crystal at his chest pulsed faintly, its azure glow merging with the warmth of his carved oaken pendant, a gift from Torin etched with a prayer: *In faith, find strength.* "The Creator has called me," Felix said, his voice steady despite the tremor in his hands, raw with the weight of leaving home. "Titania, His herald, bestowed upon me the Wind Crystal. A fallen sorcerer seeks to corrupt the elements and conquer all of Pangea. I must seek the Elemental Beasts and their crystals to thwart him and to find Rowan, if he yet lives."

Elara's breath caught, tears tracing her cheeks as she rose, clutching her own pendant, a twin to Felix's, carved by Torin in their youth. "My son," she whispered, her voice a trembling hymn, "you carry the Creator's light even in darkness." She

16

stepped forward, her healer's hands steadying as she drew a small vial of holy oil, its rich scent of Gildergrove's feverfew, a balm of faith and healing. With gentle reverence, she traced a cross upon Felix's forehead, the oil cool against his skin, its fragrance mingling with the sanctuary's frankincense. "May the Creator's renewed light guide you, shield you, and bring you back to us."

Torin's hand gripped Felix's shoulder, firm as the timber he hewed, his touch a lifeline to Eldenwold's hearth. "You carry our love and Rowan's hope," he said, his voice steady as a hammer's strike, yet heavy with unspoken fear. "When you were boys, you and Rowan carved your names into the oak by the Cragbeck, vowing to stand together. Now you must bear faith and courage, son. Return to us once you have fulfilled the Creator's calling, and if you find Rowan, bring him home." His eyes, warm yet stormy, held Felix's, a father's faith kindling his son's resolve.

Felix's throat tightened, memories surging, Rowan's laughter as they raced along the Cragbeck, Elara's songs by the hearth, Torin's hands guiding his own to shape wood into life. The weight of leaving them, perhaps forever, pressed like a stone upon his heart, yet their love and faith steeled him, a fire to match the Wind Crystal's glow. "I will," he vowed, his voice soft but resolute, a promise etched as deeply as their names in the oak. The villagers' prayers swelled, a chant of faith that filled the sanctuary with a resonant hum, echoing in Felix's chest like the heartbeat of Eldenwold itself, a chorus of hope woven into Pangea's ancient tapestry.

He turned to leave, pausing at the sanctuary's threshold, the oaken door creaking open to reveal the cool night air, heavy with the earthy scent of spring soil and the Cragbeck's silver murmur. The Cragspire Hills loomed beyond, their peaks stark against a starry firmament, a silent challenge to his quest. From the church steps, militia guards raised their spears in solemn salute, their torches crackling, casting a warm glow across their weathered faces, honoring the village's chosen champion. Above, Titania circled, her brown feathers shimmering with a golden aura, like embers sparkling in the velvet dark, a herald of the Creator guiding him toward the unknown.

Felix lingered, his gaze tracing the church's steeple, framed by the Cragbeck's sheen, its waters a sacred vein flowing alongside Eldenwold's heart. A pang of longing gripped him. Eldenwold, his hearth and home, stood now as a silhouette he might never see again, its fields and faces etched into his soul. Yet his parents' love, Elara's oil, and Torin's words kindled a fire within, a resolve to face the Elemental Beasts and restore Pangea's harmony before the fallen sorcerer's heresy could consume the land. He vowed to set forth at dawn in a village skiff, crossing the Cragbeck eastward to begin his quest. For now, he would rest in Eldenwold's embrace, drawing strength from its familiar earth until first light. The wind stirred, whispering promises of trials yet to come, and Felix stood ready, a man of humble beginnings bearing the Creator's call into the shadowed unknown.

Chapter 2: The Path of the Wind

At dawn, Felix stood at the Cragbeck's edge, the village skiff bobbing in the gentle current, its weathered wood carved with intricate Witsgarian knotwork—spirals of faith and endurance etched by Torin's own hand. The air carried the scent of dew-soaked grass and the faint tang of river silt, the Windweave Plains stretching beyond under a golden sun just cresting the horizon.

Torin, his father, stood nearby, tightening the skiff's ropes with the steady hands of a master carpenter. His eyes, weathered as the oak he worked, held a mix of pride and worry. "Do you remember, Felix, when you and Rowan used to sit by the hearth, pestering me for tales of Saint Baldwin?" he said, voice low but firm, like the creak of a well-built beam. "The crusader who crossed Pangea's wilds, purging heresy with his blessed blade. You'd swear you'd be a holy warrior like him, eyes bright as forge sparks. Now's your chance, lad. The Creator's called you, just as He called Baldwin. I'll pray for your strength and wisdom."

Elara, his mother, knelt by the water's edge, the healer's herb glowing faintly in the dawn light. Her hands, calloused from years of mending wounds and brewing salves, trembled as she tucked a sprig of sage into Felix's pouch, its sharp scent mingling with the river's breath. "Creator, weave Your light through his path," she whispered, her voice steady despite the tears glistening in her eyes. "Keep his heart true, and bring him back to us." She

19

pressed the pouch into his hand, her touch lingering, warm as the faith that bound Eldenwold's people.

Beside them stood Halric, the militia leader, his broad frame clad in a leather jerkin stamped with the Witsgarian raven. His grizzled face, scarred from a skirmish with raiders years ago, was set in a stern line, but his eyes softened as they met Felix's. "You're no boy anymore, Felix," he rumbled, resting a hand on the hilt of his shortsword. "You'll need wits as much as steel. When I trained you and Rowan with the blade, I saw your fire, but it's your faith that'll see you through. The village stands with you." He gestured to the blue banner of Witsgaria flapping gently behind, its white cross and raven stark against the azure, a symbol of vigilance forged in the kingdom's defiance against the shadow.

Tobin, Felix's childhood friend, leaned against a nearby willow, his lanky frame tense, dark curls falling over eyes that flickered with both envy and loyalty. He and Rowan had been inseparable with Felix in their youth, racing through the plains, stealing apples from Old Man Kael's orchard, and dreaming of quests under the church's stained glass. Now, with Rowan taken by Daegon's forces, Tobin's usual grin was gone, replaced by a tight jaw. "You're really doing it, eh, Felix?" he said, voice rough. "Going after the Crystals, facing those monsters... for Rowan. Wish I could come with you, like when we'd hunt deer with bows. But you're the chosen one, Wind Crystal and all." He stepped closer, clapping Felix's shoulder, his grip fierce. "Bring him back, yeah? And don't let those bastards on the hill take what's ours. Rowan's counting on you. We all are."

Felix clutched the sage pouch. He looked at them: Torin's steady hands, Elara's tearful resolve, Halric's unyielding trust, Tobin's fierce loyalty and felt the village's heartbeat in their presence. Behind them, Eldenwold's church steeple rose against the dawn, its spire catching the light like a beacon, the blue Witsgarian banner waving beneath, raven in flight. The kingdom's lore whispered in his mind: long ago, when legends told of a hero who would rise against the shadow that would creep across Pangea, the Witsgarians had bound their faith to the Creator for many centuries now.

"I'll make you proud," Felix said, voice steady, meeting each gaze in turn. "For Rowan, for Eldenwold, for the Creator's light." He pushed the skiff into the Cragbeck's current, the knotwork gleaming as the water took hold. As the skiff glided forward, Felix turned for one last look. His family and friends stood on the western bank, silhouettes against the rising sun: Elara clutching her handkerchief, Torin's hand raised, Halric's banner snapping, Tobin's fist clenched in defiance. The weight of their faith settled in his chest, kindling the Wind Crystal's glow, urging him toward the trials ahead.

Felix's heart ached with a mix of longing and determination. He was leaving behind the comfort of home, the warmth of his family's embrace, and the familiar sights and sounds of Eldenwold. Yet, he knew that his journey was necessary. The Creator had chosen him for a reason, and he could not turn away from his duty.

As the skiff drifted farther, Elara's voice rose, soft and trembling, carrying across the water like a thread of light. The *Song of the Element Hero*, an ancient Witsgarian lament, began with her alone, its Celtic-Norse melody weaving through the dawn.

Verse 1 (Elara Solo, Soft and Emotional, Torin Joins Briefly) *O winds of old, through mountains call, Where shadows creep and night does fall, My son, my light, by God's own hand,* she sang, her notes sharp as a war-harp's strings, fierce with maternal love yet radiant with divine resolve, a beacon piercing the dawn's golden haze. Torin's deep voice joined, steady and warm: *To carve thy path o'er sea and land.*

The villagers swelled behind, their harmony a battle-hymn, as if backed by unseen pipes and the thrum of a war-horn, thundering across the river.

Chorus (Villagers Join, Swelling Harmony) *Rise, Element Hero, born of light, Sent by the Lord to end the night. With faith our shield and hope our flame, Smite the dark, His holy name.*

Elara's voice carried the second verse, the village humming softly behind her, their sound like the rustle of Windweave grasses.

Verse 2 (Elara with Light Village Humming) *From Witsgar's heart, the raven flies, Beneath the cross that never dies. The Crystal hums, its power true, The chosen one shall bear it through.*

The chorus rose again, stronger now, the villagers' voices resolute, echoing off the river's surface, Torin's baritone anchoring their harmony.

Chorus (Full Village, Resolute) *Rise, Element Hero, born of light, Sent by the Lord to end the night. With faith our shield and hope our flame, Smite the dark, His holy name.*

The song built in intensity, Elara's voice intertwining with the village's as they sang of the trials ahead.

Verse 3 (Elara and Village, Building Intensity) *Through Ashen Crags, where tempests wail, By fire and tide, thy heart prevail. The evil one, with shadowed might, Shall fall before thy sacred fight.*

Elara led the bridge, her voice soaring, while the villagers chanted low, their words a prayer to the Creator, Torin's voice steady among them.

Bridge (Elara Leads, Village Chants) *O Breath of God, guide his way, Through storm and strife, through night and day. The plains will sing, the stars will gleam, For Pangea's hope, thy soul's redeem.*

The chorus swelled to a triumphant peak, the full ensemble's voices ringing like a bell across the Cragbeck, carrying Felix forward.

Chorus (Triumphant, Full Ensemble) *Rise, Element Hero, born of light, Sent by the Lord to end the night. With faith our shield and hope our flame, Smite the dark, His holy name.*

As the skiff rounded a bend, Elara's voice softened, the villagers' harmony fading like the dawn mist. Her final words lingered, a tender farewell.

Outro (Elara Softens, Village Fades) *So sail, brave heart,* *'cross river wide, With Titania's wings and truth beside. The Witsgar weeps,* *yet stands in pride, For thou art hope, where faith abides.*

Felix clutched the cross pendant, the song's strength settling into his bones. The skiff carried him onward, the Ashen Crags looming closer, Titania's wings glinting above. He etched the memory of his mother's voice, his father's steady note, and the village's faith into his heart, a beacon to guide him through Pangea's darkest hour.

The Windweave Plains opened before him, grasses swaying under a golden sun, Titania's wings glinting above, the Ashen Crags calling.

As Felix stepped onto the Windweave Plains, he pulled the hood of his cloak over his head, the fabric settling snugly as the Cragbeck's hills faded behind. His boots sank into soft earth dusted with ash. The cross charm from Torin and Elara's sage sprig pressed against his belt, their warmth mingling with the Wind Crystal's pulse. A blackened patch of grass, scorched by unholy fire, caught his eye near the riverbank, its sulfurous sting sharp in the breeze. Could a carpenter's son at twenty-two truly bear the Creator's mantle? "Creator, shield me as Elara prayed," he whispered, gripping his staff. The plains stretched vast before him, Titania soaring above, her golden wings urging him toward the Ashen Crags' fiery haze.

Titania descended, landing gracefully on a stone marker carved with crosses and ancient knotwork, its weathered surface a testament to Pangea's faithful who had stood against the shadow

24

in ages past, their prayers etched into the stone like vows against the dark. Her brown feathers shimmered like polished armor, catching the sunlight in a cascade of golden embers, and her eyes, burning with sacred wisdom, softened at Felix's distress, as if seeing the storm within his heart. The plains of Eldenwold stretched around them, their golden grasses swaying under a sky bruised with twilight, a sacred expanse where the Creator's light vied with the creeping shadow of heresy. Her voice echoed, serene yet firm, like a hymn carried on the wind that stirred the Cragbeck's silver waters. "Why so troubled, Felix Aldric?"

Felix's hands steadied, his scruffy beard brushing his jaw as he clutched the cross pendant at his chest, its oaken weight a gift from Torin, etched with a prayer for courage. The Wind Crystal pulsed faintly, its azure glow a spark of divine assurance, yet his heart pounded with the weight of her words. "Who is this fallen sorcerer?" he asked, his voice low with awe and fear, the title a shadow cast across his thoughts.

Her eyes darkened, a shadow crossing her celestial form, as if the name itself bore a curse that dimmed the plains' golden light. "Daegon," she said, her voice heavy with sorrow, a lament for a soul lost to betrayal. "Once a servant of a great order sworn to the Creator, he was among the few gifted to wield magic naturally, without need of Crystals, his power a rare spark of divine grace. But ambition and greed corrupted his heart, turning him from the Creator's light to embrace the darkness. He betrayed his Lord, forging abominations from his sin, their forms a mockery of creation, to hunt the faithful and seize the Crystals for his profane will. Sealed for his treachery in ages past, he stirs now, his heresy a blight upon Pangea, threatening to choke its sacred harmony."

Felix's breath caught, the weight of Daegon's name pressing upon him like the Cragspire Hills, its peaks looming in his mind. The Wind Crystal flared, its light weaving with the pendant's warmth, as if urging him to stand firm. "What must I do?" he asked, his voice steadying, though fear lingered like a shadow at his mind's edge. "How can I face such evil?"

Titania's gaze swept eastward, where a faint, unnatural shadow flickered in the grasses, a ripple of malice coiling like smoke under the twilight sky. "Beware, Felix," she said, her voice sharpening, a clarion call cutting through the plains' stillness. "Daegon's shadow-wrought minions already stalk these lands, their red eyes gleaming with his profane will. They are but sparks of his heresy, seeking the Crystals to darken Pangea's light. If unchecked, the Cragbeck will turn to ash, Eldenwold's fields will wither, and the Creator's light will dim across Pangea." Her wings rustled, a sacred breeze stirring the grasses, and her voice softened, a gentle hymn woven with divine resolve. "Your faith in the Creator is your strength, Felix. The Creator weaves love into courage, as He wove Pangea's heart from wind and flame. Trust that bond, and it will guide you to Daegon's defeat."

"The Creator chooses one heart to kindle many," he whispered, echoing Torin's teaching, his voice a prayer against the shadow. He bowed his head, murmuring, "Creator, let my faith be enough to face this Daegon."

Titania's eyes gleamed with approval, her wings stilling as the plains' golden grasses bowed in reverence. "Seek the Elemental Beasts, Felix, for their Crystals hold the Creator's power to restore Pangea's peace. Trials await, but His light will guide your steps, as it guides the stars above the Cragspire Hills." Felix swallowed, his awe tempered by the weight of his quest. "And the first Beast?" he pressed, his voice a mix of awe and resolve, the Wind Crystal pulsing in rhythm with his heart.

Her voice warmed, a melody of hope amidst the warning. "The Fire Lion, guardian of the Fire Crystal, dwells in the heart of the Ashen Crag's Volcano, its mane a blaze of glory vast as the Creator's flame. It tests the heart's resolve with trials of fire and truth, granting its power only to the faithful. Trust the Creator, Felix, and its flames will reveal your path." She paused, her gaze softening, a divine light that banished the plains' creeping shadow. "Your faith fuels the Wind Crystal's might. Be mindful, for Daegon's red eyes already seek its glow."

With a cry that pierced the twilight, Titania soared upward, her golden aura sparkling like embers against the starry firmament, a beacon urging Felix onward.

The plains' meadow rolled on, grasses parting under Felix's steps, his staff a steady rhythm. A ravine yawned ahead, its jagged edges dropping into shadow, too wide to cross. Doubt crept in, but the Wind Crystal thrummed, whispering whirlwinds. "Trust the Creator's gift," he muttered, stepping back, eyes fixed on the far side. He raised his hand, summoning a swirling gust that lifted him in a whirlwind, cloak flapping. He soared, dirty blonde hair whipping, landing hard—stones crunching—stumbling but catching himself with a grin. "I'm learning," he said, confidence budding.

Time stretched long and languid, measured by the sun's slow arc across the heavens and the growing ache in Felix's legs as he trod the Windweave Plains. The grasses thickened around him, their golden tips rising to brush his waist, swaying in a shimmering sea that stretched toward the horizon. The distant Cragspire Hills wavered in the heat's haze, their rugged edges smudging into the azure sky. Sweat beaded on Felix's brow, his scruffy beard prickling beneath the sun's relentless glare. He yearned for the cool whisper of the Cragbeck's waters, for a breeze to stir the stifling air, but the plains offered only their endless, sunlit expanse, unbroken save for the occasional cry of a distant hawk.

As Felix pressed onward, the meadow's character shifted subtly. The open grasslands gave way to a denser tract, where the grasses parted to reveal clusters of low, gnarled shrubs and the first scattered trees of the Windweave Plain's outlying fringes. Their twisted branches cast dappled shadows, and the air grew heavier, scented with earth and leaf-mould. The path, little more than a game trail, wound into this wooded meadow, where the trees stood like silent sentinels, their boughs whispering secrets in the faint stir of the wind. Felix's steps slowed, his boots sinking slightly into the softer earth. The Wind Crystal at his chest pulsed faintly, its warmth a steady companion, yet an unease crept into his heart, a prickling sensation, as if the very air had turned watchful.

An unnatural chill seeped through the sun's warmth, sharp as a blade's edge. The hum of insects, once a constant chorus, fell silent, replaced by a heavy, oppressive quiet that pressed against his ears. Felix's skin tingled, a shiver crawling up his spine like a spider's tread. He halted, his eyes sweeping the shadowed undergrowth and the swaying grasses beyond. The meadow lay still, the trees unmoving, yet the weight of unseen eyes tightened around him, a silent hunter's gaze that grew heavier with each heartbeat. His hand tightened on his staff, the wood warm and familiar, but his pulse quickened, the Crystal's glow flaring briefly as if sensing peril.

A faint rustle sounded to his left, sharp and deliberate, like a blade slicing through silk. Felix froze, his heart thudding against his ribs, staff raised in a trembling grip. The grasses parted, and from the shadowed thicket emerged three rough-hewn figures, their movements swift and predatory, encircling him with practiced ease. Bandits, their faces weathered and scarred by lives of hardship, stepped into the dappled light. Their tattered cloaks, patched and stained, bore the crude embroidery of a Spiral Serpent, its red coils glinting with an unnatural sheen. Their mismatched armor—leather and rusted mail—clinked softly as they moved, weapons gleaming in their hands: a notched sword, a pitted axe, and a dagger with a cruel curve. The leader, a burly man with a cruel glint in his sunken eyes, bore a pendant etched with the same Spiral Serpent, its surface pulsing with an unholy red glow that seemed to drink the sunlight. He stepped forward, his boots crunching on the earth, his voice a low, mocking growl that cut through the silence like a whip.

"Well, well, what do we have here? A lone wanderer, far from home, eh?"

Another bandit, missing a front tooth, grinned maliciously, twirling an axe in his hand. "Looks like he's lost, boss. Maybe we should help him… to our camp, after we take his coin."

The third bandit, a lanky fellow with a scarred face, chuckled darkly, hefting a heavy club. "Yeah, that staff's no match for us, boy. Hand over whatever's shining at your chest, or we'll carve it out."

Felix's pulse thundered in his ears, but he planted his feet, gripping his staff tighter. The Wind Crystal pulsed erratically at his chest, its faint hum vibrating through his trembling hands. "I'm Felix Aldric, from Eldenwold," he said, voice steady despite the fear knotting his stomach. "I'm on a quest under the Creator's protection. Let me pass, and there'll be no trouble."

The leader laughed, a harsh, grating sound that echoed across the plains. "Creator's protection? Hear that, lads? This pup thinks his prayers'll save him!" He drew a sword, its blade etched with the Spiral Serpent, the rune flickering with a faint red light. "That shiny gem at your neck, Daegon wants it. Hand it over, or we'll gut you like a deer."

The toothless bandit sneered, stepping closer, his axe glinting. "The Crystal at your chest hums with stolen light," he rasped, eyes glinting with fervor. "Daegon's will claims it, boy. Surrender it, and join the tide of his new order."

The scarred bandit spat on the ground, his club raised. "No running for this one. Daegon's promised coin for that crystal. Let's take it and be done."

Felix's heart pounded, their words cutting deep, stirring doubts about his worthiness. He remembered tales of the crusades and how their faith carried them through. "Creator, guide me," he whispered, his voice barely audible over the pounding of his heart. He raised his staff, recalling Torin's lessons—strike swift, guard low—and focused on the Wind Crystal's warmth.

The leader's smirk cut through the twilight, his eyes glinting with cruel certainty as he sensed Felix's hesitation. "Last chance, boy," he growled, his voice a low rumble like distant thunder over the Windweave Plains. He charged, his sword slashing toward Felix's chest with brutal force, the blade's edge catching the fading light in a malevolent gleam. Felix thrust his hand forward, the Wind Crystal at his chest flaring with a wild, untamed pulse. The power surged, raw and uncontrolled, erupting into a chaotic whirlwind that tore through the grasses, whipping dust and debris into a blinding storm. His footing faltered on the uneven ground, and he stumbled, the wind howling like a living beast as he fought to rein it in, his inexperience a weight as heavy as his staff. The leader staggered against the gust but pressed forward, his sword slicing through the vortex, its blade grazing Felix's arm with a searing sting. Blood welled through a tear in his sleeve, crimson rivulets trickling down, the pain a sharp jolt that snapped his senses awake.

Felix gritted his teeth, the sting sharpening his focus. "Focus," he growled to himself, wiping sweat from his brow despite the evening chill that swept across the plains. He centered himself, picturing a smaller, controlled gust. The Wind Crystal responded, its airy hum steadying into a tight whirlwind that caught the leader mid-stride, hoisting him upward. The man flailed, his sword slipping from his grip to clatter among the grasses, his curse—"Damn your tricks!"—lost in the wind's roar.

The toothless bandit seized the moment, rushing Felix with his axe raised, a wild grin splitting his weathered face, his Spiral Serpent cloak flapping like a tattered banner. Felix twisted aside, the axe whistling past his shoulder, but the bandit's elbow slammed into his ribs, knocking the breath from him in a sharp gasp. He stumbled back, his staff nearly slipping from sweaty palms, his chest heaving as he fought to steady himself. The scarred bandit circled, his club swinging in a low arc toward Felix's legs, its iron studs glinting with menace. Felix's militia training flickered to life, instincts drilled under Eldenwold's halls. He parried with his staff, the impact jarring his arms, the oaken wood splintering slightly under the force, a testament to his still-raw skill.

The toothless bandit lunged again, his axe arcing high in a reckless swing. Felix ducked, the air shivering where the blade passed, and summoned a quick, focused gust from the Wind Crystal, shoving the bandit back into the tall grasses. The man sprawled, his cloak tangling around him, his curses muffled as he thrashed in the dirt.

The scarred bandit roared, charging with his club. Felix planted his feet, channeling the Wind Crystal's power into a fierce gust that slammed into the bandit with the force of a breaking wave. The man lifted off the ground, his club flying from his hand as he crashed into a patch of windweave grass, groaning but struggling to rise, his breath a ragged wheeze.

The leader, freed from the whirlwind, scrambled to his feet, snatching his sword from the earth. His Spiral Serpent pendant pulsed red, a profane mockery of the firestones' divine glow, as if drawing strength from some unholy wellspring. "You'll pay, whelp!" he bellowed, lunging with a flurry of slashes, each strike fueled by heretical zeal. Felix dodged the first, his body twisting with desperate speed, but the second nicked his cloak.

Summoning his resolve, Felix thrust both hands forward, the Wind Crystal blazing with a clarity he hadn't felt before. A spiraling wind-shield roared to life, its gusts shimmering like a shield of starlight, deflecting the leader's next strike. Seizing the opening, Felix channeled a focused gale, a thane's battle-cry made wind, slamming the leader and the scarred bandit together. Their bodies collided with a dull thud, armor clanking as they crumpled to the ground, dazed, their weapons scattered among the grasses.

The toothless bandit, back on his feet, hesitated, his axe trembling in his grip, his eyes darting to the fallen leader. Felix fixed him with a steady gaze, the Wind Crystal pulsing with a quiet intensity. "Flee, or fall," he said, his voice low but firm, carrying the weight of a vow. The bandit's eyes widened. With a muttered curse, he turned and sprinted into the plains, his footsteps fading into the gathering dusk.

Felix stood, chest heaving, his staff trembling in his grip as blood trickled from the shallow cut on his arm, the sting a reminder of his vulnerability. The Wind Crystal's glow dimmed, mirroring his bone-deep exhaustion, its energy spent in the reckless surges of his inexperience. He'd won, but the victory felt fragile, a spark of growth amid the ashes of his mistakes, proof of his potential yet a stark warning of how much he still had to learn. The Spiral Serpent marks lingered in his mind, their red glow a chilling promise of Daegon's reach. "What is this symbol? Is this Daegon's Sigil?" he murmured, gripping his staff tighter, his resolve kindled anew.

As the last echoes of the battle faded, Felix lowered his staff, his arms trembling with exertion. The Windweave Plains stretched vast and silent around him, the whisper of the wind through the grasses a stark contrast to the bandits' earlier taunts. The sun dipped toward the horizon, painting the sky in warm hues of amber and violet, casting long shadows that danced like spirits across the meadow. The fight had drained him. Ahead, a small grove of gnarled cedar trees near a babbling stream caught his eye, their branches offering the promise of shelter amidst the boundless plains. With a weary but determined step, he started toward it, the prospect of rest a beacon as steady as the firestone pendant at his chest, its faint glow a reminder of the Creator's light guiding him forward.

He gathered dry wood from the grove's edge and knelt to strike flint and steel from his pack. A spark caught, and soon a small fire crackled to life, its warm glow pushing back the encroaching shadows. Felix sat beside it, letting out a weary sigh, the day's trials heavy on his shoulders. He was beginning to understand its airy might, each gust a step closer to the Creator's purpose.

The flames danced before him, and his thoughts drifted to Eldenwold. He pictured his mother, Elara, in her garden, blonde hair aglow as she gathered herbs, her healer's hands deft and gentle. His father, Torin, stood in his workshop, sawdust clinging to his beard, the rhythmic tap of his chisel shaping wood into prayers. A pang of longing pierced his chest, but it kindled his resolve. "I'll find you, Rowan," he whispered, the vow soft against the fire's crackle. "For you, for them all."

Lifting his gaze, Felix marveled at the star-filled sky, a celestial vault woven by the Creator's hand, its myriad lights shimmering like divine embers scattered across Pangea's ancient firmament. Each star gleamed with a timeless radiance, as if kindled by the breath of the Creator in the dawn of creation, their glow a testament to the Creator's boundless light that held fast against the creeping shadow of Daegon's heresy. The Cragbeck River murmured nearby, its silver waters reflecting the heavens— a sacred vein binding Eldenwold to the eternal. Felix's heart stirred, weary from battles fought and trials yet to come, yet kindled by a quiet hope.

"Creator, thank You for guiding me through this day," Felix prayed, his voice low, a vow rising like a hymn on the wind. "Grant me strength for the trials ahead, to wield the Crystals in Your name. Shield Rowan, Elara, Torin, and all who suffer under Daegon's shadow, that Your light may prevail over his darkness."

A gentle breeze stirred, carrying the earthy scent of Eldenwold's fields and the distant whisper of the Whispering Woods, as if the stars themselves sang of trials yet to come. Felix's heart steadied, faith weaving through his weariness like a thread in the Creator's tapestry, binding him to his divine calling. He stood beneath the celestial vault, its radiant embers a beacon in the velvet dark, ready to face the Fire Lion and the shadowed path ahead, his soul kindled by the Creator's boundless light.

He lay down on a bed of soft grass, his cloak drawn tight as a blanket. The fire's warmth mingled with the stream's gentle murmur, lulling him into peace. As sleep claimed him, dreams swirled of golden eagles and winds that carried him toward the Creator's light—a beacon in the dark.

At dawn's first light, Felix stirred, and the fire reduced to glowing embers. He rose, feeling renewed, and broke camp with a quiet prayer of thanks. The Windweave Plains stretched before him, Titania's cry echoing above as he shouldered his pack and staff, ready to follow her toward the Ashen Crags.

Chapter 3: Kirkhaven's Defiant Stand

Above the Windweave Plains, the spring sun ascended, its golden rays threading light through grasses that swayed like the tides of an ancient sea—a day and a half since Felix forded the Cragbeck's rushing waters east of Eldenwold. Felix had traversed thirty leagues of meadow and moor, his spirit unbowed though bandit-wrought wounds lingered, salved by Elara's sage beneath the stars of a fleeting encampment. Refreshed yet weary from the morn's toil, he pressed onward, Kirkhaven's faint glimmer a beacon on the horizon. As he crested a windswept rise, the rugged silhouette of Kirkhaven emerged, framed by the Ashen Crags, whose jagged peaks—scarred by eons—loomed to the northeast, their distant fires pulsing with secrets of the Elder Days. At the haven's northwestern edge, where plain met meadow, a lone watchtower stood, its weathered stones etched with firestone runes that gleamed as silent sentinels of the Fyrclad Kin's unyielding faith. Atop it, a banner unfurled against the heavens—crimson as heart's blood, adorned with a white cross and a lion rampant, its mane a flame of defiance—proclaiming the Kin's fealty to the Creator, as was the way of all Pangea's faithful since the Years of Renewed Light: to declare white crosses on all flags of those who serve Him. Felix halted, his gaze bound to the standard, its bold sigil kindling a spark within him—a memory of truths older than stone, shared by every cross-crowned banner from Eldenwold's raven to this lion's roar. Southward, fields of barley and oats gleamed like molten gold, where cows lowed softly, and chickens clucked in scattered harmony, their gentle stirrings weaving through the breeze under the sun's watchful eye. To the northeast, the Crags' shadowed maw opened, its volcanic heart aglow with a fire that whispered of creation's dawn. The tower, rising like a prayer carved in stone, guided Felix's faltering steps toward Kirkhaven's half-charred palisade, its heart nestled along the Crags' southwestern embrace. Forged by the Fyrclad Kin—descendants of miners and tillers who claimed these wilds four centuries past—the haven stood as a testament to their tartan-cloaked resolve, their firestone talismans gleaming with the light of an enduring creed.

Felix approached Kirkhaven's half-charred palisade, starting at the watchtower's northwest edge and moving toward the village heart further southeast along the southwest side of the Crags. Villagers in woolen tunics and tartan cloaks, their Scottish voices sharp, 'Who's this stranger, aye?' gripped pitchforks and mining picks, eyes wary from bandit raids. The militia, fourteen strong, in leather jerkins with cross-painted shields, stood ready, their courage forged by survival.

As Felix drew closer, an elder stepped forward from the crowd. His long white beard flowed over his tartan cloak, and his bald head reflected the firestone light. "I am Elder Bryce, leader of Kirkhaven," he said, his voice warm but cautious, with a melodic roll of his 'r's. "What brings ye to our village, stranger?" Before Felix could respond, a woman with red braided hair and a spear stepped up beside Bryce. "And I'm Captain Bryn, in charge of the militia," she added, her green eyes sharp with determination, her Scottish burr thick and fierce. "State yer business."

Felix paused, heart steadying with reverence, and raised his right hand to sign the cross, his index and middle fingers extended straight, slightly separated, the thumb tucked beneath, forming a sacred triangle, while his ring and pinky fingers folded against his palm. He touched his fingertips to his forehead, then chest, left shoulder, and right, the Wind Crystal pulsing faintly at his chest, its divine light mirroring the Fyrclad Kin's firestone glow. "I'm Felix Aldric, called by the Creator as Element Hero to face Daegon's heresy. I saw your smoke, let me help," he said, his voice steady.

Captain Bryn snorted, her freckles dusting her nose and upper cheeks as she gripped her spear tighter. "We're knackered from bandits, boy, an' nae in the mood for fancy tales!" Her tone, bold and battle-worn, carried a warrior's challenge.

Felix paused, his heart steadying as he raised his right hand to sign the cross, his fingers forming the sacred triangle. The Wind Crystal pulsed faintly at his chest, its light mirroring the glow of the Fyrclad Kin's firestone. "I'm Felix Aldric, called by the Creator as Element Hero to face Daegon's heresy. I saw your smoke, let me help," he said, his voice steady. Then, recalling his recent ordeal, he added, "On my way here, just yesterday, I encountered some bandits bearing a Spiral Serpent mark. They were after the Wind Crystal, but I managed to fend them off with the Creator's help."

Bryn's eyes narrowed, and she exchanged a glance with Bryce. "Aye, we've seen that cursed mark on the bandits plaguin' our village," she said, her voice grim, the Scottish burr thick with disdain. "It's a sign of Daegon's heresy spreadin' across the land."

A girl with brown braided hair and brown eyes, despite soot-streaked cheeks under a patched shawl, stepped forward, offering a steaming bowl of barley stew. Her calloused hands trembled slightly as she murmured, "Don't mind her, sir, ye seem kind," her voice soft as a hearth's glow, her smile shy. Felix smiled and accepted the bowl, thanking the young girl before turning and walking back toward the church.

Felix followed Bryce to the chapel, its wooden walls carved with crosses and firestone inlays, a sanctuary like Eldenwold's. Kneeling before a firestone altar, he prayed, "Creator, shield these Fyrclad Kin, guide me to defend the good." His crystal at his chest glowed, a soft hum filling the air. Bryce's wariness eased, his voice softening with the melodic roll of his 'r's. "Aye, ye're a true heart, lad. Our kin, the Fyrclad, came four centuries back, chasing firestone's glow, led by visions of the Fire Lion. We built Kirkhaven, named for the church that's our heart, its firestone altar guiding our prayers. Stone by stone, our fields and forge thrivin' despite raids. But now these bandits bear a serpent mark, coiling like the Serpent's lie in Eden, stealing firestone for Daegon's heresy whispers speak of a spire in yon Crags, rivaling the Creator's Church. We're losing hope, and lives."

Felix nodded, recalling Eldenwold's tales. "Rumors say Firestone's glow is the Creator's light, said that mages wielded them many years ago, when those with a rare gift of magic could wield it by their sheer will. Is that why Daegon seeks it?"

Bryce's eyes gleamed. "Aye, lad, it's spark's used to be a symbol for those who used to wield magic and to this day, Kings and rich folk still purchase them. But now Daegon twists it to heresy."

Felix's chest ached. "I'm no warrior born for strangers' battles," he thought, heart heavy with their trust, their talismans glinting like prayers he must answer. "Creator, am I worthy to wield Your wind for folk I've only met?" Yet their desperation reminded him of home, stirred his resolve. "I'll stand with you," he said, honor-bound to aid the Fyrclad Kin, his Crystal quest postponed, faith flaring like their forge's hearth. Bryce's eyes, weathered yet keen, studied Felix, a flicker of recognition softening his cautious gaze. "Ye've a familiar look, lad," Bryce said, voice warm as a bard's tale, rolled 'r's melodic. "That jaw, that steady gaze—are ye Torin's son, from Eldenwold? Years back, I traded with a carpenter there, fine tools for our miners' picks. Torin, aye, a man of faith and craft."

Felix's breath caught; the mention of his father grounded him like the familiar grain of his staff. "Yes, sir, I'm Felix, Torin's son," he replied, voice steady despite the ache of home tugging at his heart. "He still carves, his tools marked with the Creator's cross, each one a prayer in wood." The memory of Torin's workshop, sawdust thick in the air, the rhythmic tap of his chisel flashed vividly, steadying Felix amidst Kirkhaven's unfamiliar hearth.

Bryce nodded, a smile creasing his weathered face, his firestone talisman glinting as he leaned closer, voice dropping to a fond rumble. "Torin had some blacksmith's skill too, ye know, not just carpentry. He could forge a blade or mend a pick as deftly as he shaped a beam. Once, nigh on a decade past, he came to Kirkhaven with a cart of tools, chisels sharp as a thane's wit, and iron brackets for our forge, each etched with a wee cross for the Creator's blessing. Saved our miners a brutal season, those did. We traded firestone for his work, and he prayed with us in this very chapel, his faith as sturdy as his craft." Bryce's eyes gleamed, the memory kindling warmth in his gaze. "He spoke of his lads, then two boys, one bold as a storm, the other steady like the Cragbeck's flow. That'd be ye, I reckon, the steady one?"

Felix's throat tightened, his fingers brushing the cross pendant, its edges worn smooth by years of faith. The mention of Rowan—the bold brother, lost to strange lights in the Cragspire Hills—stirred a pang, but Bryce's recognition of Torin's broader skills sparked pride in his father. "Yes, that's me," Felix said, a faint smile breaking through, though his voice carried a tremor. "Father always said a man's hands should serve the Creator in every craft—wood or iron, it's all His work. I didn't know he'd come this far, though, trading with the Fyrclad Kin." The thought of Torin standing in this chapel, his broad hands clasping a firestone talisman, wove a thread between Eldenwold and Kirkhaven, making the haven feel less foreign.

Captain Bryn, who'd been listening nearby, her braided hair catching the firestone light, stepped forward, her spear propped, eyes narrowing with cautious respect. "If ye're Torin's blood, ye've his grit," she said, her Scottish burr sharp yet warming. "But we're knackered from bandits, lad, and Daegon's forces haunt the Crags. Prove yer father's faith in battle, and Kirkhaven's wi' ye."

Felix nodded, clutching his staff. "For the Creator, for my father's name, and for my brother," he vowed silently, his resolve a flame kindled by family and faith, ready to face the bandits' threat and the Fire Lion's trial.

Bryn's eyes, sharp as the flint of her mining kin, searched Felix's, her weathered face softened by a flicker of hope amidst the firelight's glow. "My brother, Duncan, a miner, saw a lad like ye near yon Crags, days back. Bound by wraiths, prayin' fierce wi' a cross pendant, fightin' like a warrior. They dragged him to yon Crags' lava caves, prayin' for his kin." Her voice, rough with the accent of the Fyrclad highlands, carried a weight of regret, as if the memory were a wound unhealed.

Felix's breath caught, his heart lurching as if struck by a hammer on anvil. Rowan alive, unbowed, his faith enduring amidst such torment? His hand flew to the cross pendant at his chest, its cool silver a mirror to the one Bryn described, a gift from their father, Torin, etched with a prayer for courage. "Was he fair-haired, wi' a cross like mine?" he asked, his voice urgent, trembling with a fragile hope that battled the shadow of despair.

Bryn nodded, her gaze steady, though sorrow lingered in her eyes. "Aye, just so. Fair as a field of wheat, prayin' fierce as any priest. I wanted to aid him, but wi' bandits plaguin' our mines, I couldnae leave my post. My prayers go wi' him he ken't how to fight, that lad." Her voice softened, a quiet offering of faith, and she turned her eyes to the fire, its flames casting shadows that danced like specters across the rough-hewn walls of the Kin's gathering hall.

Felix's grip tightened on his staff. The weight of Rowan's fate pressed upon him, a burden as heavy as the volcano that loomed beyond the Crags, its distant rumble a low hymn of Pangea's primal fire. He bowed his head, a whispered prayer forming on his lips, but before he could speak, Bryce stoked the fire with a gnarled hand, the embers flaring like the Lion's flame itself. His white beard gleamed in the firelight. "Our Fyrclad Kin sought firestone's wealth in ages past," he began, his voice low and resonant, like the echo of a hammer in the deep mines. "But the Lion's flame, guardian of the volcano's heart, taught us faith over greed. Our mines delve deep into Pangea's bones, our blades carry its spark, forged in the Creator's light. The Lion guards a Crystal in yon volcano's core, a trial of faith for the worthy. These bandits, curs of Daegon, seek our firestone for their dark work, to fuel their heresy in the Crags' lava caves, where ye brother may yet endure."

"Lead me to Rowan, that I may free him from the Crags and claim the Fire Crystal to thwart Daegon's madness." The fire flared as if in answer, its light casting a radiant halo across the hall, and Felix felt the weight of his calling as the Element Hero, a mantle forged in faith and fire, urging him toward the volcano's trial and the hope of his brother's salvation.

As twilight draped the Ashen Crags in a shroud of deepening indigo, a flare erupted from Kirkhaven's northwest watchtower, its firestone core blazing like a fallen star against the bruised sky. The signal cut through the dusk, a warning that rippled across the plateau, where the village of Kirkhaven clung to life amidst scorched fields and a half-charred palisade. Shouts shattered the village's fragile calm, boots pounding the earth as bandits stormed from the northwest, their torches casting jagged pools of light across the terrain. Axes and clubs glinted under the ruddy glow of Kirkhaven's firestone lamps, which hung from iron brackets along the palisade, their warm radiance flickering like the Creator's watchful gaze. Leading the marauders was Rauthar, a hulking figure whose face twisted with cruel intent, his fire-dagger pulsing with the unholy red glow of Daegon's charred serpent rune, an echo of the Serpent's lie in Eden, a blasphemous sigil that mocked the Creator's light. His eyes gleamed with the same crimson fire, his soul ensnared by the heretical promise of power. "I cast off yer Creator's chains for Daegon's might!" he bellowed, his voice a guttural roar that shook the air. "His fire feeds the selfish heart!" The dagger's flames arced wildly, igniting a patch of barley in a hungry blaze, the golden stalks curling to ash as the wind carried the acrid scent across the plateau.

The bandits—twenty in number, their ragged cloaks stained with the dust of the Crags—moved with chaotic greed, loosing fire-tipped arrows in undisciplined volleys that streaked like comets, some embedding in the palisade with dull thuds,

45

others scattering embers across the scorched earth. Their shouts were a cacophony of defiance, promising a new order under Daegon's fiery spire, a heretical dream of dominion that fueled their reckless charge.

Felix leapt to the forefront, his heart hammering against his ribs, the Wind Crystal at his chest pulsing with an airy hum that thrummed through his veins like a storm's first breath. Kirkhaven's militia rallied behind him fourteen stout Fyrclad Kin clad in leather jerkins, their cross-painted shields raised like a wall of faith, spears leveled with the precision of those who had faced the Crags' perils before. Their tartan cloaks snapped in the evening breeze, firestone talismans glinting like embers of resolve, their weathered faces set with the unyielding grit of miners who had clawed iron from the earth's bones. At their head stood Captain Bryn, her braided hair framing a fierce gaze, her spear flashing as she barked, "Hold the line, kin!" Her voice was a Highland clarion, sharp and unyielding, forged by years of leading her people against raiders and worse. "For the Fyrclad, for the Creator!"

"Creator, guide my hand in Your light!" Felix prayed, his voice a fervent whisper as he gripped his oaken staff that channeled the Wind Crystal's power from his chest. A bandit charged, his axe raised high, his voice a guttural snarl: "The spire'll rise o'er yer crosses!" Felix planted his staff into the earth, the Wind Crystal flaring with a surge that roared to life as a swirling whirlwind. The vortex erupted with a howl, catching the bandit mid-stride, his cloak tearing as the gust lifted him skyward. His scream was swallowed by the wind's fury, his fire-tipped arrows scattering like embers caught in a storm, winking out against the glow of Kirkhaven's firestone lamps.

Felix thrust his hand upward and propelled himself into the air. His cloak snapped behind him, its hem frayed from countless battles, his dirty blonde hair whipping across his face as he soared. At the whirlwind's peak, he recalled Torin's lessons— strike swift, strike sure—and gripped his staff with both hands. He slammed it down onto the airborne bandit, the impact cracking against the man's chest with a bone-jarring thud. The bandit plummeted, crashing into the scorched earth near the palisade, a cloud of dust and embers rising as he lay still, his axe clattering uselessly beside him.

The spearwall advanced, boots stomping in unison, shields locked. Three bandits fell in quick succession, blood spraying as the militia's iron-tipped spears pierced ragged cloaks, their disciplined line holding firm against the chaotic charge. The Fyrclad Kin fought with the ferocity of their forefathers, their firestone talismans gleaming like the Creator's wrath; each thrust a prayer made manifest. Felix landed, his boots crunching on the rocky ground, and sprinted forward, eyes locked on another bandit wielding a gnarled club studded with iron spikes. With a burst of wind-enhanced speed, he closed the gap in a heartbeat, thrusting his staff into the bandit's abdomen. The blunt force folded the man in half, a gasping wheeze escaping his lips as he collapsed to his knees, the club rolling free into the dirt.

Rauthar's roar cut through the chaos. "Yer wind's naught to Daegon's fire, boy!" His fire-dagger slashed forward, unleashing a searing arc of unholy flame that tore through the air, its heat warping the twilight into a shimmering haze. Felix spun, the Wind Crystal flaring brighter, and summoned a spiraling wind-shield, a vortex of compressed air that shimmered with reflected firestone light. The fiery arc collided with the shield, exploding in a burst of sparks that scattered like shattered stars, the embers winking out as they fell. Three militia fighters, their faces etched with miners' grit, countered a bandit flank, their spears thrusting in perfect unison to fell two foes, blood staining the earth as their tartan cloaks snapped in the wind.

Bryn surged beside Felix, her spear flashing as she drove it through another bandit's chest, blood spraying across her jerkin. "For our kin, gut these curs!" she snarled, her voice fierce as a Highland charge, her braided hair swinging like a warrior's banner. Behind the spearwall, in the stone-walled church at Kirkhaven's heart, the remaining Fyrclad Kin stood resolute, guarding their young. Men gripped forge-hammers, their knuckles white from years at the anvil; women clutched mining picks, their edges honed for both stone and foe; elders wielded heavy mauls, their weathered faces set with hardened resolve. Children huddled behind them, their soft voices weaving a prayer—"O Creator, shield us"—the chapel's iron cross a towering beacon of faith against the encroaching dark.

Rauthar pressed his attack, his fire-dagger slashing at Felix's arm. The blade bit deep, crimson rivulets welling through the torn sleeve of his cloak, pain searing like a brand. Yet Felix stood firm, his eyes stoic. He thrust both hands forward, channeling a focused gale that roared like a thane's battle-cry, its force toppling a charred palisade log with a thunderous crash. The log rolled, blocking three bandits' advance, their clubs thudding uselessly against the blackened wood as they cursed and scrambled. The remaining bandits, leaderless without Rauthar's fiery command, faltered in their greed-driven charge, their cohesion unraveling like a frayed rope.

Felix raised his staff, the Wind Crystal blazing with a light that rivaled the firestone lamps. He unleashed a piercing gust, a lance of air that struck Rauthar's hand with surgical precision, disarming him in a single breath. The fire-dagger skittered across the earth, its serpent runes' glow fracturing into dim sparks before fading entirely. Rauthar stumbled, his massive frame crashing hard onto the scorched ground, dust rising in a choking cloud. Bryn seized the moment, surging forward with her spear raised, its iron tip glinting like a shard of starlight. "That's for ma Fyrclad Kin, ye cur!" she roared, driving the spear through Rauthar's chest. Blood pooled beneath him, dark and viscous, as the life drained from his crimson eyes, the heretical fire snuffed out at last.

The remaining bandits, their morale shattered, fled into the twilight, their cries echoing like the wails of lost souls across the Crags. Felix panted, his arm throbbing, the Wind Crystal's pulse fading as his strength waned. He knelt briefly, whispering, "Creator, guide even these lost souls," his faith a quiet anchor amidst the victory's cost. The militia lowered their spears, their tartan cloaks still snapping in the breeze, their firestone talismans glowing softly as Kirkhaven stood unbroken, its people's resolve as enduring as the Crags themselves.

The Fyrclad Kin surged from the church, their seventy voices a chorus—"Wind-lad!"—their calloused hands raising pitchforks and hammers in salute. Bryn's eyes gleamed with respect. "Ye fought like a storm, counterin' that fire-wieldin' cur!" she said, clasping his arm, her warrior's grip firm. Felix knelt by a burnt militiaman, blistered flesh oozing, applying Elara's sage, its sharp scent soothing, the man's breathing easing. "Creator heals through faith," he murmured, tending more wounded, sage easing burns, as the fourteen militia lowered their spears, their cheers hoarse but hearty. Women with patched shawls brought water, men with weathered cloaks carried the injured, their survivalist grit a quiet strength. The chapel's cross gleamed, a beacon against the serpent's lie, as the Fyrclad Kin sang, a testament to their enduring faith.

Hours later, as twilight deepened over Kirkhaven, the sky bruised with hues of indigo and amber, painting the village square in a solemn glow, Bryce approached through the flickering light of firestone lamps that stood like sentinels along the cobblestone paths. Their warm radiance cast dancing shadows, weaving a tapestry of light and dark across the gathered Fyrclad Kin. Bryce's white beard gleamed like frost under starlight, framing a face weathered by years of wisdom and toil, his eyes alight with the steady warmth of a hearth fire kindled in the Creator's name. In his hands, he bore a single, precious gift: a longsword, its scabbard plain and unadorned, a simple sheath of blackened leather that cloaked its glory, as if forged to conceal its sacred fire from unworthy eyes, a humble vessel for a blade of legend.

"Forged by our miners, a gift for yer quest, Torin's son," Bryce said, his voice warm and wise, resonant as a chant sung in the deep halls of Kirkhaven's mountain forges, carrying the weight of the Fyrclad Kin's unyielding trust. "This is Firesong Blade, born of iron and firestone, a spark of the Lion's flame kindled in the Creator's eternal light. Its steel is meant to smite heresy, lad, and we give it to ye with our faith, as a beacon for the Elemental Hero foretold in our ancient songs."

Bryce drew the longsword from its scabbard with a slow, deliberate motion, the steel whispering against leather like a sacred hymn unveiled in a cloistered sanctuary. At first, it appeared an ordinary blade, its surface a plain, polished grey, unremarkable as any warrior's steel, worn smooth by the hands of countless smiths. Yet as Bryce turned it in the firelight, runes etched deep into the blade flared to life, their ancient script glowing with a fierce, ember-like radiance, as if the volcano's heart had been wrought into the metal itself, awakened by the touch of destiny. Shards of firestone, inlaid along the blade's cross-etched fuller, shimmered like captured flames, their pulses dancing in rhythm with the firestone lamps, a testament to the Fyrclad Kin's craftsmanship and the divine will that guided their hammers through centuries of sacred toil. The hilt, wrapped in leather tanned from the hides of mountain goats that roamed the crags of Kirkhaven's peaks, offered a sturdy yet comforting grip, its balance so perfect it seemed to sing in the hand, crafted for powerful, sweeping strikes to cleave through the shadows of heresy in the heat of battle.

Felix's breath caught, his eyes widening as the runes' glow illuminated the square, casting fleeting patterns of light across the gathered Kin, their faces alight with reverence, as if beholding a relic from the Creator's own forge. The warmth emanating from the blade was subtle yet profound, a living echo of the volcano's power, intertwined with the unwavering faith of those who had shaped it. His cross pendant, a cherished gift from his father, hung heavy against his chest, now joined by the fiery promise of Firesong Blade. Bowing his head, Felix felt the weight of the honor bestowed upon him, a mantle of responsibility that pressed upon his heart like a sacred vow, heavy with the echoes of prophecy. "This is too great a gift, Bryce," he said softly, his voice trembling with humility, raw with the awe of one who stood at the threshold of a divine calling. "Surely, there are warriors of greater renown, more worthy to bear such a blade than I, a wanderer scarred by loss."

Bryce shook his head, his eyes kind but unyielding, like the granite roots of the mountains that cradled Kirkhaven. "Nay, lad, you're the Lord's Chosen Hero, marked by the Creator's hand for this path. The runes of Firesong Blade sing of the Elemental Hero, foretold in our oldest songs—born to wield the elements, to stand as a beacon against the dark tide of heresy. Kirkhaven's faith is with ye, and this blade is yers by right, a sacred trust to wield in the Creator's name." He sheathed the longsword with gentle reverence, the runes' glow fading into the scabbard's embrace, as if cloaking their fire until called forth by Felix's hand. He extended the blade to Felix, the leather-wrapped hilt an invitation to embrace a destiny woven in starlight and flame.

Felix knelt, his heart a tumult of humility and resolve, as if the spirits of ancient heroes—those who had wielded blades of legend against the shadows of old—whispered courage into his soul. He accepted the longsword with trembling hands, his fingers curling around the hilt, feeling the faint pulse of the firestone within, as if the blade were an extension of his very purpose, a sacred covenant forged in the Creator's light. The Firesong Blade, a symbol of the Fyrclad Kin's trust and the divine mission to protect Pangea's faithful. As he rose to his feet, the blade at his side felt both a burden and a blessing, its presence anchoring him to the battles yet to come against Daegon's heresy, against the darkness threatening Thegnfast, and to the knightly duty to uphold the Creator's will with honor and sacrifice. The runes' hidden glow lingered in his mind, their ancient script a promise of power and responsibility, etched not just in steel but in the very fabric of his soul, binding him to the legend of the Elemental Hero.

Bryce's hand rested briefly on Felix's shoulder, a gesture heavy with the trust of a people who had seen their world tremble under Daegon's shadow. "Wield it in His name, lad," he said, his voice a low rumble, like the distant stir of the volcano's heart, deep and eternal. "Let Firesong Blade sing of the Creator's justice, its runes a flame to guide ye through the gathering storm, to light the path of the Elemental Hero foretold."

Felix nodded, his throat tight with the weight of the moment, the blade's warmth kindling a fire within him—a resolve to honor the Kin's faith, to bear the mantle of the Elemental Hero with unwavering courage, and to face the trials ahead with a heart steeled by divine purpose. As he stepped back, the firestone lamps cast their radiant glow upon the square, their light a beacon illuminating the path forward, where the battles for Thegnfast and the soul of Pangea awaited, and the song of Firesong Blade would resound in the clash of steel and faith.

In Kirkhaven's central hall, the firestone lamps cast a ruddy glow, their warmth mingling with the Fyrclad Kin's chant— "By Creator's light, we stand, aye, stand!"—its Scottish lilt wrapping Felix like a cloak. He sat, the Firesong Blade heavy at his side, its firestone-inlaid steel a testament to the trust of strangers. The bowl of barley stew warmed his hands. Bryn joined him, her spear propped, her fierce gaze softened. "Ye've given us hope, lad," she said, her Scottish burr warm with respect. "Kirkhaven'll rebuild stronger for it. Rest here tonight—our hearth's yers till dawn." Felix nodded, gratitude steadying his trembling hands. Bryce stoked the hearth, firestone flaring. "The Fire Lion awaits, wind-lad, but a night's rest'll steel ye for its flame. Our prayers go wi' ye to save yer brother." Titania's cry pierced the night outside, her golden wings glinting, urging patience yet purpose.

As the Fyrclad Kin's voices faded into soft murmurs, Felix lay by the hearth, the hall's warmth easing his wounds— Rauthar's slash and the wraith's scratch—soothed by Elara's sage. At dawn, Felix rose, the hall quiet save for the hymn's echo— "Shield us frae the serpent's guile." Bryn and a few Kin stood at the half-charred palisade, their firestone talismans glinting in the first light. "Godspeed, wind-lad!" Bryn called, her spear raised in salute, her voice a Highland clarion. "Find yer brother, Felix—

Kirkhaven's prayers are wi' ye!" Felix clutched his staff, the Firesong Blade firm at his side, and stepped onto the rocky path toward the Ashen Crags. The plains' grasses swayed behind, fading into the crimson haze of volcanic peaks, Titania's wings glinting above. With the Creator's light guiding his steps, Felix trekked north, heart set on the Fire Lion's trial and Rowan's salvation, the dawn sky a promise of trials yet to come.

Chapter 4: The Fires of Faith

Dawn broke over the Ashen Crags, its light struggling through a crimson haze that cloaked jagged peaks and smoldering chasms. Felix Aldric set out north from Kirkhaven, turning slightly west before veering east between the mountain the village nestled against, and the watchtower to his far left, entering the Ashen Crags' eastward-turning entrance. The volcano's peak loomed, its fissures flaring red—the Fire Lion's domain, a forge of divine trial. The people of Kirkhaven echoed in his heart, mingling with Bryn's fierce salute and Duncan's tale of Rowan's defiance. "Creator, prepare me for Your flame," Felix prayed, gripping his staff, the Wind Crystal's airy pulse sharpening his senses as he neared the ledge where the Element Guardian awaited, his resolve forged by faith and family.

Titania's golden wings glinted above, her cry cutting through the haze. She descended, landing on a scorched outcrop, feathers shimmering like polished armor, eyes burning with sacred wisdom. Felix paused, catching his breath. "Titania, how does Daegon grant magic to mortal men?" he asked, voice steady, Firesong Blade's hilt firm in his grip. "His bandits wield fire, their serpent runes pulsing—how can heresy rival the Creator's light?" Titania's gaze darkened, wings rustling. "Daegon was a student of a monastic order on an island southeast of Pangea, Felix Aldric," she said, voice serene yet grave. "There, the Creator's faithful trained, and a rare few, gifted with magic even without Crystals, were called to serve. Daegon was such a one, his talent honed in prayer, sacred texts, and discipline, dedicated to our Lord. But greed and pride twisted him, as the Serpent's lie in Eden deceived. He betrayed his order, turning sacred knowledge to heresy, forging serpent runes to bind mortals' greed to his will. His magic, a shadow of the Creator's, corrupts, not creates. Trust in your faith, for only the Creator's light prevails." Felix nodded, resolve firm, the serpent's deceit a shadow he'd face with the Fire Lion's power. "Creator, keep me true," he prayed, Titania's wings flaring, urging him upward.

The path from the Ashen Crags' eastward-turning entrance steepened into a treacherous climb up the volcano's rough slopes, jagged rocks biting Felix's boots, the air heavy with sulfur. Sweat stung his eyes, matting his hair, his beard flecked with ash. Above, Titania's wings sliced the crimson sky, her cry a clarion call. The peak loomed ahead, its fissures glowing like the Fire Lion's promised mane. Each step honed his focus, the Creator's light his guide. Eldenwold's warm hearth and Kirkhaven's tartan-clad hope steadied him, the trial ahead a forge for his faith. "Creator, let Your wind and fire guide my hand," he whispered, staff firm.

The path opened to a narrow ledge jutting from the south side of the volcano's rim—a solemn stage carved by ancient eruptions, its blackened stone etched with radiant veins of firestone that pulsed like the Creator's heartbeat. The ledge, roughly thirty feet long and ten feet wide, barely accommodated two men standing abreast, its surface uneven with shallow cracks and scorched runes, half-erased by time, marking it as a sacred arena where faith was forged. Jagged spires, their tips crowned with glowing embers, framed the ledge like sentinels, rising ten feet high and casting shadows that danced with the caldera's ruddy glow to the north. To the south, a sheer drop plunged into a shadowed ravine, its depths lost in volcanic haze. Scattered claw marks crisscrossed the stone, evidence of past trials. The ledge's western edge, closest to Felix's approach, crumbled slightly, loose stones skittering into the molten depths below. The eastern end tapered to a point, where a single spire stood like a beacon, its firestone veins flaring brighter, as if awaiting the Lion's arrival. The air hummed with heat, sulfur stinging Felix's lungs, yet the Wind Crystal's pulse steadied his breath, its airy warmth a counterpoint to the volcano's fire. He stepped onto the ledge, boots scraping the uneven stone, staff planted firmly, eyes tracing the firestone veins toward the eastern spire. "This is Your arena, Lord," he murmured, the south-side stage a testament to the Creator's fiery judgment.

Titania landed on the eastern spire, her golden feathers shimmering, eyes burning with sacred wisdom. "Felix Aldric, the Fire Lion's trial awaits," she said, voice serene yet urgent. Her eagle gaze shifted east, piercing the haze to a small, flat, wide hill just beyond the Crags, where a compact camp stood stark against the open expanse, its handful of tents circled by unholy red torches flickering like wounds in the dawn light. "There, on that hill, Daegon's wraiths hold their camp. With my eyes, I see him— Rowan, your brother, bound yet unbowed, his cross pendant glinting as he prays." Felix's heart leapt, his staff trembling as he peered over the ledge. The camp's red fires flickered on the hill's broad crest, shadowed figures moving within, one bearing a spiral serpent on his forehead—a mage, Titania's gaze confirmed. "Rowan," Felix gasped, stepping toward the eastern edge, the caldera's heat singeing his cloak. "I could go to him now, Titania—fight those wraiths and free him!"

His mind raced, torn between duty and family. The Fire Lion was his first true test as Element Hero, a divine guardian whose flame could forge his path to Rowan. Yet his brother was so close, captive on that hill, his prayers fading with each passing hour. "Creator, guide me to save Rowan before it's too late," he thought, urgency heavy as the volcano's heat. He turned to Titania, voice raw. "Titania, the Lion's a beast of divine fire—its power could end me! Rowan's down there, sufferin' on that hill. What if I'm too late?" Titania's wings rustled, her voice a hymn on the wind. "Felix Aldric, the Creator's light weaves love and duty as one. The Fire Crystal is the key to break Daegon's chains—without it, Rowan remains lost, and Pangea falls. Face the Lion, prove your faith, and the path to your brother opens." Felix's breath hitched, the camp's red glow taunting him from the hill. "But a guardian, Titania—its strength could crush me," he pressed, Firesong Blade's hilt slick in his grip. "Trust the Creator's choice," she replied, eyes kind yet resolute. "Your heart, forged in Eldenwold's church and Kirkhaven's trust, is your strength. My prayers go with you, Element Hero."

The roar shook the mountain like a forge's bellows kindled by the Creator's breath—primal, divine, unyielding. Ignis, the Fire Lion, emerged from the volcano's heart, stepping onto the ledge with the deliberate grace of an ancient sentinel. Tall as a massive rhino, its tawny hide rippled over muscles hewn from divine fire, its mane a blazing crown of flame where each strand twisted like a molten whip against the firestone veins etched into the stone. Its eyes, vast as a thane's shield and glowing like embers from the ledge's core, locked onto Felix's, piercing through flesh to soul with stoic judgment. Felix stood unwavering, gripping Firesong Blade, the Wind Crystal's pulse steadying his chest, his breath calm under the weight of that gaze. Claws like forged steel scraped the stone, sparking against the radiant veins, yet Ignis did not lunge—it stood tall, a furnace of trial and fate.

"I am Ignis, Guardian of the Fire Crystal," it declared, voice deep and stoic, resonating like iron struck on an anvil, tempered by a beast's calm resolve. "Felix Aldric, chosen of the Creator, thou standest before me, a humble son clad in faith's mantle. The camp on yonder hill holds a mage, marked with Daegon's spiral serpent on his brow, a captain of his unholy forces. He sought my Crystal, his greed faltering before my flame, and fled. Dost thou dare claim what he could not?"

Felix steadied himself, the Wind Crystal pulsing like a heartbeat of resolve. "Ignis, I'm no mage, just a man called by the Creator," he said, voice firm against the heat. "I stand for Pangea, for my kin, for His light—to wield Your flame against Daegon's heresy."

Ignis's eyes narrowed, flames dancing in their depths. "Thy brother's fate drives thee, chosen one. Yet the Crystal is not won by haste. Prove thy faith here, or Daegon's forces will claim all."

Felix nodded, the camp's glow on the hill a spur to act. "The Creator's will comes first—His light will free Rowan. I'll face your trial."

Ignis tilted its head, a flicker of approval in its gaze. "A heart resolute. But know this, boy—the mage's serpent rune stirs even now on that hill, plotting to seize what thou might win. Earn my Crystal, then face him, or thy brother's hope fades."

Titania circled above, her cry piercing the haze. "Ignis speaks true, Felix—his flame burns away doubt. Claim the Crystal, and Daegon's captain falls."

Felix's resolve flared. "For You, Lord, and for Rowan," he vowed, eyes fixed on Ignis. "I'll earn it, then save him."

Ignis roared, flames surging from its mane, but it held its ground, testing Felix's will like a smith eyeing flawed ore. Felix planted his feet, raising Firesong Blade, its firestone glowing in harmony with the sacred stone. He knew from the old scrolls— fire guardians like Ignis drew strength from heat and earth, their flames feeding on stillness, vulnerable to motion and chill. The ledge was his ally: jagged spires for cover, firestone veins that could be stirred or shattered, and the ever-present sulfurous winds that could be bent to his command. No potions like the witchers of legend, but the Wind Crystal was his sign, his preparation—the air itself his blade against the blaze.

Ignis leapt first, claws slashing downward, flames trailing like a comet's tail across the ember-crowned spires. Felix dodged left, channeling a precise gust from the Wind Crystal to blur his steps, his cloak snapping as he pivoted behind a spire. The claw struck stone, cracking a rune and sending molten sparks flying. Felix countered swiftly, thrusting his hand to summon a focused whirlwind—not a broad gale, but a tight vortex aimed at Ignis's mane, drawing in the sulfur haze to smother the flames like dousing embers with foul air. Embers scattered like fireflies, the mane dimming for a heartbeat, exposing the hide beneath.

The Lion roared, undeterred, shaking its head to reignite the blaze brighter. It charged, breath unleashing a torrent of flame that scorched the ledge's edge, the firestone veins flaring in defiance. Felix anticipated it—fire beasts always led with breath when pressed—and raised a shimmering wind-shield, angling it not just to block but to redirect the heat upward, superheating the air above Ignis and forcing it to rear back from the backlash. Heat stung his face, singeing his brow, but he pressed the advantage, spinning Firesong Blade in a wind-sharpened arc. The blade clashed against Ignis's claws, sparks erupting like shattered stars over the firestone etchings. The impact jarred his arms, but the wind's momentum carried through, nicking the Lion's foreleg and drawing a hiss of divine ichor that sizzled on the stone.

The ledge shook, a fissure cracking through a rune, molten rock bubbling below. Ignis pressed, its mane lashing out like whips, one strand grazing Felix's arm where a bandit's old slash lingered. Pain flared hot as forge-iron, blood welling, but Felix twisted away, using the environment: he channeled a gust to lift loose stones from the crumbling edge, hurling them like shrapnel into Ignis's eyes. Dust and embers clouded the air, buying him a moment to circle right, toward the southern brink where the sulfur vents were thickest.

"Thy heart holds, but dost thou falter?" Ignis rumbled, voice steady as stone, probing like a witcher's silvered trap.

Felix's mind flashed—Eldenwold's church, Kirkhaven's people, Rowan's prayers fading in Daegon's grip on that hill. "I stand for His light—to save my kin!" he shouted, thrusting both hands to summon a gale like a thane's battle-cry. It pushed Ignis back, claws scraping for purchase, but Felix didn't stop there—he wove the wind through the vents, stirring a choking cloud of sulfur that clung to the Lion's flaming mane, weakening its blaze like acid on hide. Ignis staggered, flames guttering, and Felix lunged, Firesong Blade slashing a shallow gash across its flank. The cut smoked, the wind amplifying the strike to bite deeper than steel alone.

Ignis shook free, roaring as it leapt again, faster, a claw grazing Felix's shoulder in a spray of crimson. He winced, boots slipping on loose stones that skittered into the ravine's shadowed drop, firestone veins flaring hot underfoot. Sulfur burned his lungs, but he prayed, "Creator, guide my strength!" The Wind Crystal hummed, steadying him as he thrust upward, summoning a whirlwind to lift him above the ledge. At its peak, he twisted, channeling a sharp downdraft laced with vent fumes directly into Ignis's maw mid-roar, turning its own breath against it in a choking backlash.

He landed near the eastern spire with a crack, a rune flaring gold beneath his boots. Ignis quaked the ledge in pursuit, cracks splitting another rune that bled molten light. "Thy faith burns bright, boy!" Ignis declared, its voice a deep rumble tempered by divine calm. "One final test!"

It unleashed its torrent—a wall of flame scorching the center, runes glowing fiercely. Felix, leaning on his staff, met the gaze of those ember eyes. This was the crux: fire guardians tested not just strength, but harmony—the willingness to merge with the element rather than conquer it. He thrust both hands, the Wind Crystal flaring, summoning a roaring gale that didn't oppose the flame but encircled it, feeding oxygen to heighten the blaze while steering it into a contained vortex. Embers and wind swirled in a divine storm, the ledge trembling as if the mountain itself judged. Ignis leapt through the maelstrom, claws slashing, but Felix dodged with wind-blurred grace, his blade striking true once more—a deeper cut across the Lion's chest, wind and firestone harmonizing in a spark that illuminated the runes like a prophecy fulfilled.

The storm peaked, Ignis's flames clashing against Felix's gale in a final, cataclysmic burst that cracked the ledge's heart, molten veins pulsing in rhythm with Felix's pounding heart. Ignis landed heavily, its mane flickering low, gaze softening—not in defeat but in recognition. The Lion bowed its massive head, breath steadying as the storm ebbed. "Thou hast proven thyself, Element Hero—not by domination, but by faith. Thy wind tempers my fire, as the Creator intended."

The Fire Crystal materialized, floating before Felix, its molten glow pulsing like the volcano's heart, warm and radiant.

He reached out, and it merged with his chest alongside the pendant in a flash of divine light, fiery power coursing through his veins to join the Wind Crystal's airy pulse—a union that restored much of his stamina, leaving only scars of trial. Ignis rose, mane flaring one last time. "Seek thy brother in the camp on yonder hill, where the serpent-marked mage lurks. Wield the Crystals wisely against Daegon, and his heresy falls. But remember, boy: true guardianship is eternal vigilance."

With a final roar echoing like a forge's pulse, Ignis turned and leapt into the volcano's heart, vanishing into the molten depths. The caldera flared in reverence, the ledge's sacred scars humming with purpose. Felix stood, breath heaving, the twin Crystals' glow kindling his soul. The sun neared midday, piercing the haze as Titania soared above, her cry sharp. "The Creator's light prevails, Felix. Fire and wind unite in you—look now to the hill, where unholy torches burn."

Felix peered east, the camp's red flickers on the flat hill beyond the Crags—a short trek across ash-strewn slopes, less than a league away. Rowan's prayers echoed faintly in his heart, urging him despite aching limbs. "Creator, let Your wind and fire lead me to Rowan," he prayed, sheathing Firesong Blade, its edge warm with Kirkhaven's trust. With a final glance at the volcano's fading heat, he descended the treacherous path under the late morning sun, each step resolute, faith and fraternal love driving him toward the serpent-marked mage in the Creator's sacred light—the midday sky a beacon for trials yet to come.

Chapter 5: The Flaming Winds of Vengeance

Midday's harsh light pierced the Ashen Crags' crimson haze, casting jagged shadows as Felix Aldric descended the volcanic path, his boots grinding against ash-strewn stone, each step a testament to his weary resolve. The sulfurous air stung his lungs and burned his eyes, yet the twin glows of the Wind Crystal and Fire Crystal pulsed warmly against his chest. Firesong Blade hung sheathed at his side, its firestone-inlaid steel a silent vow of the Fyrclad Kin's trust, its weight a steady anchor. Titania's golden wings glinted above, her cry cutting through the haze like a clarion call, urging him toward a smaller hill within the Ashen Crags east of the volcano ledge, where unholy red torches flickered like open wounds against the noon sky—visible yet too distant to discern individuals. "Creator, guide me to Rowan," Felix prayed, gripping his staff, as he descended the volcano and ascended slightly toward the camp atop the hill, his legs aching from the night's climb. Rowan's grin by the Cragbeck, daring him to skip stones farther, flashed in his mind—a tether to hope amidst the Creator's trial.

A smaller hill rose within the Ashen Crags east of the volcano ledge, its broad, barren crest ringed by a compact camp of tattered tents, their canvas stained with soot and ash, flapping in the sulfurous breeze—visible from the ledge but too distant for clear detail. Six wraiths, Daegon's minions, patrolled the perimeter, their smoky forms writhing like shadows torn from the Creator's light, their eyes blazing with a coiling red glow sharp as the Ashen Crags' haze. Their obsidian claws, long as scythes, slashed the air, trailing unholy mist that stung Felix's lungs with a sour, cold bite. At the camp's heart stood a cage of twisted iron, its bars pulsing with profane runes that glowed like molten embers, sealing a figure within. Though too far to see clearly, Titania's keen eyes had revealed Rowan shirtless, slumped against the bars, his body a map of suffering: whip scars, deep and festering, crisscrossed his back like cruel runes, mingling with old battle scars from fights long past; his face, once bright with a riverbank grin, was gaunt, bruised, and streaked with dried blood, his fair hair matted with ash. Yet his lips moved in whispered prayer, unbowed despite days of torture. Felix's heart clenched, rage surging like a storm. "Creator, let Your light burn away this evil," he murmured, the Crystals flaring, their warmth a divine spark—but Rowan's suffering kindled a darker fire within him.

The wraiths turned, their red eyes locking onto Felix, hissing in a chilling chorus, "The Crystals belong to Daegon. Give them to us." Their smoky forms surged forward, claws slashing with predatory grace. Felix planted his feet, the Wind Crystal's airy pulse surging through his veins, steadying his trembling hands. He thrust out his hand, summoning a roaring gust that caught the first wraith mid-lunge, its form fraying like burnt cloth, embers scattering across the ash-strewn hill. The second wraith darted left, its claws raking his cloak, tearing fabric with a sharp rip. Felix spun Firesong Blade, the Fire Crystal flaring, and unleashed a burst of flame that engulfed the creature, its shriek fading into ash as it dissolved. Two more wraiths flanked him, moving in eerie unison, their red eyes coiling like serpents in shadow. Felix darted with wind-enhanced speed, his cloak snapping, but a claw grazed his arm, reopening the bandit's old scratch, blood welling in crimson rivulets. Pain seared, yet he pivoted, channeling a whirlwind that hurled one wraith skyward, its form splintering in the gust, embers raining like fireflies. The other lunged, claws arcing toward his chest, but Felix raised his staff, a fiery blast incinerating it, the heat singeing his beard as ash drifted down.

The final two wraiths circled, their hisses a low, menacing drone, their smoky forms weaving through the tents like specters. Felix's breath quickened, his legs trembling from the strain, sweat matting his dirty blonde hair. One wraith lunged, claws slashing at his side, but Felix twisted, summoning a gust that pushed it back, its claws scraping the earth. The other struck from behind, its obsidian claws grazing his shoulder, drawing a sharp sting of blood that soaked his cloak. Felix grunted, pain lancing through him, but he spun, Firesong Blade flashing with firestone glow. He channeled a focused flame and struck, incinerating the wraith in a burst of embers. The last wraith hissed, its red eyes flaring, and charged with unnatural speed, claws aimed at his heart. Felix planted his staff, the Wind Crystal flaring, and summoned a vortex that trapped the wraith, spinning it high above the hill. With a thrust of his hand, he ignited the vortex with fire, the creature shrieking as it burned to ash, its remains scattering across the barren crest. Felix stood panting, the Crystals' warmth pulsing erratically, his body aching but resolute, determination forged in

Rowan's suffering. "For you, brother," he whispered, eyes fixed on the cage, its runes flickering faintly.

From the camp's heart, a figure emerged: Valthor, the serpent-marked mage, his forehead bearing Daegon's spiral rune glowing like molten iron. Taller than Rauthar, his lean frame thrummed with profane energy, dark robes billowing as if stirred by an unseen, unholy gale. His serpentine eyes fixed on Felix, a cold smile curling his lips—sharp and deliberate. "Ze Element Hero," he said, voice low, precise, carrying the faint German accent of Kroneburg's ancient halls, each syllable measured, edged with arrogance honed by years of betrayed faith. "A boy, clutching at divine sparks he cannot comprehend." No trace of mockery softened his tone; it was a blade, cutting through the sulfur-choked air with calculated disdain.

"I am Valthor, once a priest of ze Creator's light, now battlemage and herald of Daegon's vill," he continued, his words deliberate, laced with bitter pride, the German lilt subtly shaping his speech. "Ze Creator offered mercy, veak and fleeting. Daegon granted power eternal, unyielding. His rune binds my soul to flame and shadow, and through me, his dominion rises." The serpent rune pulsed—a twisted mockery of his forsaken vows—as his hands wove arcs of unholy flame, the air crackling with malevolent heat.

Felix lunged, Firesong Blade slicing the air, trailing a gust of wind. Valthor moved like a specter, blurring with unnatural speed, countering with a lance of unholy flame that grazed Felix's arm, blood welling from the bandit's earlier slash. Felix spun, summoning a whirlwind to parry Valthor's next strike, their clash sparking like shattered stars across the barren hill. Valthor's smile didn't falter, his movements fluid, precise, dodging Felix's fiery slashes with an ease that bordered on disdain. The rune flared as he unleashed a volley of lightning, one bolt striking Felix's shoulder. Pain seared through the Fire Lion's wound, driving him to one knee, his cloak smoldering.

Valthor pressed forward, his speed a blur, a fiery arc slicing Felix's side, tearing cloth and flesh in a thin, burning trail. The battle surged across the hill's crest, Valthor's power relentless. He conjured a sphere of unholy flame, its heat scorching the earth, pinning Felix against a charred tent frame, canvas curling into ash. "Your Creator forsakes you," Valthor said, his voice calm, cutting, the faint German accent underscoring his words like a ritual chant. "Faith crumbles before Daegon's might." He hurled a blazing spear, its tip grazing Felix's chest, missing his heart by a breath.

Felix's vision blurred, legs trembling under the weight of wounds and exhaustion. Sulfur and blood choked his lungs as he slumped, staff slipping, Rowan's cage looming in his sight—his brother's scarred form motionless within. "I won't fail him," Felix rasped, voice barely audible, body shaking. "Creator, lend me strength." The Wind and Fire Crystals pulsed faintly, their divine light flaring against the darkness, coursing through his veins. Pain dulled, resilience surged, as if the Creator's hand steadied his faltering frame.

Valthor towered upon the barren hill, unscathed amidst the smoldering wreckage of his camp. His rune-scarred face twisted into a sneer, his voice cold and precise. "Your brother's screams vere sweeter zan your prayers!" he taunted, his words a venomous blade. He raised a hand, summoning another fiery burst, its heat singeing the air.

Felix's heart pounded, a storm of rage and faith surging within him, drowning the chill of doubt that Valthor's words sought to kindle. The memory of Rowan's bloodied form—whip scars crisscrossing his back, his anguished cries echoing through the night—seared Felix's mind, fueling a fire that threatened to consume his soul. He pushed himself up from the ash-strewn ground, trembling, his eyes blazing into Valthor's, unfazed by the mockery that sought to unravel him. "The Creator's light prevails," he declared, his voice a defiant hymn, gripping both fists as the Elemental Crystals at his chest flared brighter, their azure and crimson glow pulsing like twin stars awakened from ancient slumber. The air stirred, a restless whisper across the hill, and twin tornadoes roared into being beside him, their winds howling like the wrath of the Creator's elemental guardians, swirling dust and ash in their wake, scouring the earth as if to cleanse it of Daegon's taint.

Valthor's grin widened, a predator's delight glinting in his serpentine eyes. "Zo, you still have some fight in you," he mocked, his voice a blade's edge. But Felix, driven by Rowan's suffering and a surge of divine will, felt the Crystals' warmth course through him, a sacred fire kindling his resolve. Flames erupted within the tornadoes, merging wind and fire into blazing

71

whirlwinds that roared across the hill, their heat charring the earth, their light casting jagged shadows across Valthor's rune-scarred face. His sneer faltered, awe and fear flickering in his eyes like a candle caught in a gale. "No one has merged ze elements except Master Daegon!" he gasped, his bravado crumbling, his voice trembling as the firestorm's radiance illuminated the hill—a divine rebuke to his heresy.

Felix extended both arms, the flaming tornadoes surging forward, their relentless pull consuming the camp's tattered tents in a blaze of divine wrath, the earth blackened beneath their fury like a canvas seared by the Creator's judgment. Halfway to Valthor, the twin whirlwinds merged into one massive fire tornado, its roar a thunderous hymn of retribution, its flames spiraling upward like a pillar of light piercing the heavens. Valthor screamed, clawing at the air, his dark robes incinerating as the tornado dragged him toward its molten heart, the serpent rune on his face pulsing weakly—a fading ember of his master's power. "Mercy, Hero!" he begged, his voice breaking, a wretched plea swallowed by the firestorm's din.

High above, a sharp, urgent cry pierced the sky, and Titania descended, her golden wings glinting like a beacon of the Creator's light, her celestial form radiant against the smoke-choked heavens. Her voice, clear as a clarion call, cut through Felix's rage. "Felix, abandon vengeance! End his suffering in the Creator's light, not the shadow of wrath!" Her words struck like a hammer on anvil, stirring the scriptures etched in Felix's heart: *Vengeance is mine, saith the Creator, and justice shall be wrought in mercy.* His soul wavered, torn between the consuming fire of retribution and the quiet call of faith. Rowan's scars flashed in his mind, but so too did the teachings of his father, Torin.

Struggling, Felix whispered, "Lord, cleanse my heart of this fury," his voice a trembling prayer, barely audible above the firestorm's roar. He thrust his hands upward, the Crystals flaring with a final, blinding burst of light, as if the Creator Himself had answered. The fire tornado erupted in a radiant conflagration, consuming Valthor in a surge of divine flame, his form reduced to ashes that scattered across the hill, borne away by the wind like chaff from a sacred threshing floor. The serpent rune's glow extinguished, its dark power broken, leaving only silence in its wake.

Felix stood, breath heaving, the Crystals' warmth fading to a gentle pulse, their light dimming as the hill fell still, the air heavy with the scent of charred earth and fading smoke. His soul was clouded with the weight of his near-fall to vengeance—a shadow that lingered like a wound unhealed. He looked to Titania, her golden wings folding as she alighted upon the hill, her eyes kind yet solemn, a guardian of the Creator's will. "You chose mercy, Felix," she said softly, her voice a balm to his troubled heart. "The path of the Element Hero is not vengeance, but redemption." Felix nodded, his throat tight. The hill, scarred and silent, bore witness to his victory and his struggle, as the path to Thegnfast loomed ahead—a crucible of faith and fire yet to be faced.

Adrenaline ebbed, and Felix staggered, his legs nearly giving way, vision swimming with ash and blood. The Crystals' divine energy pulsed faintly, sustaining his battered body, their light knitting his strength just enough to keep him upright. Emotions churned: anger at Valthor's cruelty, regret for his vengeful impulse, joy at Rowan's imminent freedom. He turned to the cage, its profane runes flickering like dying embers, their unholy glow wavering under the Crystals' radiant power. Felix raised his hand, the Wind and Fire Crystals flaring in unison, their light weaving a surge of divine energy. He channeled a focused gust laced with flame—the wind slicing through the iron bars like a blade, the fire melting their rune-etched surfaces. The cage groaned, its structure buckling, then collapsed into a heap of smoldering metal, the runes extinguished in a final hiss of unholy mist. Rowan stumbled forward, barely conscious, his gaunt frame trembling, whip scars raw and deep across his back, festering and untreated. "Felix," he rasped, voice a faint thread as he reached out. Felix's throat tightened, tears burning as he saw the brutal scars—a map of suffering etched into his brother's flesh. He knelt, steadying Rowan, and lifted him over his shoulder, the weight heavy but resolute. "I've got you, brother," he murmured, the Crystals' warmth a faint comfort against his clouded mind.

The trek back to Kirkhaven began under the fading light of late afternoon, each step a battle against exhaustion down the ash-strewn slopes. Rowan's frail form grew heavier, his shallow breaths fading into silence. Halfway down the hill, as dusk painted the sky in hues of amber and crimson, Rowan's body went limp, his consciousness slipping, the weight of his tortured frame dragging at Felix's wounded shoulder. Felix stumbled, pain lancing through him, blood soaking his cloak. His legs trembled, the sulfurous air choking his lungs, each breath a struggle. "Creator, lend me strength," he prayed, gripping Rowan tighter, his brother's cross pendant glinting faintly against his chest. The ash-dusted path stretched endlessly, the Crags' crimson haze blurring his vision. Felix's knees buckled, and he sank to one knee, Rowan's weight nearly toppling him. He clutched his staff, its familiar grain grounding him, and whispered, "Rowan, stay with me." Memories surged: Rowan's grin by the Cragbeck, daring him to skip stones; Elara's steady hands tending wounds; Torin's firm grip teaching him to wield a staff. "I won't lose you again," Felix vowed, pushing himself up, his wounded arm screaming in protest. The Crystals pulsed softly, their divine light coursing through his veins, easing the agony in his shoulder and arm, granting him the strength to rise. He adjusted Rowan's limp form, blood from his own wounds mingling with the ash, each step a testament to his resolve.

The path wound through jagged rocks, volcanic ash dusting Felix's boots, stinging his eyes as night fell, the stars emerging faintly through the sulfurous haze. The weight of Rowan's unconscious body tested his endurance. His shoulder burned, now caked with dust. Felix's breath came in ragged gasps, his vision wavering as exhaustion clawed at him. He paused, leaning against a blackened outcrop. "Creator, guide us home," he prayed, Rowan's shallow breaths a faint rhythm against his back. The distant glow of Kirkhaven's firestone lamps flickered on the horizon—a beacon through the haze—but the path seemed to stretch forever. Felix's legs trembled, his wounds aching, yet Rowan's weight anchored his purpose. He pressed forward, each step heavier, the Crystals' warmth a fading spark against the sulfurous air.

A shout broke the silence under the night sky, sharp and fierce. Captain Bryn, her braided hair swinging, led three Fyrclad Kin scouts, their tartan cloaks catching the starlight, firestone talismans glinting at their chests. Her fierce gaze softened, joy and shock mingling in her Scottish lilt. "Felix, ye're alive—and yer brother!" she cried, rushing forward. "Why'd you come, Bryn? I thought you couldn't leave Kirkhaven," Felix rasped, his voice weary, strength fading as he swayed under Rowan's weight. Bryn's eyes gleamed with resolve. "One o' our scouts saw a flamin' tornado in the distance at dusk, lad, blazin' like the Creator's wrath. I couldnae sit idle—I gathered the lads to be sure ye were alive!" She gestured to the scouts, their weathered faces set with purpose as they stepped forward. "Let us help ye back to the haven," Bryn said, her voice firm yet warm, her warrior's resolve a beacon. One scout, a lanky youth with soot-stained hands, took Rowan's limp form, easing the burden from Felix's wounded shoulder. Another offered a waterskin, its cool contents soothing Felix's parched throat. Felix nodded, gratitude steadying his trembling limbs, as the scouts supported Rowan.

The group trekked toward Kirkhaven under the starlit night, the ash-strewn slopes giving way to the Windweave Plains' swaying grasses, their golden hues faintly visible in the moonlight. Felix's wounds throbbed, blood crusting his cloak, but Bryn's presence and the scouts' strength bolstered him. Rowan's unconscious form swayed gently, carried by the scouts, his whip scars raw and angry under the starlight. Felix's heart ached, the sight of his brother's suffering fueling his resolve. "Creator, heal him as You've guided me," he prayed. Kirkhaven's firestone lamps grew brighter, their ruddy glow a testament to the Fyrclad Kin's enduring faith. Bryn marched beside him, her spear propped, voice gruff yet warm. "Ye fought like a storm, lad, savin' yer brother. Kirkhaven's prayers were wi' ye." Felix's throat tightened, Rowan's faint breaths a reminder of his vow. "I'll bring him home," he said, voice firm despite his exhaustion. The haven's half-charred palisade loomed ahead, its firestone lamps a beacon of hope, as Felix carried his brother toward healing—his heart heavy with the Creator's light and the shadow of vengeance, the Windweave Plains stretching behind in the sacred starlight.

Chapter 6: A Time for Healing

The group trudged wearily through the half-charred palisade of Kirkhaven, the firestone lamps casting a warm, flickering glow on the stone paths. Captain Bryn led the way, her spear propped on her shoulder, her braided hair catching the light. Behind her, the scouts carried Rowan's limp form, his cross pendant glinting faintly in the dim light. Felix stumbled alongside, his legs heavy with exhaustion, his wounds throbbing with each step. The air was thick with the scent of ash and herbs, a reminder of both the battles fought and the healing that awaited.

As they approached the healer's quarters—a sturdy stone building with a cross etched above the door—Bryn called out, "Fiona! We've got wounded!" The door swung open, and a woman stepped out, her long dark brown hair tied back, her green eyes sharp with concern. She was slightly taller than average. "Bring them in," she said, her voice calm and authoritative.

Felix barely registered the interior of the healer's quarters—shelves lined with jars of herbs, a firestone lamp burning brightly—before his vision blurred. He felt hands guiding him to a bed, the softness of the mattress a stark contrast to the hard ground he'd slept on for days. His eyes closed, and he sank into darkness.

When Felix awoke, the room was bathed in the soft light of midday. He blinked, disoriented, and tried to sit up. Pain lanced through his shoulder and arm, and he winced, looking down to see his torso wrapped in bandages. His shirt was gone, and the scent of sage and other herbs filled the air.

To his left, on another bed, lay Rowan. His brother's chest rose and fell with shallow breaths, his face pale and bruised, but he was alive. Felix's heart clenched at the sight of the whip scars crisscrossing Rowan's back, still raw and untreated. Yet, despite the wounds, Rowan's cross pendant rested on his chest, a symbol of the faith that had sustained him.

The door creaked open, and the woman from earlier entered, her smile brightening as she saw Felix awake. "Ye're awake already, lad," she said, her voice soft and warm, with a gentle Scottish lilt. "I didn't expect you to mend so quickly from those wounds."

She approached, checking his bandages with practiced ease. "I'm Fiona, healer and servant of the church here in Kirkhaven. You're Felix, aye? Bryn spoke of you." Felix nodded, his throat dry. "Yes, ma'am. Thank you for helping us." Fiona's eyes twinkled with kindness. "It's the Creator's guid hand that's brought you here, safe and on the mend, lad. Your brother's a strong soul, too. He's not yet awake, but his wounds are tended, and he's holding steady." Felix's gaze drifted to Rowan's cross pendant, identical to his own, carved by their father, Torin. The sight of it brought a flood of memories, and Felix closed his eyes, letting them wash over him.

He was ten years old, kneeling beside Rowan in Eldenwold's church, the air thick with incense. Their mother, Elara, stood at the front, leading the congregation in prayer.

79

"Creator, renew our hearts in Your light," she intoned, and the villagers echoed her words. Rowan nudged Felix, whispering, "Do you think the Creator hears us?" Felix frowned, serious even then. "Of course He does. Mother says He's always listening." Rowan grinned, his eyes sparkling with mischief. "Then I'll ask Him for a new fishing rod." Felix rolled his eyes but couldn't help smiling. Even in prayer, Rowan found a way to be himself.

The memory faded, replaced by another.

The Feast of the Creator was the highlight of the year in Eldenwold. The village square was adorned with garlands of wildflowers, and tables groaned under the weight of food—roasted meats, fresh bread, and bowls of fruit. At the center, a large loaf of bread and a jug of wine sat on a table draped with a white cloth, symbols of the Creator's sacrifice and covenant.

Felix, now fifteen, helped his father carve the bread, while Rowan poured the wine into cups. "Remember, boys," Torin said, his voice deep and steady, "this feast honors the Creator's gift of life and redemption. We share this meal as one family under His light." Rowan nodded solemnly, but as soon as Torin turned away, he whispered to Felix, "I bet I can eat more bread than you." Felix laughed, the sound mingling with the chants rising from the church. Those were simpler times, before the strange lights and Rowan's disappearance.

Fiona, who had been tending to Rowan, glanced over. "He'll come round, Felix. The Creator's guid hand is upon him, just as it's upon you, keeping you both safe." Felix nodded, drawing strength from her gentle words. "Thank you, Fiona. For everything." She smiled, her green eyes warm and reassuring. "Rest now, lad. Ye both need it. The Creator's work isn't finished yet, but for now, ye're in guid hands."

As the afternoon wore on, Felix drifted in and out of sleep, his mind a tapestry of memories and prayers. Each time he woke, he checked on Rowan, whose breathing grew steadier with each passing hour. The healer's quarters were quiet, save for the occasional murmur of voices from outside or the soft hum of a hymn from the church. In those moments of stillness, Felix reflected on his journey, the divine summons, the battles fought, and the trials yet to come. But above all, he thought of the Creator's grace, which had carried him through the darkest hours and led him to this place of healing. And as the sun dipped below the horizon, casting a golden glow through the window, Felix whispered a prayer of gratitude. For though the road ahead was uncertain, he knew he was not alone. The Creator's light would guide him, just as it always had.

Exhaustion weighed heavily on Felix, his body aching from the trials he had endured. He glanced once more at Rowan, whose steady breathing brought a sense of peace. With a final, weary sigh, Felix allowed himself to drift into a deep, healing sleep.

The next morning, the soft light of dawn filtered through the window, gently rousing Felix from his slumber. He blinked, disoriented for a moment, before the familiar surroundings of the healer's quarters came into focus. His body still ached, the wounds from his battles protesting as he shifted, but he found he could slowly lift himself up, propping his back against the headboard.

The door creaked open, and Fiona entered, her big smile lighting up the room despite the dull pain that lingered in Felix's limbs. Her long, dark brown hair was tied back, and her green eyes sparkled with kindness.

"Guid mornin', lad," she said, her voice soft and melodic, carrying that gentle Scottish lilt. "Ye're lookin' a wee bit stronger today."

Felix managed a small smile in return, though the effort tugged at his sore muscles. "Thank you, Fiona. I'm… getting there." He hesitated, his gaze drifting to Rowan's bed. "How's my brother doing?"

Fiona followed his gaze, her expression softening. "Rowan's makin' a slow but steady recovery. The Cragmoor folk are known for their resilience, aye? He's provin' that true."

Felix nodded, a faint chuckle escaping his lips. "Rowan's always been bold, stubborn, too, at times. I suppose that's what's kept him fighting."

Fiona chuckled warmly, the sound a soothing balm. "Aye, a touch o' stubbornness can carry ye far."

Just then, the door opened again, and Elder Bryce stepped inside. His big white beard framed a warm smile, his eyes twinkling with relief and joy at seeing Felix upright. He wore his tartan cloak, the firestone talisman glinting at his chest.

"Aye, it's good to see ye alive and up, lad," Bryce said, his voice rich with a warm Scottish burr. "Ye had us worried."

Felix inclined his head respectfully. "I'm grateful for your care, Elder Bryce." He paused as Bryce's gaze settled on the glow around his chest, which glowed faintly with the power of both the Wind and Fire Crystals.

Bryce's smile widened. "How did the trial go, lad?"

Felix looked down at the chest, the twin glows a testament to his victories. "It went well," he said. "I was able to claim the Fire Crystal and rescue Rowan afterward." His voice grew somber as he continued. "But I faced a mage named Valthor, marked by Daegon. He had a southeastern accent, spoke of power and dominion."

Bryce's brow furrowed, his expression turning thoughtful. "Valthor, ye say? I don't know the name. It's not common anymore to see folk from the southeastern reaches this far up the northwestern side of Pangea—not since the crusades of the third century, when the lands were purged of pagans. Their capital, Kroneburg, lies on the southern coast, near the eastern corner of the continent. Its harbor sails the Ocean of Cordelia."

Felix's interest sharpened. "Kroneburg, I've heard of this place."

"Aye," Bryce replied, his voice taking on a storyteller's cadence. "A grand city, vibrant with scholars, dedicated knights, and a fierce devotion to the Creator—more so than most in Pangea. A bastion of faith and knowledge."

Felix's mind drifted southward, away from the rugged northwest of Pangea where Kirkhaven stood. He thought of Thegnfast, the grand city of his people, nestled on the northwestern shore of Gildermere. The lake shimmered in his memory, its vast, tranquil waters fed by the Cragbeck River, which flowed down from the north, curving slightly west before opening into Gildermere's wide expanse. The lake then narrowed again, its waters winding toward the sea on the southwestern edge of the continent. Thegnfast, down south from his village, stood as a vibrant testament to his people's heritage—its halls alive with scholarly works, famed warriors, and literature steeped in tradition. He recalled the towering spires piercing the sky, the bustling markets, and the great library where ancient scrolls whispered tales of valor and faith.

As a boy, Felix had stood in awe of Thegnfast's training grounds, watching warriors spar with a grace that belied their strength. It was a city where the Creator's light burned brightly, a beacon of resilience and wisdom bordering the southern half of Gildermere. That memory warmed him now, a fleeting comfort amidst the storm brewing in his heart.

But the warmth faded as his thoughts darkened. If Daegon's forces, marked by heresy and ambition, were already striking this far north, then even Thegnfast—mighty and wise— was not beyond their reach. The realization struck him like a blade: no sanctuary would stand if Daegon's shadow grew unchecked. *I must recover swiftly. I cannot fail them.*

He met Bryce's steady gaze, resolve hardening his voice. "I need to heal soon," he said. "Daegon's plans are advancing, and I have to stop him."

Bryce nodded solemnly. "Rest now, lad. Gather yer strength. When ye're ready, we'll stand with ye."

Fiona finished tending to Rowan's wounds, her hands steady and practiced as she adjusted the final bandage. Standing up, she brushed her hands on her apron and looked at Felix with a warm, reassuring smile. "I expect him tae make a full recovery quick enough, lad," she said, her gentle Scottish lilt softening the words. "But he'll need tae eat and rest proper. I'll send for some food for ye both."

Bryce, who had been lingering near the doorway, gave a nod of agreement. "I must be going to help the village keep rebuilding after the battle," he said, his deep voice carrying a mix of warmth and duty. "I'll tell Bryn ye're doing well, Felix. She might visit later, though she's a workaholic, that one." He let out a hearty chuckle, his big white beard bouncing slightly as he grinned.

Felix managed a small smile, his first in what felt like ages. "Thank you, both of you," he said, his voice still faint but filled with gratitude.

As Fiona and Bryce stepped out of the room, Felix's gaze drifted back to Rowan. He noticed a slight color returning to his brother's pale cheeks—a subtle but welcome sign of recovery. Relief washed over him, loosening the tight knot of worry in his chest. Exhausted but comforted, he lay back down on his own bed, his body aching but his spirit lighter. Closing his eyes, he whispered a quiet prayer: "Creator, watch over Rowan and all who've helped us. Guide me to protect them, as You've protected me."

His mind wandered to home—Eldenwold's familiar thatched roofs, the soothing rush of the Cragbeck River, and the unshakable faith of his parents. Then, his thoughts shifted to his quest, the weight of it settling over him once more. He wondered when Titania would appear again, her divine presence a beacon on this uncertain path.

A soft knock broke his reverie. The door creaked open, and a familiar face stepped inside—the young girl who had offered him food when he first stumbled into Kirkhaven. She carried a tray laden with a steaming bowl of meat, fresh bread, and a cup of milk, the rich aroma filling the room. She looked about eleven, with brown hair tied back and bright brown eyes that sparkled with quiet cheer.

"I'm happy ye're okay," she said, her voice sweet and genuine as she set the tray down beside him. "I'm Isla. I help my mother, Fiona, around here."

Felix smiled warmly, his stomach growling in anticipation. "Thank you, Isla. This smells great."

She beamed shyly. "I'll pray for ye to get well soon," she said before slipping out of the room, her footsteps light and quick.

Felix ate slowly, the hot meal warming him from the inside out. The tender meat and fresh bread filled him with a comforting energy, and by the time he finished, he felt noticeably better. His eyelids grew heavy, and soon he drifted into a deep, restful sleep.

Later that night, Felix stirred awake. The room was dim, lit only by the faint glow of a firestone lamp. His body still ached, but the soreness had dulled, and he felt stronger. Carefully, he swung his legs over the side of the bed and stood, wincing at the initial stiffness. He glanced at Rowan, still sleeping peacefully, and decided to step outside for some fresh air.

The night air was cool and crisp as he walked slowly toward the fields of Kirkhaven. The moon hung high, bathing the landscape in silver light. As he breathed deeply, a familiar silhouette appeared against the sky—Titania, her golden wings glinting as she descended gracefully to the ground before him.

"Felix Aldric," she said, her voice calm yet resonant, "your resilience in faith strengthens you."

Felix's heart lifted at the sight of her, but a shadow of shame crossed his face. He looked down, the memory of his last encounter with her flooding back—the rage that had burned in him as he faced Valthor, the vengeful fury she had pulled him back from. "I would've lost myself if not for ye," he admitted, his voice thick with regret. "I nearly gave in."

Titania's expression softened, her wings rustling faintly. "I am your guide, Felix. Your repentance and remorse are why your faith led you away from such sinful actions, even in the hardest moments."

Her words eased the guilt gnawing at him. Felix took a steadying breath and met her gaze, resolve hardening in his chest. "When do we begin the journey to the next Crystal?" he asked. Titania replied, "The Earth Crystal lies to the southeast of here." She inclined her head. "Soon, Felix. The path awaits, but you must be prepared."

Felix's jaw tightened, his thoughts turning to the growing threat looming over the land. "I have to stop Daegon quick," he said, his voice firm with determination. "Before his forces spread through the land."

Titania's eyes shone with quiet approval. With a graceful sweep of her wings, she rose into the moonlit sky, leaving Felix standing alone in the field, his purpose clearer than ever.

Felix stood in the moonlit field, his eyes fixed on Titania as she soared into the night sky, her golden wings catching the silver light. The sight filled him with renewed determination and faith, a quiet strength blooming in his chest. The cool breeze carried away his doubts, leaving only the clarity of his purpose.

As Titania vanished into the distance, Felix turned back toward the healer's quarters. The village of Kirkhaven lay silent, bathed in the gentle glow of firestone lamps. His steps were slow but sure, each one a testament to the battles he'd endured and the resolve he'd gained.

Entering the room quietly, he glanced at Rowan, still resting peacefully. The sight eased his heart. Felix settled into his bed, his body weary but his spirit steady. He closed his eyes, ready for the rest he needed, prepared for whatever the next day would bring.

Chapter 7: The Deserter's Arrival

The first light of dawn crept through the small window of the healer's quarters in Kirkhaven, casting a soft, golden glow over the stone walls and wooden beams. Felix Aldric stirred, his body heavy from days of deep, restorative sleep, yet his spirit hummed with a quiet, resolved determination. He blinked, the remnants of dreams—Eldenwold's church steeple, Rowan's grin by the Cragbeck, and the fiery glow of the Ashen Crags—fading into the stillness of the early morning. For a moment, he lay still, listening to the steady rhythm of his brother's breathing beside him. The air carried the faint scent of sage and firestone, a reminder of the battles fought and the healing that had followed.

Felix turned his head, his gaze settling on Rowan, who lay in the bed to his left. His brother's chest rose and fell in a slow, peaceful cadence, his face still pale and bruised but softened by sleep. The whip scars crisscrossing Rowan's back, though bandaged and beginning to heal under Fiona's care, remained a stark testament to his suffering. Felix's heart clenched with a mix of relief and lingering worry. He had rescued Rowan from Daegon's grasp, but the road to full recovery stretched ahead, and Felix's own path called him elsewhere.

The door creaked open softly, and Fiona stepped inside, her long dark-brown hair tied back, her green eyes sparkling with warmth. She carried a small tray of herbs, and her presence filled the room like the dawn light itself. Seeing Felix awake, her smile brightened. "Ye're awake already, lad," she said, her gentle Scottish lilt a soothing melody. "Ye're lookin' much better— mendin' faster than I'd have thought, after all ye've been through."

Felix managed a small smile, though his body ached as he shifted slightly. "Thank you, Fiona," he said, his voice still rough from sleep but warm with gratitude. "I'm truly blessed to have such a great healer looking after me and my brother."

Fiona chuckled softly, her humility shining through as she waved off the praise. "Och, it's nae just me, lad. Ye've a strong spirit, and the Creator's guid hand has been upon ye. That's what's pullin' ye through so quick."

Felix sat up slowly, wincing as the scabs on his wounds pulled tight and the soreness in his muscles protested. He swung his legs over the side of the bed, steadying himself with a hand on the mattress. His gaze drifted to Rowan again, concern deepening his tone. "How's he doing? How long until he wakes up?"

Fiona moved to Rowan's bedside, her hands deftly checking the bandages with practiced ease. "He's mendin' well, Felix," she said, her voice calm and reassuring. "I expect him to open his eyes any day now—could be today, could be tomorrow. But he'll need time to regain his strength. A week or two, perhaps, before he's back on his feet proper."

Felix nodded, a wave of relief washing over him. Rowan would wake soon—that was a mercy he clung to. Yet a pang of sadness followed, sharp and bittersweet. His quest loomed like a shadow on the horizon, its urgency pressing against his heart. The Earth Crystal awaited to the southeast, as Titania had revealed, and Daegon's forces would not rest. Felix couldn't linger in Kirkhaven, not even for Rowan's recovery. He glanced toward the left corner of the room, where his staff and Firesong Blade leaned against the wall. The staff's familiar grain and the sword's firestone-inlaid steel glinted faintly in the dawn light, calling him back to his purpose.

With a deep breath, Felix stood, stretching his arms above his head. Soreness lingered in his shoulders and legs—a dull ache from the Fire Lion's claw and Valthor's fiery assaults—and he could feel the taut pull of scabs on his wounds. Yet beneath the stiffness, he sensed his strength returning; his body was beginning to feel like his old self again, tempered by faith and the Creator's grace. He took a few steps, testing his balance, and found he could move with relative ease. The days of rest had woven their healing magic, preparing him for the trials ahead.

Fiona watched him with a knowing smile, setting the tray of herbs on a nearby table. "Ye're a quick healer, Felix," she said, her tone warm but laced with gentle caution. "But don't push yerself too hard. Ye've carried a heavy burden to get this far."

"I know," Felix replied, his voice steady, his dirty-blonde hair falling slightly into his eyes as he met her gaze. "But I have to be ready. The quest isn't finished—there's still much to do."

Fiona nodded, her expression softening with understanding. "Aye, lad. The Creator's timing is perfect, though. Trust in that, and ye'll find yer strength when ye need it most."

Her words settled over him like a prayer, and Felix took them to heart. He would rest a little longer, gather his strength, and then answer the call that tugged at his soul. For now, he was grateful for the sanctuary of Kirkhaven, for Fiona's care, and for the chance to see Rowan safe. The dawn light grew brighter, painting the room in hues of gold, and Felix stood in its embrace, his resolve firming like steel in a forge.

Dawn light bathed the healer's quarters in gold, and Felix stood in its glow, his resolve firm as forged steel. He took a deep breath, feeling the need for fresh air and sunlight after days confined to rest. With a final glance at Rowan, still sleeping peacefully, Felix stepped outside, the cool morning air greeting him like an old friend. Kirkhaven stirred quietly around him, the scent of woodsmoke and dew-kissed grass mingling in the breeze. His muscles ached with each step, the soreness a reminder of battles won and strength regained, but the sun's warmth on his skin lifted his spirits.

As he walked toward the village square, a familiar figure caught his eye. Captain Bryn, her red braided hair glinting in the sunlight, was overseeing repairs near the half-charred palisade. She spotted him and strode over, her warrior's gait confident yet softened by a warm smile. "Well, look who's up and about," she said, her Scottish burr thick and teasing. "Last time I saw ye, ye were half-dead, lad. Thought we'd have to bury ye alongside those bandits."

Felix chuckled, though the movement tugged at his healing wounds. "Thanks to you, Bryn, and your people, I'm still here. And so is Rowan." He gestured back toward the healer's quarters, gratitude warming his voice.

Bryn waved it off, her eyes gleaming with pride and humility. "Don't mention it. Ye risked yer life for us, so it's only fair we do the same for ye. Besides, anyone willing to aid my people is a friend and ally to me." Her words carried sincerity, and Felix felt a deep sense of connection, as if Kirkhaven's hearth had woven him into its fabric.

Bryn's gaze sharpened with curiosity. "Speakin' of aid, one o' my scouts mentioned a flamin' tornado blazin' like the Creator's wrath. Care to tell me about that?"

Felix paused, the memory of his battle with Valthor surging back—the rage, the merging of wind and fire, the moment he nearly lost himself to vengeance. He took a steadying breath. "It was… intense," he said, choosing his words carefully. "I faced a mage named Valthor, one of Daegon's captains. He was powerful, but with the Wind and Fire Crystals, I merged the elements. The tornado… it was like nothing I've ever felt. It consumed him, but it almost consumed me, too."

Bryn's eyes widened, a mix of shock and admiration crossing her face. "Wow, so ye can do all that with just two crystals? Maybe I should get one for myself to rid these lands o' bandits," she said with a sarcastic lilt, though a hint of seriousness lingered in her tone. She sobered quickly, her voice dropping. "Bryce mentioned what ye told him about this Valthor and his accent. It's troublin', Felix. Daegon's reach is growin', and I'm scared for my people. We're tough and loyal folk, but we're few in number. This Daegon… he's a damn blight on the land."

Felix noticed the frustration in her clenched fists and the tightness of her jaw. He stepped closer, his voice gentle yet firm. "I understand, Bryn. I've seen what his forces can do. But I won't let him win. I have to stop him, for all of us. That's why I need to head southeast to find the Earth Crystal."

Bryn's expression softened, though worry lingered in her green eyes. "Southeast, huh? I guess that means ye'll be leavin' us soon."

Felix nodded, a pang of regret tugging at his heart. "Yes, even though Rowan hasn't awakened yet. I can't stay here and let Daegon's forces consume Pangea. But… I trust you, Bryn. Will you look after him? Make sure he gets home safely once he's able to travel?"

Bryn placed a hand on his shoulder, her grip strong and reassuring. "Of course, lad. Rowan's in good hands. We'll see him back to Eldenwold—ye have my word."

Felix felt a wave of relief, his trust in Bryn deepening. "Thank you, Bryn. That means more than I can say."

Before they could continue, two of Kirkhaven's militiamen approached, escorting a stranger whose appearance set him apart. He wore a padded gambeson emblazoned with an oak tree, its fabric torn and stained with dirt and blood. His armour was battered, an empty sheath dangling at his side, and his face was gaunt, eyes hollow with exhaustion. One of the militiamen stepped forward, addressing Bryn. "Captain, this man appeared on the southeastern side near the village. He claims to have witnessed forces raiding and destroying villages of the Derwgorians."

Bryn's gaze sharpened, her warrior instincts flaring. "Speak up, man. What's yer name, and what do ye know o' these attackers?"

The man straightened, his voice trembling yet carrying a soft Welsh lilt. "I'm Ewan of Derwgor, from Meadowbrook. We were preparin' to flee to Oakridge when mercenaries hit us. They bore shields with a spiral serpent, burnin' and takin' all we had. I barely escaped."

Felix's gut twisted, the spiral serpent a chilling sign of Daegon's spreading influence. Bryn's jaw clenched, her gaze darkening with recognition and anger. "Meadowbrook? That's a good stretch southeast o' Kirkhaven—a day's ride or two on foot, sittin' right where the Windweave Plains border Vineland Vale. I've traded there meself, swapin' our firestone for their oak carvings. Fine folk, livin' along a riverbend, their homes tucked amidst fields and groves." Her voice grew heavy. "The Derwgorians have a gift—songs that echo in yer soul, hands that craft wood like it breathes, their midsummer feasts glowin' with torchlight. Oakridge, their city, lies farther east, near the Whisperin' Woods—two days' march from here. Never thought I'd hear o' Meadowbrook in flames."

Ewan nodded, his hands unsteady. "It's gone, Captain. What's left o' us are headin' to Oakridge, but those raiders—they're not done."

Felix's mind raced, stirred by his father's old stories. "The Derwgorians—I remember my father speaking of their bards, how their voices could calm a tempest, and their feasts that drew travellers from afar. But Vineland Vale—that's the land of grapes, isn't it? Stretchin' from Oakridge all the way west to Thegnfast along Pangea's southern beaches?"

Bryn gave a curt, sombre nod. "Aye, Vineland Vale's a treasure o' Pangea, famed for its vineyards and the best wines ye'll ever taste. It runs from Oakridge in the east to Thegnfast in the west, huggin' the southern coastline. Rows o' grapes as far as the eye can see, their scent fillin' the air—a land o' bounty. But now Daegon's shadow looms over it." She locked eyes with Felix, her tone sharp with urgency. "This is a storm brewin', Felix. If they've struck Meadowbrook, Kirkhaven's in their path."

Her words settled like stones in Felix's chest, mingling with the ache of Rowan's suffering and the fire of his purpose. "I can't stand idle," he said, his voice steady despite the turmoil within. "If I don't go, more'll fall. I'll head to Meadowbrook, Bryn. I'll face them."

Bryn placed a firm hand on his shoulder, her grip a grounding force. "Ye've got a lion's heart, lad. We'll gear ye up—my best can ride with ye, if ye'll have 'em."

Felix shook his head, a faint smile breaking through. "Thank you, but I can't accept. If Daegon's forces reach Kirkhaven, ye'll need your men to help defend your people. The Creator's guiding me—I've got to trust that. I'll take the horse, though—every hour counts."

Her grip tightened for a moment before releasing. "Then go with His light, Felix. Kirkhaven stands with ye, whatever comes."

With a final nod, Felix turned toward the healer's quarters to gather his gear. His staff rested against the wall, its worn grain a familiar comfort, while Firesong Blade lay nearby, its firestone-inlaid steel catching the morning light. He secured the sword at his side, its weight a quiet vow, and took up his staff. Fiona approached, her hands offering a folded tunic and a sturdy cloak, both dyed in the Fyrclad Kin's earthy hues.

"Ye'll need these, lad," she said, her voice warm with care. "A hero cannae face the world half-clothed." The tunic was practical yet durable, and the cloak bore subtle knotwork along its hem, a testament to Kirkhaven's faith and strength.

Felix took them with a grateful smile, pulling the tunic on and fastening the cloak about his shoulders. "Thank you, Fiona. For all you've done." He cast a lingering glance at Rowan's bed, his brother's steady breaths easing his heart. "And Bryn," he added, turning to the captain, "I owe you more than words for keeping him safe."

Bryn clasped his arm, her hold firm and sure. "We'll guard him well, Felix. Ye have my oath."

Geared and resolute, Felix stepped outside. The sun rose higher, bathing the rocky outcrops and swaying grasses of the Windweave Plains in golden light. At the edge of Kirkhaven, a sturdy horse awaited—a gift from Bryn to speed his journey. Its coat gleamed like burnished copper in the morning sun, sturdy and sure-footed, a testament to the Fyrclad Kin's resilience. Its mane, streaked with hints of dawn's light, seemed to carry a quiet strength, as if blessed by the Creator Himself. Felix approached, running a hand along its flank, grateful for the strength it would lend him.

He paused the moment he reached the horse, kneeling on the dew-kissed grass, his staff planted beside him. "Creator, guide my steps," he murmured. "Shield Meadowbrook's survivors, and watch over Rowan and Kirkhaven. Let Your light show me the way." Rising, the prayer fortified him like armour, and he swung into the saddle, securing his staff and Firesong Blade within easy reach.

With a final nod to the village, he urged the horse forward. The path stretched southeast toward Meadowbrook—a village a day's ride away, perched at the border where the Windweave Plains met Vineland Vale. Beyond lay the famed Vineland Vale itself, a land rich with vineyards, its grapes fuelling the finest wines in Pangea, stretching from Oakridge to Thegnfast along the southern coastline. He could almost taste the air thick with ripening fruit, carried on the breeze from that distant shore.

As he rode into the plains, Titania's golden wings flashed overhead, her cry a piercing note of courage. Felix's cloak billowed in the wind, the horse's hooves striking the earth in a steady rhythm, carrying him swiftly toward his destiny. The Windweave Plains unfurled before him, their vast grasses whispering secrets of the journey ahead. Meadowbrook lay waiting—smoke on the horizon marking Daegon's wrath—and with it, the next step in Felix's fight against the encroaching dark.

Chapter 8: The Fate of Meadowbrook

The sun dipped low, painting the fields in hues of gold as Felix rode toward Meadowbrook from the west. The steady clop of his horse's hooves against the dirt path did little to ease the tension coiling in his chest. After a long day's ride from Kirkhaven, his body protested, but his mind remained alert, driven by the weight of his purpose.

As he neared the outskirts of Meadowbrook, the village's edge came into view, nestled close to the boundary where fields met the river. Before he reached the bridge that marked the village's western limit, a chilling sight stopped him short: two bodies lay sprawled in the grass beside the road. One was a man, his pitchfork still gripped in lifeless hands; the other a woman, her blood-soaked apron a stark contrast to the peaceful earth beneath her. Felix's stomach lurched, his grip tightening on the reins. These were no warriors—just villagers, struck down in the shadow of their home.

Titania appeared at his side, her golden wings glinting in the fading light. "We cannot linger, Felix," she urged, her voice firm yet heavy with sorrow. "The village awaits, and every moment counts."

Felix nodded, forcing his gaze away from the fallen. With a nudge to his horse, he pressed forward, the short distance to the bridge feeling endless. The structure spanned the river just ahead, its wooden planks weathered by years but standing solid and unshaken. Beneath it, the river flowed serene and untouched, its gentle ripples mocking the violence that framed its banks.

The wood creaked softly as Felix guided his horse across, the sound a quiet reassurance of the bridge's strength. He couldn't shake the thought that the raiders had spared it, perhaps crossing it themselves to wreak their havoc. When he reached the other side, Meadowbrook unfolded before him, its nearness to the river's edge making the devastation all the more immediate. Smoke curled from the ruins of homes, and the air thickened with the stench of ash and death.

Felix rode into the village, his heart sinking at the sight. Charred husks of cottages lined the streets, their roofs collapsed into piles of smoldering debris. Bodies littered the square—some clustered together in a final, futile stand, others fallen where they stood. Near the well, a small group bore the marks of desperate resistance: a hammer, an axe, a knife, all broken and useless now.

Rage and grief warred within him. Who could do this? he thought, his jaw tight. What kind of evil leaves nothing but ruin?

His gaze snagged on a splintered cross half-buried in the dirt, its charred edges a cruel mirror to the pendant at his throat. The sight anchored him, pulling his mind to Eldenwold—the church steeple aglow, the Cragbeck's gentle rush, his family's steady faith. But the image twisted: the river choked with ash, the church in ruins, his parents lost. No, he vowed silently, gripping the reins until they bit into his palms. I won't let that happen. The broken cross before him tied Meadowbrook to his home, fueling his resolve. He was the Element Hero, chosen to stand against this darkness, and he would not falter.

A soft rustle of wings broke his reverie. Titania descended beside him, her golden feathers catching the fading light, her presence a quiet balm amidst the chaos. Felix turned to her, his voice raw with the weight of what he'd seen. "Titania, this…" He swept a hand toward the destruction, his words faltering as emotion thickened his throat. "What could Daegon possibly gain from wiping out an entire village?"

Titania's eyes met his, steady and sorrowful, yet resolute. "Daegon seeks to crush the lands of Pangea into fear, Felix. He hopes for submission through destruction. There are many in Pangea willing to fight him, but he is cunning. He knows that if he can win a battle of submission rather than conventional warfare, he can crush their spirits. By razing villages like Meadowbrook, he sends a message: resistance will be met with annihilation. Fear is his weapon, as much as any blade."

Felix's fists tightened at his sides, knuckles whitening. "He's a coward," he said, his voice low but fierce. "Hiding behind terror instead of facing us head-on."

Titania nodded, her tone measured yet firm. "Yes, the hearts of men like Daegon prefer fear tactics to demonstrate their terrorizing reach. But that is why your quest matters, Felix. You are not yet ready to face him directly—there are still two crystals you must claim. The Earth Crystal is the next step, and its power will bring you closer to challenging Daegon's tyranny."

"Where do I find it?" Felix asked, his resolve hardening as he held her gaze, the fire of purpose reigniting within him.

"The stag who guards the Earth Crystal dwells in the forest east of Oakridge," Titania replied. "He is Terranus, the Earth Stag, a noble guardian whose presence anchors the land itself. Seek him there, Felix, and prove yourself worthy of the crystal's strength."

Felix drew a deep breath, the name Terranus settling into him like the solid earth beneath his feet. "Terranus, the Earth Stag," he murmured, committing it to memory. "I'll find him. I'll stop Daegon, no matter what it takes."

Titania's wings rustled softly, a faint, encouraging smile touching her features. "I know you will. The path ahead is perilous, but you carry the Creator's light within you. Go now— east to Oakridge and face the trials that await."

Her golden wings glinted as she hovered beside him, her voice cutting through the heavy silence. "We cannot linger, Felix," she urged, her tone resolute yet tinged with sorrow. "The Earth Crystal awaits, and Daegon's shadow grows with every passing hour. Move forward—your purpose lies ahead."

Felix nodded, his chest tight with grief and determination. He turned his horse to face the devastation one last time, his eyes tracing the charred husks of homes and the broken bodies strewn across the square. The splintered cross lay half-buried in the dirt, a silent plea from the fallen. Closing his eyes, he bowed his head, performing a signing of the cross, his voice a whisper carried on the wind.

"Creator, I pray for the souls of Meadowbrook. May they find peace in Your light, free from suffering, cradled in Your embrace where pain and fear are no more. Grant me the strength to carry on, to stop this evil from claiming more lives."

The prayer lingered in the air, a solemn vow to the lost, a hope that they rested with the Creator now. With a deep breath, Felix urged his horse eastward, leaving the village behind as the sun dipped lower, painting the sky in hues of orange and gold.

The path to Oakridge stretched before him, winding through the edge of the Windweave Plains and Vineland Vale toward the Whispering Woods. The late afternoon light faded into twilight as he rode, the steady rhythm of hooves against earth a counterpoint to the restless churn of his mind. He thought of Rowan, safe in Kirkhaven, healing under Fiona's care—his brother's grin by the Cragbeck a fleeting comfort amidst the darkness. He thought of the people of Meadowbrook, their lives snuffed out by Daegon's cruelty, their fate a warning of what could befall Witsgar, Kirkhaven, and all of Pangea if he failed. The weight of his quest pressed against him, urgent and unyielding, driving him onward even as exhaustion tugged at his limbs.

Night fell, the stars emerging like sentinels in the vast sky. The path grew dim, shadows pooling beneath the grasses, and Felix's body ached from the long ride. His horse slowed, its breath visible in the cool air, and he realized he could go no further without rest. Oakridge lay ahead, but the darkness and his own fatigue demanded a pause. Spotting a cluster of trees off the path, he guided his mount toward them, finding a small clearing sheltered from the wind.

Dismounting, he tethered his horse to a sturdy branch and gathered dry wood from the forest floor. With a focused breath, he extended his hand, the Fire Crystal at his chest pulsing faintly. A spark flickered in his palm, growing into a steady flame that ignited the wood, casting a warm glow over the clearing. The fire crackled softly, its light dancing on the surrounding trees, creating a haven of warmth and safety amidst the night.

Felix settled by the fire, his back against a tree, the heat seeping into his tired muscles. He stared into the flames, their hypnotic dance easing the restlessness that had plagued him. The sounds of the night—the rustle of leaves, the distant hoot of an owl—wrapped around him, a quiet symphony that soothed his spirit. His eyelids grew heavy, the day's weight slipping away as the fire's warmth cradled him. With a final murmured prayer— "Creator, guide me to the Earth Stag"—he surrendered to exhaustion, drifting into a deep, restorative sleep beneath the starlit sky.

The first rays of dawn pierced the forest canopy as Felix slept by the dying fire, its warmth a faint comfort against the morning chill. A distant rumble stirred him—hooves, pounding the earth, drawing closer with every beat. His eyes snapped open, his pulse quickening as he bolted upright, shaking off the haze of sleep. He gripped his staff, peering into the shadows beyond the clearing.

The sound swelled, a thunderous rhythm of horses galloping toward him. He rose, heart hammering, and backed against a tree, watching the path. Who's coming? he wondered, his mind racing with possibilities—friend or foe, he couldn't tell.

From the gloom emerged a band of riders, their silhouettes sharpening in the pale light. At their head rode a knight, his chainmail armor gleaming, the oak symbol on his chest catching Felix's eye—the same mark Ewan had borne. Six cavalrymen followed, their hands poised on sword hilts, faces set in grim lines. The knight's armor—sturdy and well-crafted chainmail beneath a dark green surcoat—spoke of quality even in the dimness.

The knight raised a hand, halting his men. They fanned out, encircling Felix, their horses snorting clouds of mist in the cool air. The knight's gaze locked onto him, sharp and suspicious. His medium-length brown hair was pulled back, a thick beard framing a face that suggested he was in his upper thirties. He leaned forward in his saddle, his voice cutting through the stillness with a faint Welsh lilt.

"Who might you be, and what brings you to rest on these roads, then?"

Felix steadied his breath, meeting the knight's stare. "I'm Felix Aldric, from Eldenwold. I'm on my way to Oakridge, then east to the Whispering Woods."

The knight's eyes narrowed, his brow furrowing. "The Whispering Woods, is it? And why would you be wanting to go there?"

Felix gripped his staff, the Wind and Fire Crystals pulsing faintly at his chest, their warmth grounding him. "I'm on a quest," he said, his voice firm yet tinged with humility. "The Creator has chosen me as the Element Hero to stop Daegon, a fallen sorcerer whose heresy threatens all of Pangea. He seeks the Elemental Crystals—ancient relics of the Creator's power—to corrupt the land's sacred balance and enslave its people. I've claimed the Wind and Fire Crystals, but I must find the Earth Crystal, guarded by Terranus the Earth Stag in the Whispering Woods, to grow strong enough to face him. I saw what his forces did to Meadowbrook—burned to ash, its people lost. I won't let that darkness spread to Oakridge or beyond."

The knight's expression darkened like storm clouds gathering over ancient hills, his gauntleted hand tightening on the reins of his sturdy destrier, whose flanks gleamed with the sweat of a long ride through mist-shrouded forests. "Meadowbrook, you say? And why should I be believing you? For all I know, you could have had a hand in that attack, now."

Felix's chest tightened, a vise of sorrow squeezing his heart as memories of Meadowbrook's ruins surged forth like a bitter tide—timber homes reduced to smoldering skeletons, their thatched roofs collapsed into ashen heaps; streets once alive with the laughter of children now silent and strewn with the lifeless forms of villagers, their simple woolen garments charred and torn.

A child's wooden toy, carved in the likeness of a bounding deer, lay half-buried in the soot, its innocent form a stark emblem of the horror. He shook his head, grief etching deep lines on his youthful face, shadowed by the hood of his travel-worn cloak. "I didn't attack Meadowbrook. I came from Kirkhaven after a man named Ewan, with his weathered face, told me of the peril. Captain Bryn gave me this horse to hasten my path, but I arrived too late, the flames already devouring all in their path. Daegon's forces, those shadow-cloaked marauders with blades forged in unholy fires, will keep burning villages unless I find the Crystals— those ancient gems said to pulse with the light of forgotten stars—and stop him."

The knight paused, his keen eyes—sharp as a falcon's, framed by a helm adorned with oak-leaf engravings—studying Felix intently beneath brows furrowed like ancient furrows in the earth. Then, a flicker of recognition softened his gaze, like sunlight piercing through the canopy. "You know Captain Bryn, do you?"

"Yes," Felix said, nodding firmly, his voice steady despite the ache in his soul. "She helped me in Kirkhaven, amid its sturdy stone walls and bustling market squares. A good warrior—tough as they come, honorable as the oaths of the greatest of warriors."

The knight's lips curved into a faint smile, revealing teeth white against a beard streaked with the silver of many winters. "She is that, indeed. I've met her a few times, even sparred with her once in the training yards of Oakridge, where the clash of steel rang like thunder. One of the toughest soldiers I've known, with a heart of gold beneath her mail, she has." He glanced at his men—hardy riders clad in chainmail, their spears tipped with gleaming iron—who eased their grips on their weapons, the tension in the air dissipating like morning fog under the rising sun.

"I'm Arthur, Knight-Captain of Oakridge, House Gwynfor," the knight said, his tone warming with a subtle Welsh cadence, rolling like the gentle brooks of verdant valleys. "Tell me, what's the state of Meadowbrook? Any survivors?"

Felix's gaze fell to the leaf-strewn path beneath them, his voice grim as the tolling of a funeral bell. "None. Almost nothing's left. Everything's destroyed—the once-fertile fields blackened to barren waste, the mill by the river a crumpled ruin of stone and splintered wheel. Even the innocent didn't survive; elders and young alike felled by cruel blades, their blood soaking the earth that once nurtured their crops."

Sadness clouded Arthur's eyes, deep pools reflecting the sorrow of ages, and he looked down for a moment, his broad shoulders slumping under the weight of his chainmail as if bearing the grief of a hundred lost kin. The wind whispered through the surrounding oaks, their leaves rustling like hushed laments, carrying the faint, acrid hint of distant smoke. "I understand," he murmured, his voice thick with unspoken loss. "Our kin tilled those lands, under skies painted with the hues of dawn. Thank you for trying to help them, stranger." He straightened, resolve hardening his features like forged steel cooling in the forge. "We're heading back to Oakridge to prepare our defenses. These dark forces will come for us next, drawn like moths to the flame of our resolve, and we need every warrior we can muster, we do. Will you join us, then?"

Felix nodded, his determination unwavering. "Yes, I'll come with you."

Arthur signaled his men, who turned their horses toward the path. Felix mounted his own steed, falling in behind them as they rode toward Oakridge, the rising sun casting long shadows across the land.

Under the midday sun, its golden rays spilling across the verdant expanse of Vineland Vale, Felix and Arthur led their small band of riders along a winding road tracing the northwestern edge of the vale, their path bearing eastward from the shadowed western hills. The landscape unfurled like a tapestry woven by ancient hands—rolling hills cloaked in emerald grasses, dotted with wildflowers that swayed in the gentle breeze, their petals bright as scattered jewels. To their south, beyond the road's dusty verge, a shimmering river carved its sinuous path from west to east, its waters catching the sunlight in fleeting glints like the scales of some great, unseen serpent.

As they rode closer, a faint tremor stirred the earth beneath their horses' hooves, a whisper of unease that set Felix's heart to quickening. A distant haze of smoke curled above the horizon, faint as a specter's breath, and the air grew thick with the acrid tang of burning pitch. Then came the sounds of conflict, sharp and unyielding—harsh shouts like the cries of carrion birds, the metallic clash of steel on steel, and the deep, rhythmic thuds of siege engines unleashing their fury, each impact resounding like the heartbeat of some fell beast. Arthur's jaw tightened, his eyes narrowing beneath the brim of his oak-leafed helm. "Faster, men!" he bellowed, his voice rising above the clamor like a warhorn's call. "Our people need us now!" Felix's pulse surged, a storm of fear and determination roiling within him as he spurred his bay mare onward, her hooves pounding the earth in rhythm with Arthur's desperate command.

They crested a low hill, and the scene below struck Felix like a hammer's blow to an anvil. Oakridge stood defiant, its towering stone walls hewn from the grey granite of the vale's ancient bones, their surfaces scarred yet unyielding. To the south, the river curved in a gentle arc, its serene waters flowing past the western gate, untouched by the chaos, a silent guardian of the city's flank. But to the southeast, Daegon's forces launched their assault, a disciplined menace some few hundred strong. Infantry clad in dark mail wielded spears beneath spiral serpent banners that writhed in the wind like living shadows. Archers, their bows drawn taut, loosed arrows in deadly arcs that hissed through the air like vipers. A half-dozen siege engines—crude trebuchets and ballistae, their timbers blackened as if kissed by fire—hurled flaming pitch and jagged stones, each missile crashing against the walls with a roar that shook the earth. The thick stone battlements absorbed the onslaught, but the defenders atop them, clad in green cloaks, strained under the relentless pressure, their cries echoing across the vale like a lament for fading hope. Dark green banners snapped in the wind, their white crosses bold beneath the embroidered oak tree, its branches spread wide as if to shelter

Derwgor, a testament to their unyielding faith and resilience forged in the fires of countless trials.

Felix had studied battles in his dusty tomes—tales of valor and ruin scribed by scholars long dead—but the raw chaos before him dwarfed those faded words. His grip tightened on his sword, its hilt worn smooth by years of use, as the Wind and Fire Crystals flared with sudden light, their twin glows pulsing like twin stars awakened from slumber. Not again, he thought, the devastation of Meadowbrook searing his mind's eye—smoldering homes, lifeless streets, the broken form of a child's toy deer half-buried in ash. His hands trembled on the reins, doubt creeping like a chill mist, but Arthur's steady presence, a rock amidst the storm, anchored him. I won't let Oakridge fall, he vowed silently, the Crystals' warmth spreading through his chest, as if kindling his resolve with their ancient fire.

"I didn't think they'd strike Oakridge this soon," Arthur muttered, his voice taut with a blend of shock and iron resolve. His gaze lingered on the city, where smoke rose in dark plumes above the southeastern walls, and for a moment, his hand tightened on his sword's hilt, as if steadying himself against the weight of his people's peril. "My sister's children dwell within those walls," he said softly, almost to himself, then shook his head as if casting off despair. He drew his sword in a swift, gleaming arc, the blade flashing like a signal fire kindled in defiance and wheeled his steed to face his men. "The western gate holds strong! We charge for it—keep them from breaching our walls! For the Creator! For Oakridge!"

A roar erupted from the riders, their weapons drawn in a gleaming chorus of steel as they urged their mounts into a gallop, hooves thundering like a gathering storm. Felix unsheathed his sword, its blade singing as it cleared the scabbard, and the Wind and Fire Crystals surged brighter, their light weaving ribbons of azure and crimson that danced across his mail like a storm of elemental fury. Their power thrummed in his veins, a song of ancient might that steadied his trembling hands. With a shout that tore from his throat, raw and defiant, he kicked his horse forward, joining Arthur and the knights in their desperate race toward the embattled city, where Oakridge's fate teetered on the edge, and the battle loomed ever closer, a crucible of fire and steel.

Chapter 9: The Battle for Oakridge

The midday sun hung high above Oakridge, its light glinting off the battlements as the serpent-marked horde of Daegon stormed the southern wall. Ladders rose like claws against the stone, but the Derwgorians stood firm, their arrows slicing through the air in deadly arcs. Atop the wall, a line of archers stood resolute, their longbows—carved from the heartwood of the Whispering Woods—gleaming faintly in the sunlight. These were no mere weapons; they were the pride of a people forged by generations of skill and faith.

"Draw!" roared the archer captain, his voice cutting through the clamor of the enemy below. As one, the archers pulled back their bowstrings, the tension singing in the air like a hymn. Their eyes, sharp as the arrowheads they wielded, tracked the first wave of soldiers scrambling up the ladders. Then, with a unified cry of "Loose!" they released.

The air erupted with a chorus of whistles as arrows streaked downward, a storm of feathered death unleashed with devastating force. The longbows' power was unmatched; each arrow punched through the enemy's crude armor as if it were parchment. A soldier clad in blackened mail took an arrow through the chest mid-climb, the shaft burying itself so deep that only the fletching remained visible; he fell silently, dragging the ladder askew. Another, raising a shield in vain, cried out as an arrow pierced through the wood and into his arm, sending him plummeting into the chaos below.

The defenders watched as the volley thinned the enemy ranks, bodies piling at the wall's base like fallen leaves. The southern wall held firm, its stone unyielding under the archers' deadly rain. "Nock again!" the captain bellowed, and the archers obeyed, their movements swift and sure. The ladders kept coming, but so did the arrows—each one a testament to the skill that made Oakridge's walls a fortress not even Daegon's numbers could easily breach.

The enemy recoiled from the archers' deadly volleys and the scalding oil, but their retreat was brief. With a guttural roar from their Lieutenant, they rallied, dragging forward a new wave of ladders—each crowned with rough-hewn wooden shields hastily lashed to the rungs. As the ladders slammed against the southern wall, a series of clay pots shattered at their bases, spilling smoldering embers and damp hay that birthed a thick, acrid smoke. The haze rolled upward, swallowing the climbers in a murky veil, and the archers' next volley faltered—arrows thudding into shields or vanishing into the gloom.

Below, the enemy infantry surged, their spiral-serpent banners fluttering as spears thrust toward the wall's base. The archer captain spat a curse, his voice cracking over the din: "Water! Clear the smoke!" Soldiers tipped cauldrons over the edge, sending streams of steaming water to cut through the haze. Visibility flickered back as the smoke thinned, revealing shielded figures clawing up the ladders, inches from the top. "Reserves!"

the captain bellowed, and a ragged line of defenders rushed to the battlements, their shields clashing into place. The wall trembled under the weight of the assault, every heartbeat a test of the Derwgorian people's resolve.

From the western gate, Felix caught the sound of the archers' volleys—a steady rhythm of defiance that bolstered his own resolve. The Derwgorians were not just holding the line; they were carving it in the enemy's blood, proving that this city would not fall while its people still drew breath.

Felix, charging alongside Arthur's knights, ducked as a fire-tipped arrow hissed past, its serpent-marked fletching grazing his cloak as they galloped toward Oakridge's western gate. The city's walls shuddered under the barrage of Daegon's trebuchets, their flaming stones arcing like fallen stars. "Hold fast!" Arthur bellowed, his oak-emblazoned shield raised, his Welsh voice cutting through the din. Felix's Wind Crystal flared, summoning a gust to scatter a volley of arrows, while Firesong Blade's firestone glowed, hungry for battle. "Creator, be my strength!" he prayed, charging into the fray, the serpent banners looming closer with every stride.

The enemy archers froze, their bows slackening as Felix's gale tore their fiery volley into a whirlwind of shattered shafts and scattered embers, the serpent-marked fletching's dissolving like ash in the Creator's light. Their shocked eyes, glinting with fear under crude helms, met Felix's for a fleeting moment, their disciplined ranks faltering before the divine power of the Wind Crystal. Arthur seized the chaos, his sword flashing as he led the knights through the western gate, their hooves pounding the stone like a war drum. Felix gripped Firesong Blade and summoned a spiraling wind to shield the defenders atop the battlements, their shields etched with the sacred cross entwined with an oak tree—the Derwgorian emblem of faith and unyielding roots. "For Pangea!" he roared, his voice a carpenter's son's vow forged in faith, as he plunged into the siege's heart, Daegon's heresy a shadow he would shatter.

The western gate's iron-bound timbers trembled as Daegon's army surged forward, their jagged blades glinting with unholy fire, battering the oak-reinforced barricades with axes and torches. Oakridge's defenders, clad in oak-embroidered tunics, braced behind the gate, their cross-and-oak shields locked in a desperate wall, the cobblestone ground beneath them slick with blood and ash. A trebuchet's flaming boulder roared overhead, its heat searing Felix's face, his scruffy beard flecked with embers. He thrust his hand forward, the Fire Crystal blazing at his chest, and unleashed a searing whip of flame that lashed through the spearmen's ranks, their cloaks igniting as they screamed, reeling back from the gate's threshold. "Creator, hold this gate in Your light!" Felix prayed, Firesong Blade flaring in his grip, as Arthur's roar rallied the knights, their swords slashing to keep the serpent's tide at bay.

Felix's fiery whip crackled, its divine blaze scattering the serpent-marked spearmen as Arthur and his knights surged forward, their oak-emblazoned swords carving through the faltering enemy ranks to secure the western flank. The cobblestone ground shook under charging hooves, littered with shattered spears and smoldering cloaks, the air thick with the stench of charred flesh and sulfurous smoke. Defenders atop the gate cheered, their cross-and-oak shields raised like a forest of faith, their voices rising defiantly against the trebuchets' thunder. Felix, heart pounding, pressed toward the southern wall, his Fire Crystal flaring as he summoned a roaring fireball to blast a knot of archers, their serpent-marked bows snapping like kindling.

But a bellowing cry halted his advance—a towering Lieutenant, a beast of a man astride a snorting warhorse, his heavy armor clanking, black beard framing fierce brown eyes. Brandishing a broadsword and a metal shield painted with a coiling serpent, he roared, "Push the ram forward! To the west gate, ye curs! Break their spine! Make them tremble before the new order of Master Daegon!" His voice was a thunderclap, rallying Daegon's troops as they heaved a massive battering ram toward the gate, its iron-capped head gleaming ominously.

Felix's eyes widened at the sight of the ram, its presence a dire threat to Oakridge's defenses. He knew that if the gate fell, the city would be overrun. With a shout, he thrust both hands forward, the Wind and Fire Crystals blazing at his chest. A swirling fire tornado roared to life, its molten core scorching the earth as he hurled it into the enemy line's center. The fiery vortex tore through the spearmen, their formation shattering in a chorus of screams, but its true target was the battering ram. Flames licked hungrily at the wooden structure, igniting it in a blaze that sent the enemy crew scattering, their cries of panic mingling with the crackle of burning timber.

The Lieutenant's face twisted into a mask of rage, his brown eyes blazing with heretical zeal as he watched his prized siege weapon—reduced to a roaring pyre. "You'll rue that fire, Chosen! I'll cut you down, take the crystals, and deliver your head to Master Daegon personally!" he snarled, his voice a guttural roar that cut through the din of battle, sharp as volcanic glass. Spurring his warhorse—a massive beast clad in crimson barding emblazoned with Daegon's charred serpent rune—he charged down the ash-slick dirt road, his broadsword raised in a deadly arc. Felix stood his ground, the Wind Crystal at his chest flaring with a pulse that thrummed through his veins like a storm's first breath. His body blurred with divine speed, a gust of wind propelling him sideways as the broadsword's arc sliced through empty air, the blade's heat singing the frayed hem of his cloak. But the ash-slick ground betrayed him; his boots slipped, and he stumbled, thrown from his own momentum. He hit the dirt hard, pain jarring through his shoulder as he rolled to his feet, dust and embers rising in a choking cloud.

The Lieutenant wheeled his warhorse for another charge, the beast's hooves pounding the earth like war drums, its eyes wild with the same fervor that burned in its rider's gaze. Felix scrambled upright, his staff gripped tightly, when Arthur spurred his own steed forward. "For Oakridge!" Arthur bellowed, his voice a clarion call that echoed across the battlefield, his shield raised high. His longsword clashed against the Lieutenant's massive shield in a shower of sparks, the impact ringing like a forge hammer on an anvil. The Lieutenant's attention snapped to the new threat, his serpent-painted shield swinging with brutal force to meet Arthur's strike, the collision sending a tremor through the air.

Felix seized the moment, his heart pounding as he channeled the Wind Crystal's power. A surge of divine energy coursed through him. He thrust his staff skyward, summoning a gust that roared to life with the fury of a highland gale. The wind struck the Lieutenant like a battering ram, tearing him from his saddle and sending him flailing into the air, his crimson cloak whipping like a tattered banner. The beast of a man's eyes widened in shock, his massive frame helpless against the vortex, his warhorse rearing below with a panicked whinny. Felix didn't hesitate; tapping the Fire Crystal, its heat surged through his veins like molten iron—a searing reminder of Mount Ignis' sacred flames. He unleashed a blazing fireball, a comet of divine wrath that streaked through the twilight and engulfed the airborne foe. The flames wrapped around the Lieutenant like a shroud, their golden radiance a stark contrast to the profane red of his serpent rune, searing through his armor with a hiss of melting steel.

The Lieutenant crashed back to the ground in a heap of scorched plate, his helmet clattering free to reveal sweat-matted black hair plastered across a scarred forehead. Deep burns seared his side, his armor charred black, and his once-fierce gaze clouded with pain, his breath ragged. Yet, with a defiant snarl, he struggled to rise, slamming his serpent-painted shield into the earth with a force that sent cracks spiderwebbing through the dirt. The shield's coils pulsed red, as if drawing strength from some unholy source—a profane echo of the firestones' sacred glow. With a guttural roar, he lunged at Felix, his broadsword swinging in a desperate, arcing stab.

Felix reacted on instinct, the Wind Crystal flaring once more. He thrust his hand forward, summoning a force push—a rippling wall of compressed air that struck with the precision of a spear. The impact deflected the Lieutenant's blade, sending it skittering across the dirt, the air shimmering with the force of the blow. With a cry of "For the Creator!" Felix drove Firesong Blade—its firestone-inlaid steel glowing with a radiant warmth, pulsing like embers of divine will—through the Lieutenant's chest. The steel pierced armor and bone with a sickening crunch that echoed in the sudden hush of the battlefield. The Lieutenant's eyes locked onto Felix's, a storm of pain and disbelief clouding his gaze, his lips trembling as he choked out a final, whispered plea: "Master Daegon…" His massive frame collapsed, the serpent shield's glow fading to dull, lifeless metal, its runes extinguished like a snuffed candle.

Felix, chest heaving, turned to see the serpent-marked front line faltering, their spears wavering as Arthur's knights pressed forward, their cross-and-oak shields a bulwark of faith. Suddenly, a thunderous roar rose from the south—a banner bearing a vine-wreathed oak led a charge of cavalry along the road east of the river, their lances gleaming as they raced toward the western gate and swung northeast, crashing into the enemy's flank. The serpent-marked soldiers, caught between Arthur's knights and the riders, buckled under the dual assault. Refusing to let another soul fall, Felix dug deep, the Wind and Fire Crystals flaring like twin stars at his pendant. With a shout, he lunged skyward, propelled by a divine gust, and unleashed a roaring gust of flames that tore behind the enemy line, cloaks and banners igniting in a blazing crescent, the ground blackening. The enemy ranks broke, their screams mingling with the defenders' Welsh songs, as Arthur and his knights, bolstered by the newcomers, seized the chaos, their swords cutting down the fleeing spearmen. Felix landed, his gaze fixed on the southern wall, where ladders rose like claws. He thrust his hand forward, the Wind Crystal surging, and hurled a gale that swept across the wall, toppling ladders and scattering climbers into the dust below.

From a distant tent southeast of the battlefield, a figure in red armor and a billowing black cloak stood, arms crossed, his intense gaze piercing the haze. Mounting a steed, he waved a serpent-etched banner, his voice a low command: "Retreat! Fall back!" The enemy army echoed the cry, their lines dissolving into a chaotic withdrawal.

Oakridge's defenders erupted in cheers, their cross-and-oak shields raised like a forest reborn, their voices singing praises of the Creator's light. Arthur, his armor dented but unbowed, rode to Felix's side, his weathered face breaking into a smile. "You truly are the Creator's Chosen Hero," he said, his Welsh lilt warm with awe, bowing his head in gratitude. "Your fire and wind saved our city." Felix, exhausted, his scruffy beard dusted with ash, shook his head humbly, his voice steady despite trembling limbs. "I'm just glad I could help save innocent lives, Arthur." The knight lifted his head, his smile deepening. "You're a humble soul, Felix. I see why the Creator chose you." The knights and defenders continued to cheer, their voices echoing across the scarred courtyard, the western gate standing firm under the fading smoke. Felix's gaze lingered on the southeast, the distant red-armored figure's retreat a shadow on his heart, the Wind and Fire Crystals pulsing with the promise of battles yet to come.

The smoke began to clear over Oakridge's scarred fields, the western gate standing resolute under the fading sun, its oak-reinforced timbers etched with the cross-and-oak emblem of the Derwgorians. Felix leaned on Firesong Blade, his chest heaving from the battle's toll, ash dusting his scruffy beard and torn cloak. Arthur dismounted, his armor clanking, his weathered face softened by a warm smile. "We couldn't have done it without you, Felix," he said, his Welsh lilt thick with gratitude. "Oakridge and her people owe you a debt deeper than the Whispering Woods. Our King must meet the Creator's Chosen—you deserve a kingly reward, and aid for your quest, I reckon." Felix bowed his head, exhaustion weighing his limbs, but his voice held steady, warmed by humility. "I'm honored, Arthur, and I'll meet your King, if he'll have me." The Wind and Fire Crystals pulsed faintly at his chest, a reminder of the Creator's call, as Arthur clapped his shoulder, his nod a silent vow of brotherhood.

From the battlements, Oakridge's soldiers gazed down, their cross-and-oak shields glinting in the twilight, their eyes wide with awe at the Creator's Hero who had turned the serpent's tide. Whispers rippled among them, tales of Felix's fire tornado and wind-felled ladders already weaving into legend, their voices soft with reverence. A young archer, his oak-embroidered tunic stained with soot, signed the cross, murmuring a prayer to the Creator, while others raised their spears in silent salute, their faith a forest rooted in the cobblestone below. Felix felt their gazes, his heart stirred but heavy, the memory of Meadowbrook's fallen sharpening his resolve to press on. The distant serpent banners, now retreating beyond the southern wall, cast a shadow on his thoughts, the red-armored General's silhouette a specter of battles yet to come. He gripped Firesong Blade, its weight grounding him, as the city's great gate creaked open, its oak-carved panels swinging wide to reveal a new chapter.

The King's Guard emerged—six warriors in polished armor adorned with oak-leaf inlays, their shields bearing the sacred cross entwined with an oak tree, their steps measured yet proud. Their leader, a grizzled man with a silver-streaked beard, raised a gauntleted hand in greeting. "Knight-Captain Arthur, we're gladdened to see you and your men alive," he said, his Welsh accent formal but warm. "The city stood by your valor." Arthur shook his head, gesturing to Felix, his smile faint but earnest. "Thank you, Owain, but I'd not be here without Felix Aldric. His fire and wind broke the serpent's back." The Guard's leader, Owain, turned to Felix, his eyes assessing yet respectful. "Indeed, we owe you our lives, Chosen Hero. The King wishes to speak with you both. If you're able, we'll escort you to him now." Arthur glanced at Felix, his faint smile encouraging, and asked, "Ready? Do you need a moment?" Felix gathered his strength, his body aching but bolstered by faith and duty, nodded. "I'm ready." Owain saluted, and the Guard formed ranks, their oak-inlaid armor gleaming as they led Felix and Arthur through the gate, the cheers of Oakridge's defenders echoing along the walls.

As Felix and Arthur were escorted through Oakridge's western gate by the King's Guard, Felix's eyes widened at the sight of the city unfolding before him. The craftsmanship of Oakridge was breathtaking—stone arches soared overhead, their surfaces etched with intricate oak tree motifs, while wooden beams carved with delicate knotwork framed the streets. Banners bearing the sacred cross entwined with an oak tree fluttered in the breeze, a testament to the Derwgorians' skill. Yet this beauty stood in stark contrast to the city's current state. The streets, once a symbol of prosperity, were now crowded with refugees—men, women, and children displaced by Daegon's merciless raids. Their homes reduced to ashes, they huddled in makeshift shelters of tattered cloth and scavenged wood, their faces etched with exhaustion and despair. The air carried the mingled scents of smoke, sweat, and resilience—a proud city brought low but not broken.

Amid the chaos, Felix's gaze softened as he observed acts of compassion piercing the gloom. Priests in dark green robes moved through the throngs, their hands distributing bread and blankets, their voices offering murmured prayers of comfort. Nearby, healers tended to wounded soldiers, their deft fingers applying salves and wrapping bandages with practiced care, their presence a lifeline amidst the suffering. Felix's heart lifted slightly as he saw soldiers—some leaning on crutches, others kneeling in the dirt—signing the cross with trembling hands, their lips moving in silent thanks to the Creator for sparing their lives. The sight stirred him deeply, a pang of pain tightening his chest. He thought of Eldenwold, of Meadowbrook's smoldering ruins, and

126

imagined his own village facing such a fate. His hand rose instinctively, tracing the sign of the cross—forehead, chest, left shoulder, right—a quiet prayer escaping his lips: "Creator, ease their suffering. Let me be Your light against this darkness."

Arthur, walking beside him, noticed Felix's pause and placed a steady hand on his shoulder. "It's a hard thing to see," he said, his Welsh lilt softened by empathy. "But you've given them hope today. That's no small gift."

Felix nodded, though his eyes lingered on a young boy clutching a broken toy, his hollow stare mirroring the loss Felix had witnessed in Meadowbrook. "I just wish I could do more," he murmured, his voice thick with resolve.

"You will," Arthur replied firmly. "Your quest isn't done, and neither is our fight."

The King's Guard, led by Owain, guided them onward through the city, their oak-inlaid armor gleaming faintly in the fading light. As they approached the inner castle, Felix marveled at its sturdy stone walls, adorned with tapestries depicting Oakridge's history—scenes of faith and triumph woven in vibrant threads. The halls were rich with the scent of polished wood and flickering torchlight, casting a warm glow over the stone floors. Yet, compared to the tales he'd heard of Thegnfast's towering grandeur, Oakridge's castle felt more modest—impressive, but rooted in the humility of a smaller kingdom.

They entered the throne hall, a spacious chamber where a large hearth crackled at one end and a stained-glass window spilled colorful light across the floor. At the far end stood a man in royal armor, the Oakridge banner—a white cross beneath an oak tree—emblazoned proudly on his chest. He appeared to be in his early forties, his shoulder-length brown hair framing a face weathered by leadership, his beard streaked with the first signs of silver. He stepped forward from the throne, his presence regal yet approachable, exuding a quiet strength.

Owain bowed deeply, his voice resonating with respect. "My king, here is Knight-Captain Arthur and the Chosen Hero, as you requested."

Arthur followed with a bow, his posture reflecting the loyalty of a seasoned knight. Felix, though weary from battle, mirrored the gesture, his heart pounding with a mix of awe and duty.

The king raised a hand, his voice deep with a faint Welsh accent that rolled warmly through the hall. "Thanks, Owain. Rise, both of you. I am King Cedric, House Morcant, and I bid you welcome." He turned to Arthur first, his tone laced with pride. "Knight-Captain, your valor has once again proven why you're the backbone of Oakridge's defense."

Arthur shook his head humbly. "It wasn't I alone, Your Majesty. Without Felix Aldric, the western gate would've fallen."

King Cedric's gaze shifted to Felix, his eyes warm yet piercing with gratitude. "Felix Aldric, the Chosen Hero. Rumors had spread a hero was chosen. You've saved Oakridge, and for that, you have our deepest thanks."

Felix straightened, his voice steady despite the exhaustion tugging at him. "It was my duty, Your Majesty. The Creator guides my path, and I couldn't stand by while your people suffered. I only wish I'd reached Meadowbrook in time."

Cedric's expression softened, a shadow of sorrow crossing his face at the mention of Meadowbrook. "Your heart speaks as loudly as your deeds, Felix. We've lost much to Daegon's shadow, but your presence here renews our hope. Oakridge stands with you in your quest—whatever aid you need, be it men, supplies, or refuge, you shall have it."

Felix met the king's gaze, a flicker of gratitude warming his chest. "Thank you, Your Majesty. I'll need every strength I can gather to face what lies ahead."

King Cedric's posture shifted subtly, his regal bearing softening into a more somber demeanor as he regarded Felix and Arthur in the throne hall. The warm light from the hearth flickered across his face, casting shadows that deepened the lines of concern etched there, while the stained-glass window spilled a mosaic of colors across the stone floor. "This attack came quicker than any of us expected. Yet, they came in smaller numbers than we feared. It seems Daegon hoped to crush our spirits swiftly, to break us from within before we could rally a proper defense."

Felix nodded, his thoughts aligning with the king's assessment, though exhaustion weighed heavily on him after the battle. "Daegon's tactics are indeed to destroy the spirit of a nation," he replied, his voice steady despite the fatigue tugging at his limbs. "He seeks to make the people fall from the inside,

129

sowing fear and despair so deeply that resistance crumbles before his forces even arrive."

The king's eyes gleamed with a mixture of respect and shared understanding. "Yes, you've the right of it, Felix. But there's more to this. Our scouts have returned with reports that the regions to the southeast have not yet been touched by his shadow. It suggests Daegon lacks the strength to strike at his closest enemy, at least for now."

Felix's attention sharpened, his gaze locking onto the king's. "You know where Daegon is?" he asked, a note of surprise threading through his words.

Cedric nodded gravely, his expression resolute. "Yes. He has made his stronghold on an island southeast of Pangea, off the coast from Kroneburg."

Felix's brow furrowed in confusion. "But if Kroneburg is closest, why wouldn't Daegon attack there first?"

Arthur stepped forward, his oak-emblazoned armor catching the hearth's glow as he spoke. "Kroneburg's armies are some of the finest in all the land," he explained. "Their years of crusades have honed their tactics and forged their equipment into something formidable. Daegon knows he cannot take them head-on, not yet."

The king agreed, his voice resonating with quiet certainty. "Indeed. By striking at smaller kingdoms like ours, Daegon seeks to spark fear across Pangea, to make examples of those who dare to stand against him. He is not ready to conquer the whole of the land, but he is cunning enough to weaken us through terror."

Felix's resolve hardened, his hand instinctively brushing against the Wind and Fire Crystals at his chest, their faint pulses a reminder of his purpose. "Then I must go to the forest east of Oakridge," he said, his voice firm with determination. "I need to find the Earth Crystal and grow strong enough to stop him before his shadow spreads any further."

King Cedric's gaze softened, his eyes tracing the lines of weariness on Felix's ash-dusted face. "I can see the fire in you, lad, but I also see the toll this day has taken. You've fought bravely, but even the Creator's Chosen needs rest. I insist you stay in the king's chambers tonight. Rest, gather your strength, and leave at first light."

Felix hesitated, his sense of urgency warring with the king's wisdom. The memory of Meadowbrook's ruins and Oakridge's near fall fueled his drive, but his body ached, his mind clouded with fatigue. He knew Cedric spoke truth—without rest, he'd be no use to anyone. "You're right, Your Majesty," he conceded, bowing his head slightly. "I'll rest here tonight and set out at dawn. Thank you for your kindness and aid."

The king smiled, a warm, paternal expression that eased some of the tension in the room. "It is the least we can do for the one who has saved our city. I'll have food and drink sent to you both. Arthur, see to it that Felix is shown to the chambers."

Arthur bowed deeply, his loyalty evident in every movement. "Of course, Your Majesty."

Felix followed suit, his bow a gesture of respect and gratitude. "Thank you, King Cedric. Your hospitality means more than I can say."

With a final nod, the king dismissed them, and Arthur led Felix from the throne hall, their footsteps echoing softly against the stone floors. The castle's corridors blended sturdy stone with intricate woodwork, the air thick with the scent of polished oak and flickering torchlight—a stark contrast to the chaos beyond the walls. As they walked, Arthur glanced at Felix, his voice low and encouraging. "Get some rest while you can. There's a big day ahead tomorrow."

Felix managed a tired smile, his scruffy beard catching the light. "I will, Arthur. Thank you for everything."

They reached the quarters—a spacious room with a large, canopied bed, its wooden frame carved with delicate oak leaves. A hearth crackled softly in the corner, casting a warm glow over the stone walls, offering a sense of comfort and safety that felt worlds away from the battlefield. Felix's gaze drifted to the window, where the first hints of dusk began to darken the sky, a promise of renewal after a long night of rest. He set his staff and Firesong Blade against the wall, their familiar weight a quiet reassurance.

Less than an hour later, a soft knock sounded at the door. A servant girl entered, her dark hair tied back, carrying a tray laden with food and drink. "Compliments of the king, sir," she said, her voice gentle as she placed it on a small table. Felix thanked her warmly, his stomach rumbling at the sight of roasted meat still steaming, a loaf of crusty bread, a pitcher of water, and a decanter of deep red wine. She offered a shy smile before departing, leaving him to his meal.

He sat at the table, tearing into the bread and meat with a hunger he hadn't fully realized. The wine, rich and smooth, danced on his tongue with the unmistakable flavor of Vineland Vale's finest grapes—a taste renowned across Pangea, a fleeting luxury amidst his trials. As he ate, the warmth of the food and the comfort of the room eased the tension from his muscles, his spirit settling into a rare moment of peace.

With his belly full and his heart at ease, Felix moved to the bed, sinking into its soft embrace. He clasped his hands together and whispered a prayer. "Creator, thank You for guiding me through this day. Watch over Rowan, my family, and all who suffer under Daegon's shadow. Grant me the strength to continue, to be Your light in this darkness."

His prayer complete, Felix lay back, his eyes closing as sleep claimed him. The dawn light would creep through the window, bathing the room in a gentle glow—but for now, he rested, gathering his strength for the journey ahead.

Chapter 10: The Roots of Faith

The first light of dawn slipped through the window of the king's quarters, its gentle rays filtering through the intricate woodwork framing the glass. Felix Aldric stirred beneath the heavy blankets, the warmth and softness of the bed cradling him in a way he hadn't known since the Creator's call had set him on his quest. For the first time in weeks, he felt truly refreshed—his body rested, his spirit renewed. The deep sleep, born of the comfortable bed and the safety of Oakridge's castle, was a gift he hadn't realized he'd needed so desperately. The echoes of Meadowbrook's ruins, the clash of battle at Oakridge's gates, and the weight of his brother Rowan's fate all seemed to fade, if only for a moment, in the quiet peace of the morning.

He opened his eyes slowly, letting the golden light wash over him, and stretched his arms, feeling the lingering aches of his trials ease from his muscles. Rising from the bed, his bare feet met the cool stone floor, grounding him in the stillness. The room around him bore the marks of Oakridge's craftsmanship— delicate oak leaves carved into the bed frame, a hearth now simmering with glowing embers, and tapestries whispering tales of faith and resilience. Felix took a steadying breath, the faint scent of polished wood filling his lungs, and began to ready himself for the day ahead. The trial of the Earth Stag, Terranus, loomed in his mind, the Earth Crystal a vital step toward facing Daegon's shadow. He secured the Firesong Blade at his side and gripped his staff, its familiar weight a comfort in his hand. His cloak, mended by the castle's staff, settled over his shoulders, the subtle knotwork along its hem a reminder of the faith that carried him.

A soft knock at the door broke the silence. Felix turned as the servant girl from the previous night entered, her dark hair tied back neatly, carrying a tray laden with food. The hearty aroma of roasted meat, fresh eggs, and warm bread wafted toward him, joined by a pitcher of water and a small jug of milk. She set the tray on the table with a gentle smile, her voice soft but kind. "Good morning, sir. The king wishes you well-fed for your journey."

Felix's heart warmed at the gesture, his voice earnest as he replied, "Thank you—this is a kindness I won't forget." The girl's smile widened, and with a slight curtsy, she slipped out of the room, closing the door quietly behind her.

He sat at the table, the tray before him a small feast that spoke of Oakridge's generosity. The meat was tender and savory, the eggs cooked to perfection, and the bread still carried the heat of the oven. He ate slowly, savoring each bite, the cool water and rich milk refreshing him further. As he ate, his thoughts turned to the road ahead—the Whispering Woods east of Oakridge, where Terranus guarded the Earth Crystal. The path would be long and perilous, fraught with Daegon's minions and the trials of the Elemental Beast, but this meal was a moment of respite, a chance to gather strength for what lay beyond the castle walls. Gratitude swelled within him, and he murmured a quiet prayer: "Creator, thank You for this provision, and for the hands that prepared it. Guide me in the trials to come."

When the last bite was finished, Felix rose, his resolve firm. He gathered his belongings—staff in hand, the Firesong Blade at his hip, and cloak fastened securely. With a final glance at the room that had offered him such rare comfort, he stepped into the corridor, the scent of polished oak and torchlight greeting him as he made his way toward the throne room. The castle's halls were quiet in the early hour, the flickering light casting long shadows across the stone. His boots echoed softly with each step, his heart steadying as he prepared to speak with King Cedric one last time before departing.

The throne room was as Felix remembered it, with its large hearth crackling at one end and the stained-glass window spilling colorful light across the floor. King Cedric stood near the throne, speaking quietly with a woman of regal bearing. She had striking blue eyes, sharp and intelligent, and wore a beautiful dark green dress that flowed gracefully around her. Her long, wavy brown hair cascaded down her lower back, catching the light in soft ripples. As Felix entered, both the king and the woman turned to face him, their conversation pausing.

Cedric's face lit up with a warm smile. "Ah, Felix, come closer," he beckoned, his voice carrying the faint Welsh lilt Felix had come to recognize.

Felix approached, bowing deeply, his heart swelling with respect for the royal presence before him. "Your Majesty," he said, his tone steady and reverent.

Cedric gestured to the woman beside him. "Felix, allow me to introduce my wife, Queen Elowen."

The queen stepped forward, her posture poised yet warm. Felix inclined his head again, his voice humble. "Your Grace, it's an honor to meet you."

Elowen's blue eyes softened, and she offered a gentle smile. Her voice was soft but filled with sincere gratitude. "The honor is mine, Felix. We owe you a great debt for your bravery yesterday. Your actions saved our kingdom, and for that, we are eternally thankful. I wish you strength and safety on your quest, wherever it may lead."

Felix bowed his head once more, touched by her words. "Thank you, Your Grace. I'm grateful for your kindness and your prayers."

Cedric's expression grew earnest as he stepped closer. "Felix, how may we assist you further?"

Felix shook his head gently, his humility evident. "Your Majesty, you've already done so much by providing me with food and a place to rest. I'm deeply grateful. Now, I must continue my journey to the Whispering Woods."

Cedric nodded, a flicker of hope in his eyes. "We understand. May you find success in your quest and rid our lands of Daegon's dark forces swiftly."

Felix's gaze hardened with determination, his voice resolute. "I will do everything in my power to stop him, Your Majesty. The Creator guides my path, and I will not falter."

Cedric's face softened with approval. "Very well. I'll have my men ready your horse for the journey."

Felix bowed once more, his gratitude clear. "Thank you, Your Majesty, Your Grace." With that, he turned and left the throne room, his heart heavy with the weight of his mission but lifted by the support of Oakridge's rulers.

As Felix made his way through the castle and toward the city gate, he observed the men of Oakridge hard at work repairing the damage from the recent battle. Hammers rang against stone, and wooden beams were hoisted into place, their industrious spirit a testament to the resilience of the Derwgorians. The sight stirred a quiet pride in him, though it was tinged with the urgency of his departure.

When he reached the western gate, he found Arthur waiting for him, a familiar smile on his weathered face. "Felix, I wanted to see you off," Arthur said, clasping Felix's hand firmly, his Welsh lilt warm with camaraderie.

Felix returned the smile, relief washing over him at the sight of his friend. "It's good to see you too, Arthur, before I go. I wish I could stay and help with the repairs, but my quest calls me to the Whispering Woods."

Arthur nodded understandingly, his grip steady. "Don't worry, my friend. The Derwgorians are skilled craftsmen; we'll have the city restored in no time. And thanks to you, we'll be better prepared for any future threats."

Felix's smile widened, the weight on his shoulders lightening slightly. He mounted his horse, which had been brought to him by one of the stable hands, its copper coat gleaming in the morning light. "Thank you, Arthur, for everything. I hope to see you again soon."

Arthur stepped back, raising a hand in farewell. "You go with the prayers of all Derwgor, Felix. May the Creator guide and protect you."

With a final nod, Felix urged his horse forward, riding out of the western gate and around the city walls. The fields stretched out before him, leading to the Whispering Woods, which lay only an hour's ride away. As he rode, the wind whispered through the trees, carrying with it the promise of new challenges and the hope of victory.

As Felix rode toward the Whispering Woods, the forest loomed larger with each stride of his bay mare, its presence rising against the horizon like a living monument to Pangea's ancient heart. The beauty of the woods unfurled before him—towering trees stretched skyward, their strong, majestic branches laden with lush green leaves that shimmered in the spring sunlight, each leaf catching the rays like emeralds kissed by the Creator's grace. The canopy, dense as a woven tapestry, cast much of the forest floor into cool, dappled shadow, exuding an ancient, timeless aura that seemed to hum with life, as if the woods themselves breathed with the pulse of Pangea's primal spirit. A faint whisper stirred the air, a chorus of leaves and wind that spoke of secrets older than the hills, guarded by the Elemental Beast in ages long faded into legend.

Felix drew his horse to a halt at the forest's edge, his breath catching as he lifted his gaze to the mighty trees that stood like sentinels, their thick, gnarled trunks etched with the scars of centuries, hinting at a quiet watchfulness that had endured since the Creator shaped the world. Their roots sprawled across the earth, gnarled and vast, like the veins of Pangea itself, pulsing with the lifeblood of a land both sacred and imperiled. Could this be the Whispering Woods, the sacred grove whispered to be the cradle of the Earth Crystal? The Elemental Crystals at his chest warmed, their azure and crimson glow a quiet affirmation, as if the Creator Himself urged him forward.

Felix dismounted, his boots sinking slightly into the soft, moss-laden soil, the scent of earth and dew rising to meet him, a stark contrast to the smoke and ash of recent battles that still clung to his cloak. He approached the forest's entrance on foot, each step deliberate, feeling the weight of the moment settle over him like a mantle woven of wind and light. The air was rich with the fragrance of moss, pine, and ancient loam, and a gentle breeze carried the whispers of the woods—soft, sibilant voices that seemed to speak his name, as if the trees themselves recognized the Element Hero foretold in their ancient boughs.

From behind him, Titania descended, her golden wings glinting as she landed gracefully at his side. Her presence was a steadying force, her voice calm yet imbued with purpose. "The

Stag lies at the heart of the forest, Felix," she said. "It is there you must go to claim the Earth Crystal."

Felix turned to her, his brow creasing with both curiosity and unease. "Is there anything I should know about the Stag?" he asked, his voice steady but tinged with the weight of the unknown.

Titania's gaze met his, her eyes reflecting a quiet reverence. "The Stag is a creature of immense power, Felix—Terranus, the Earth Stag, guardian of the Earth Crystal. He stands nearly as large as the Fire Lion you faced, a being of awe and strength. His antlers are golden, sharp as the finest spears, capable of piercing flesh with little hesitation. He is not merely a beast but a judge of worthiness, testing those who seek the crystal's power. Approach him with respect and courage, for his trial will demand both."

Felix nodded, absorbing her words as his heart quickened. He glanced back at the forest entrance, the shadowed path ahead whispering of mystery and peril. Closing his eyes, he clasped the cross pendant at his chest and murmured a swift prayer: "Creator, guide my steps and strengthen my heart." The familiar warmth of the pendant steadied him, and with a deep breath, he stepped into the Whispering Woods.

The moment Felix crossed the threshold, the world shifted. The air grew cooler, the sunlight filtering through the thick canopy in thin, golden shafts. The forest was alive with sound—the rustle of leaves overhead, the distant trill of birds, and a soft, eerie whisper carried on the wind, as if the trees themselves were speaking. His steps were cautious, his boots pressing into the damp earth, each movement deliberate as he ventured deeper into the woods.

The path wound between towering trees, their sprawling roots forcing him to navigate carefully. Shadows flickered at the edges of his vision, and the air grew heavy with an otherworldly presence. The deeper he went, the more the forest seemed to test him. The trail twisted unexpectedly, doubling back on itself or narrowing until he had to squeeze between gnarled trunks. At times, the branches above seemed to reach down, brushing his cloak with a touch that felt almost intentional. The whispers intensified, a chorus of voices weaving through the leaves: *You are not ready. A carpenter's son cannot bear this burden. Turn back.*

Felix's grip tightened on his staff, the Wind and Fire Crystals pulsing faintly at his chest. "I am the Creator's chosen," he whispered to himself, his voice a quiet defiance against the doubt. "I will not falter." He pressed onward, his faith a shield against the forest's murmurs.

After what seemed hours of wandering through the Whispering Woods' shadowed depths, the trees began to thin, and a soft, golden light pierced the canopy ahead, casting radiant beams across the moss-laden earth. Felix's breath caught as he stepped into a clearing—the heart of the Whispering Woods, a sacred grove where the air was still, thick with anticipation, as if Pangea itself held its breath. In the center stood Terranus, the Earth Stag, an avatar of the Creator's primal might, his presence a living monument to the earth's enduring strength.

The creature was breathtaking, nearly as vast as the Fire Lion, his coat a deep, earthy brown that shimmered faintly in the dappled sunlight, each hair gleaming like the rich loam of Pangea's ancient fields. His golden antlers, broad and branching like the roots of the world, gleamed like molten metal, their razor-sharp tips catching the light in a dance of divine fire. His eyes, ancient and wise, locked onto Felix, assessing him with a gaze that pierced through to his soul, as if weighing his worth against the scales of eternity. The clearing pulsed with a quiet power, its mossy floor etched with faint spirals—runes of the Earth Crystal, whispered to lie hidden within the grove, guarded by Terranus's unyielding vigil.

The Whispering Woods pressed in around Felix, the air heavy with an unnatural stillness, the towering trees looming taller, their gnarled branches twisting like claws of ancient sentinels. Shadows deepened, swallowing the faint sunlight, and the ground quivered beneath his boots, a subtle tremor that warned of the trial to come. The whispers of the woods, once soft, grew sharp and venomous, slithering through the leaves like serpents: *You are not ready. You cannot bear this burden. Turn back.* Felix's hands tightened around his staff, the wood slick with sweat, the Wind and Fire Crystals at his chest flickering weakly, their glow dimmed by the forest's oppressive weight. His heart thudded wildly, each beat a drum in his ears, and a cold sweat prickled across his brow, stinging his eyes as doubt took root like a weed in his soul.

Visions flickered at the edges of his sight—Eldenwold burning, its fields choked with ash, its people screaming under

Daegon's shadow; Rowan, his brother, bound in the Cragspire Hills, his fair hair matted with blood, his fate a gnawing void; Burhgard's smoldering ruins, the Spiral Serpent banners mocking the fallen. *What if I fail?* The question clawed at him, relentless, threatening to unravel his resolve. His legs trembled, threatening to buckle, and his grip on the staff faltered, the Firesong Blade at his hip heavy with the Fyrclad Kin's trust, yet silent in the face of his fear. He was no hero—just Felix Aldric, a carpenter's son who knew the weight of a hammer better than a weapon, whose hesitation before the Wind Crystal in Eldenwold had nearly cost him everything. *What if I fail?* The whispers swelled, a cacophony of mockery, and the trees seemed to close in, their roots rising like a cage forged by the forest's ancient will.

Terranus shifted, pawing the ground with a hoof that sent tremors rippling through the earth, the moss quivering as if stirred by Pangea's heartbeat. "Fear binds you, Felix Aldric," the Stag rumbled, his voice deep and resonant, like the groan of shifting stone in the depths of the world. "The earth does not yield to the timid, nor does the Creator's light shine through a heart shackled by doubt." The words struck Felix like a blow, amplifying the panic clawing at his throat, his vision blurring as his pulse raced.

Yet amidst the storm, a faint warmth bloomed at his chest. He closed his eyes, shutting out the taunting visions, and whispered, "Creator, renew my heart. Let Your light guide me, as it did my father and brother, to bear this burden for Pangea." The whispers faltered, their venom dulled, and a flicker of calm pierced his soul, like sunlight breaking through a storm cloud. He thought of his mother, Elara, her steady hands mending broken

144

lives; of Torin, his faith unshakable as the oak he shaped; and of Rowan, whose courage Felix carried like a torch in the dark. *I won't let them down.*

Felix opened his eyes, meeting Terranus's ancient gaze with a shaky but growing resolve. "I am the Creator's chosen," he said, his voice trembling yet firm, echoing through the grove like a vow carved in stone. "My faith will hold me, for Eldenwold, for my family, for all of Pangea." The Stag's eyes gleamed with a hint of approval, and the forest's oppressive weight lifted slightly, the shadows retreating as if cowed by his defiance. The Crystals flared brighter, their azure and crimson light dancing across the clearing, as if the Earth Crystal, hidden within, stirred in recognition.

Terranus lowered his antlers, their golden tips glinting with menace, and the ground trembled anew, the runes in the moss glowing faintly, as if the grove itself braced for the trial's climax. "Prove your worth, Element Hero," the Stag intoned, his voice a challenge that shook the air. Without warning, he charged, his massive form a blur of power and intent, antlers lowered like twin spears forged by the Creator's hand. Panic flared anew, sharp and blinding, urging Felix to flee, but the pendant's warmth and his prayer's echo held him fast. *Trust in the Creator.* In that heartbeat, his fear shattered like glass. He dove aside, the Wind Crystal surging with power, the air whistling as the antlers grazed his cloak, tearing a shred of fabric. He landed hard, rolling to his feet, staff raised, breath ragged but eyes blazing with determination, the Firesong Blade at his hip pulsing as if ready to sing in the trial's crucible.

Terranus turned, his gaze piercing yet proud. "You have faced your fear," he said, voice warm with respect. "Now, prove your courage."

The ground rumbled again, and before Felix could respond, a ramp-like hill erupted from the earth, its slope steep and jagged. Terranus bounded up it with graceful power, hooves pounding the soil. At the peak, he leaped into the air, his massive form soaring, antlers gleaming like spears aimed at Felix's heart.

Felix's pulse thundered, but his faith surged, drowning out fear. He felt the Creator's presence, the warmth of the Wind and Fire Crystals pulsing in rhythm with his resolve. "For You, Creator!" he shouted, planting his feet. As Terranus descended, Felix summoned the Wind Crystal's might, channeling a massive gust that roared like a tempest. The force struck Terranus mid-air, sending the Stag hurtling sideways. He crashed into a towering tree at the clearing's edge, the trunk shuddering under the impact, leaves raining down.

Felix stood, chest heaving, the Wind Crystal's glow fading, but his resolve burning brighter. He gripped his staff, ready for another charge, but Terranus rose slowly, unharmed, his golden antlers catching the light. The Stag's eyes shone with approval, his voice warm with respect. "You have not only countered my strike, Felix Aldric, but conquered your fear. It is the brave and bold in faith who are called to serve the Creator."

Felix lowered his staff, relief and awe washing over him. "I only wish to honor His will," he said, voice steady but humble.

Terranus stepped closer, his presence no longer a threat but a blessing. "The earth requires sacrifice," he said. "You have offered your fear, releasing the doubt that lingered in your heart. Trust the path you walk and the strength the Creator has bestowed."

Closing his eyes, Felix recalled every moment of uncertainty—facing wraiths, standing before the Fire Lion, witnessing Meadowbrook's ruin. Each time, he had prevailed by the Creator's grace. "I trust in You," he whispered, sincerity trembling in his voice. "I let go of my fear."

A warmth surged through him, radiating from the crystals at his chest. When he opened his eyes, Terranus nodded, his expression solemn. "You have proven yourself worthy, Felix Aldric. The Earth Crystal is yours."

From the earth at the Stag's feet, a glowing gem emerged—deep, rich green, pulsing with the land's steady heartbeat. It floated toward Felix, merging with his chest alongside the Wind and Fire Crystals. As it settled, a surge of power grounded him, connecting him to Pangea's roots, a strength as unyielding as the forest.

Terranus bowed his head, voice softer. "Go forth, Element Hero. The earth stands with you, as do the winds and flames. Wield their power wisely, and may the Creator's light lead you to victory."

Felix rose, gratitude swelling in his heart. "Thank you, Great Stag. I will honor your gift and the trust you've placed in me."

He turned, making his way back through the forest. The path seemed clearer, trees parting as if honoring his passage. The whispers that once taunted now murmured encouragement, urging him onward.

Emerging from the heart of the Whispering Woods, Felix Aldric felt the Earth Crystal's steady pulse at his chest, its deep green glow harmonizing with the Wind and Fire Crystals. The forest, once a maze of taunting shadows and twisting paths, now seemed to guide him. The towering trees stood as silent sentinels, their branches parting to ease his passage, and the eerie whispers that had challenged his resolve softened into murmurs of encouragement. Each step felt more certain, as if the earth itself recognized him as its champion, the combined power of the three crystals thrumming at his chest, anchoring his soul with purpose and strength.

The journey back through the forest took hours, the dense canopy filtering sunlight into thin, golden shafts that lengthened as the day waned. By the time Felix reached the western edge of the Whispering Woods, where he had left his horse tethered, the sun hung low, casting a warm amber glow across the landscape. The air carried the rich scent of moss and the faint coolness of early evening.

From the fading light, Titania descended, her majestic form gliding gracefully to meet him. Her wings caught the last rays of the setting sun, shimmering like molten gold, and her eyes glowed with pride and sacred wisdom. She landed softly near the forest's western edge, her presence a steadying force, a beacon of the Creator's guidance.

"Felix Aldric," she said, her voice resonant and serene, "you have come far. The Earth Crystal is yours, earned through courage and faith. Only one remains—the Water Crystal, guarded by the Leviathan on an island at the heart of the Cordelia Ocean, far to the south."

Felix stepped closer, his heart swelling with determination as he glanced toward the southern horizon, where the ocean's distant sheen beckoned. "The Cordelia Ocean," he echoed, visions of its boundless waves stirring both awe and resolve. "It's a long journey, but I'll face it. Daegon's forces must be stopped before they bring more ruin to Pangea."

Titania nodded, her gaze steady and approving. "The path to the ocean is fraught with peril, Felix, and the Leviathan is a formidable guardian. Yet your bravery and steadfastness have grown with each trial. Trust in the Creator and the power He has bestowed upon you. You do not walk alone."

Felix bowed his head slightly, humility tempering the eagerness burning within him. "Thank you, Titania. I feel stronger now, ready for what lies ahead. With the Creator's guidance and these crystals, I'll do all I can to succeed."

A faint smile touched Titania's lips, her expression softening with warmth. "You have grown much since Eldenwold,

Felix. The Creator chose wisely in you. Go now, and may His light guide your path."

With that, she spread her golden wings and ascended into the twilight sky, her form blending with the deepening hues of orange and purple until she vanished from sight. Felix watched her go, a renewed inner strength coursing through him—brave yet humble, eager yet grounded. He turned to his horse, its copper coat gleaming faintly in the evening light, and untethered it with a steady hand. As he prepared to mount, he considered his options. The sun was nearly set, and Oakridge lay just an hour's ride to the west. Camping in the wilderness offered little safety compared to the city's sturdy walls, and he could use the rest and perhaps learn more about Daegon's movements from King Cedric or Arthur.

With a decisive nod, Felix mounted his horse, the saddle creaking softly beneath him. "Oakridge it is," he murmured, nudging the steed westward. The ride was swift, the fields blurring past as the last light faded from the sky. By the time he reached the city's western gate, twilight had settled, the stars beginning to pierce the velvet dark.

The gate guards spotted him, their faces breaking into grins of recognition. "Felix Aldric!" called one, a grizzled man with a cross-and-oak shield at his side. "Back so soon? Word was you'd gone toward the Whispering Woods—didn't expect to see you this night!"

Felix dismounted, patting his horse's flank as he stepped onto the cobblestone. "I've claimed the Earth Crystal," he said, a tired but proud smile tugging at his lips. "But it's late, and I'd rather rest here tonight. Besides, I need to know more about Daegon's forces—how they've reached so far inland."

The guard's expression sobered, but he nodded. "Wise choice, sir. The king'll want to hear of your victory. Come on in—Arthur's at the castle, and he'll be glad to see you."

Felix led his horse through the gate as it creaked open, the familiar sights of Oakridge washing over him—the stone arches, the wooden beams etched with knotwork, the banners of the sacred cross and oak fluttering in the breeze. The city hummed with quiet resilience, its people undeterred by the recent battle. As he stepped into the warm glow of Oakridge's streets, the weight of the Earth Crystal pulsed steadily at his chest, a reminder of his purpose. The road to the Cordelia Ocean loomed ahead, but for now, he found strength among allies, readying himself for the trials yet to come.

Chapter 11: The Call of the Sea

Felix Aldric rode through the twilight streets of Oakridge, the rhythmic clop of his horse's hooves echoing off the cobblestones. The city hummed with quiet resilience, its people still mending the scars of battle under the fading light. As he approached the inner castle, its sturdy stone walls rose before him, adorned with intricate oak motifs carved into the gates. The gates stood open, flanked by guards who nodded in recognition as he passed. Dismounting, Felix handed the reins to a stable hand and stepped into the courtyard, his cloak swaying lightly in the evening breeze.

At the entrance, he was met by Owain, the grizzled leader of the King's Guard. Owain's polished armor gleamed faintly in the torchlight, the oak-and-cross emblem prominent on his chest, his silver-streaked beard catching the glow. "Felix Aldric," Owain greeted, his voice warm yet formal, tinged with a Welsh lilt. "Welcome back to Oakridge."

Felix offered a tired but genuine smile, brushing a hand through his ash-dusted, dirty-blonde hair. "Thank you, Owain. I'd like to inform the king, if he's not too busy, that I've been successful in claiming the Earth Crystal. And, humbly, I'd request to rest here tonight."

Owain's stern expression softened, a flicker of pride in his eyes. "A fine success indeed. I'll inform His Majesty at once."

With a crisp turn, he strode into the castle, his armored steps echoing on the stone.

Felix lingered in the courtyard, the weight of the Earth Crystal pulsing steadily at his chest alongside the Wind and Fire Crystals. The trials of the Whispering Woods still clung to him—Terranus's golden antlers, the forest's taunting whispers—but he stood taller now, his weariness tempered by triumph. Moments later, the castle doors swung open, and King Cedric emerged, a broad smile lighting his weathered face. His royal armor bore the Oakridge banner—a white cross beneath an oak tree—and his brown hair, streaked with silver, framed eyes bright with joy.

"Felix!" Cedric called, his voice rich with warmth and a faint Welsh accent. "Owain tells me you've returned victorious. The Earth Crystal is yours?"

Felix bowed his head, humility grounding his words. "Yes, Your Majesty. The Creator guided me through the Whispering Woods, and Terranus deemed me worthy. I'm grateful for your hospitality—it means more than I can say."

Cedric's smile deepened, his hand gesturing dismissively. "Nonsense, lad. You're always welcome in Oakridge. This castle is your home whenever you need it."

The king's tone shifted, growing somber as he stepped closer, his brow furrowing. "But there's more pressing news. We've updates on how Daegon's forces pierced so deep into the lands of Derwgor."

Felix straightened, his exhaustion giving way to eagerness. "Please, Your Majesty, tell me."

Cedric sighed, his gaze distant. "A city on the border between Derwgor and the Kronemark was attacked—a major trade hub on Pangea's southern coast, called Parelkaap. It's a place of Kaapvaarders spirit, its harbors bustling with ships. Daegon's forces struck from the sea, raiding their vessels and harbors, while an army landed on the western shores. The Kronemarkers sent aid to keep Parelkaap from falling, but a small contingent of Daegon's troops slipped past."

Felix's eyes widened, his mind racing. "And now?"

"Reports say Daegon's navy is wreaking havoc in the Cordelia Ocean," Cedric continued, his voice grave. "They're raiding trader ships, making the southeastern shores perilous. The waters there are a battleground."

Felix shook his head, a wry smile tugging at his lips as the irony sank in. "It's almost too fitting. My quest pulls me south, Your Majesty—to cross the Cordelia Ocean and reach its heart for the final Water Crystal."

Cedric's eyes gleamed with recognition, a faint smile returning. "The Creator works in mysterious ways, doesn't He? It seems the chessboard has aligned for you, Felix Consumer. Parelkaap's traders have some of the finest ships on the southern coast. Perhaps you're meant to aid them and secure passage across the sea."

Felix paused, reflecting on the king's words. The steady pulse of the Earth Crystal grounded him, its strength mingling with the Wind and Fire at his chest. "You're right," he said, resolve firming his voice. "I must head there as soon as I can—tomorrow, at first light."

Cedric nodded approvingly. "Then it's settled. You'll use the same room as before. Parelkaap lies southeast from Oakridge, directly south from the western edge of the Whispering Woods. Rest well—you'll need your strength."

Felix tilted his head, a flicker of curiosity in his gaze. "Is there anything else you know, Your Majesty?"

The king's expression darkened briefly. "Not at present, I'm afraid. We're stretched thin with these recent attacks, but if anything comes up before you leave, I'll see you're informed."

Felix bowed deeply, gratitude softening his features. "Thank you again, Your Majesty. I'll head to my room now to rest."

Cedric clapped a hand on his shoulder, his smile returning. "Good lad. I'll have food sent up—sustain yourself for the road ahead."

With a final nod, Felix turned and made his way through the castle's torchlit halls, the scent of polished oak and stone enveloping him. The familiar room welcomed him—its canopied bed carved with oak leaves, the hearth crackling softly in the corner. He set his staff and Firesong Blade against the wall, their weight a quiet reassurance, and sank onto the bed's edge.

The canopied bed, adorned with carved oak leaves, and the crackling hearth offered a rare moment of calm. His gaze drifted to the window, where stars shimmered over Oakridge, a quiet testament to the Creator's watchfulness.

Moments later, a soft knock sounded at the door, pulling him from his thoughts. The door creaked open, and Felix's eyes lit with recognition as the same servant girl from the night before stepped inside. Her dark hair was neatly tied back, and she carried a tray brimming with food—roasted meat, fresh bread, a pitcher of water, and a bottle of Vineland Vale's famous wine. Her face brightened as she met his gaze.

"Praise the Creator for your victory, sir," she said warmly, her voice carrying genuine relief. "I'm so happy to see you back safe."

Felix smiled, touched by her kindness. "Thank you for your words and your service. It means a lot."

She set the tray on the table beside the bed, her movements steady and practiced. Glancing at her, Felix tilted his head slightly. "May I ask your name?"

Her eyes sparkled as she replied, "It's Nia, sir."

"Nice to meet you, Nia," Felix said, his tone warm. "I hope Oakridge stays safe while I'm gone."

Nia nodded, her expression softening with faith. "It's all in the hands of the Almighty Creator. We trust in Him."

They shared a quiet smile, a moment of understanding passing between them. With a slight curtsy, Nia stepped back. "Enjoy your meal, sir," she said before slipping out, closing the door softly behind her.

Felix turned to the tray. The roasted meat glistened, the fresh bread steamed faintly, and the rich red wine from Vineland Vale gleamed in its bottle, promising a taste of comfort. He ate slowly, savoring the meal, the flavors grounding him after the trials of his journey. The roasted meat melted on his tongue, the fresh bread crumbled warmly between his fingers, and the rich Vineland Vale wine left a lingering sweetness that eased the day's trials. He sipped the water last, its coolness refreshing him as he finished the meal.

With a full belly, he leaned back in the chair, the crackling hearth casting a soft glow across the room. The bed, with its carved oak leaves, beckoned him, and he rose, setting the empty tray aside.

Kneeling beside the bed, Felix clasped his hands, his cross pendant warm against his chest. The Wind, Fire, and Earth Crystals pulsed faintly, their combined glow a quiet testament to his journey. "Creator," he whispered, his voice steady yet reverent, "thank You for this day, for the strength to claim the Earth Crystal, and for the shelter of Oakridge. Watch over Rowan, my family, and all who stand against Daegon's shadow. Guide me to Parelkaap and the Water Crystal, that I may serve Your will." The prayer settled his spirit, and he climbed into bed, pulling the heavy blankets over him. The softness enveloped him, and within moments, sleep claimed him, deep and dreamless, a rare peace washing over the Element Hero.

Dawn broke gently, the first rays of light slipping through the window to rouse Felix from his slumber. He stirred, blinking against the golden glow, and stretched his arms, the rest having knit together the weariness of his bones. Rising from the bed, his bare feet met the cool stone floor, grounding him as he began to ready himself for the journey ahead. The trial of the Water Crystal loomed in his mind, its guardian the Leviathan waiting across the Cordelia Ocean. He fastened Firesong Blade at his hip, its firestone-inlaid steel glinting in the morning light, and took up his staff, its familiar weight steadying his resolve. His cloak, mended and cleaned by the castle staff, settled over his shoulders, the subtle knotwork along its hem a reminder of the faith that carried him.

A soft knock interrupted his preparations. The door creaked open, and Nia, the servant girl with dark hair tied neatly back, stepped in, carrying a tray laden with breakfast—roasted meat, fresh bread, a pitcher of water, and a small jug of milk, just as she had the morning before. Her face brightened as she saw him, her voice warm. "Good morning, sir. The king wishes you strength for your journey."

Felix smiled, gratitude softening his features. "Thank you, Nia. This is more than I could ask for."

She set the tray on the table, her eyes sparkling with quiet pride. "Safe travels to Parelkaap, sir. May the Creator guide you."

"I hope so, too," Felix replied, his tone earnest. "Please thank the king for me."

With a slight curtsy, Nia slipped out, leaving him to his meal. He ate slowly, savoring the tender meat, the crusty bread, and the rich milk, each bite fueling him for the road ahead. The Earth Crystal pulsed steadily at his chest, its deep green glow harmonizing with the Wind and Fire Crystals, a reminder of the power he wielded and the responsibility it carried. When the last morsel was gone, he gathered his belongings—staff in hand, blade at his side, cloak secure—and stepped into the corridor, the scent of polished oak and torchlight guiding him toward the throne room.

The throne room was bathed in the soft light of dawn, the large hearth crackling at one end, the stained-glass window spilling colorful patterns across the floor. As Felix entered, a familiar figure turned to greet him—Arthur, clad in his oak-emblazoned armor, his weathered face breaking into a warm smile.

"Felix!" Arthur called, striding forward to clasp his hand firmly, his Welsh lilt thick with camaraderie. "I heard of your victory in the Whispering Woods—well done, my friend. I'm sorry I missed you yesterday; duty kept me at the walls."

Felix returned the smile, relief washing over him at the sight of his friend. "There's no need, Arthur. I'm just glad to see you again before I leave for Parelkaap."

Arthur's eyes widened slightly, his grip tightening. "So you've heard the news, then—of what's happened there?"

Felix nodded, his expression resolute. "Yes, King Cedric told me last night. Daegon's forces struck Parelkaap from the sea, and his navy's causing havoc in the Cordelia Ocean. It's where my quest leads me next—the Water Crystal lies on an island at its heart, guarded by the Leviathan."

Arthur's gaze turned thoughtful, his voice lowering. "I hope you can find a way across those waters, Felix. Daegon's made them treacherous—raiding ships, blocking trade. It won't be an easy crossing." He paused, then added, "And be careful on the road to Parelkaap. Our scouts say the forces that attacked Oakridge might still linger in the southeast. We don't know where they've gone or what they're planning."

Felix's brow furrowed, the warning settling heavily on his shoulders. "I'll stay vigilant. Thanks for letting me know, Arthur."

Before Arthur could reply, the throne-room doors swung open, and King Cedric entered, his royal armor gleaming with the Oakridge banner—a white cross beneath an oak tree. His brown hair, streaked with silver, framed a face warm with recognition. "Felix, Arthur," he greeted, his faint Welsh accent rolling through the hall. "I'm happy to see you both this morning."

Felix bowed his head, respect and gratitude in his stance. "Your Majesty, I've come to say farewell. I'm ready for the journey ahead and will leave at once."

Cedric's eyes gleamed with approval. "Good lad. The road to Parelkaap is a two-day ride on horseback across the Southern Marches—a rugged land south of the Whispering Woods, along the southern coast. You've proven yourself capable, Felix, but take care. Daegon's shadow stretches far."

Felix nodded, his resolve firm. "I will, Your Majesty. Thank you for everything—your hospitality, your support. Oakridge has given me strength for this quest."

Cedric stepped closer, placing a hand on Felix's shoulder, his smile paternal. "And you've given us hope, Felix. The Creator guides you, and the prayers of Derwgor ride with you."

Arthur stepped forward, his voice steady. "Pangea will be safe, Felix. We'll hold the line here, keep Daegon's forces at bay until you can strike the final blow."

Felix's chest tightened, humbled by their faith in him. "I won't let you down," he said, his voice thick with emotion as he bowed his head once more.

With their words echoing in his heart, Felix made his way through the castle to the western gate. The morning air was crisp, the sky a pale blue streaked with the promise of a clear day. The people of Oakridge were already at work—hammers rang against stone, wooden beams rose to mend the battle's scars, their resilience a quiet inspiration. He reached the courtyard where his horse waited, its copper coat gleaming in the sunlight, and mounted with a steady hand.

Glancing back, he saw Arthur and Owain at the gate, raising their hands in farewell. Felix returned the gesture, then urged his horse forward, riding out of the western gate and turning southeast along the southern side of the Whispering Woods. The forest loomed to his left, its dark silhouette a stark contrast to the open fields stretching toward the horizon. The road wound through the Southern Marches—a land of rolling hills and coastal cliffs, the distant shimmer of the Cordelia Ocean calling him onward.

As he rode, Felix reflected on the faith placed in him by Cedric, Arthur, and the people of Derwgor. Their trust bolstered his spirit, mingling with the steady pulse of the crystals at his chest. The journey to Parelkaap would be long, and the dangers Arthur warned of lingered in his thoughts, but he felt the Creator's presence guiding him. With a murmured prayer— "Creator, strengthen my heart for what lies ahead"—he spurred his horse onward, the promise of the sea and the final crystal pulling him toward his destiny.

Hours later, as the sun dipped below the horizon, casting a warm glow of orange and purple across the Southern Marches, his journey to Parelkaap weighed heavily on his mind. But for now, the fading light and the steady clop of hooves kept him grounded.

As he rounded a bend, a flicker of light caught his eye—a campfire, its glow stark against the encroaching dusk. Curiosity stirred within him, tempered by caution. Felix dismounted, securing his horse to a gnarled tree half-shrouded by a boulder, and crept forward, staff in hand. Peering from his vantage point, he spotted six soldiers in serpent-marked armor gathered in a small clearing, their weapons glinting in the firelight. At their center paced a tall captain, twin swords strapped to his back, his presence commanding and deliberate.

Felix crouched in the underbrush at the edge of the clearing, the salty tang of the nearby sea mingling with the acrid smoke of the campfire. Twilight draped the coastal forest in shades of bruised purple and fading gold, where ancient cedars whispered secrets to the wind, their gnarled roots twisting like the veins of the earth itself. The camp below was a ragged affair: a dozen tents stitched from weathered hides, clustered around a central fire pit where skewers of salted fish sizzled over flames. These were Daegon's men—hardened remnants of the shattered Legion, their armor still gleaming faintly under the dying light. Scars of old battles marked their faces, and their eyes held the hollow gleam of soldiers who had lost a battle but not their edge.

Felix's breath hitched in his throat, a knot of resolve tightening in his chest. He couldn't let them push further south; the fishing villages along the jagged shoreline were already reeling from raids, their thatched roofs no match for marauders like these. The crystals at his sternum—Wind, Fire, and Earth—pulsed faintly against his skin.

With a deep, steadying breath, Felix drew upon the Wind Crystal. A low hum built in his core, like the distant roar of a storm, and he unleashed it in a focused torrent. The gust exploded into the camp like an invisible battering ram, ripping tent stakes from the soil and scattering embers in a chaotic whirlwind. Dust and leaves spiraled upward in a blinding veil, choking the air and muffling shouts of alarm. Seizing the moment, Felix channeled the Fire Crystal next, its heat blooming in his veins like molten iron. A spark leaped from his outstretched hand, igniting the stacked crates of dried rations and oil flasks in a voracious blaze. Flames roared skyward, painting the trees in flickering orange and devouring supplies.

The soldiers snapped to action with the precision of a well-oiled machine, forged in the crucible of Daegon's campaigns. They shook off the surprise, shields clanging as they formed a phalanx, their eyes sharp as flint, sweeping the encroaching shadows. Crossbows were shouldered, bolts nocked with mechanical efficiency, while others drew blades.

At the forefront strode the captain, a towering figure clad in blackened plate armor. His face was a map of old wounds: a jagged scar bisecting his left eye, which glowed faintly with an inner fire, a remnant of the pyromantic rituals that bound his soul to flame. His forehead bore the serpent's mark. "The Element Hero," he growled, his voice a gravelly rumble that cut through the chaos like a blade through silk. He drew his twin swords with a theatrical flourish, the blades igniting in unison—flames coiling along the edges like living serpents, fed by his Master's innate affinity for fire magic, drawn from the wicked heart of Daegon's magical mark branded upon his head. The fiery dance cast elongated shadows across the clearing, twisting like tormented spirits.

Felix's heart thundered against his ribs, but he planted his feet wide, drawing a surge of unyielding calm from the Earth Crystal's steady thrum—a deep, resonant vibration that rooted him like the ancient cedars around them. He'd faced greater threats. Survival demanded not just power, but cunning. With a swift upward gesture of his staff, he channeled Earth again, sending a seismic ripple through the soil. The ground buckled and split in a jagged line toward the captain, uprooting ferns and flinging clods of earth like shrapnel.

The captain leaped aside with predatory grace, his boots barely skimming the fracturing terrain, and retaliated in a blur. His twin swords slashed forward, trailing arcs of searing flame that scorched the air, the heat warping reality like a mirage. Felix ducked low, the edge of his travel-worn cloak singed black, the acrid smell of burning wool stinging his nostrils. He needed strategy over brute force.

Channeling Earth once more, Felix raised a barrier of jagged stone from the forest floor, a makeshift wall veined with quartz that shimmered in the firelight, buying him precious seconds. The soldiers, sensing opportunity, split to flank him— half circling left through the underbrush, the other right, their boots crunching over fallen leaves. But Felix had anticipated the maneuver. He summoned a cascade from the Earth Crystal, loosening the soil beneath their feet into a treacherous mire. The ground gave way in a shallow pit, swallowing boots and eliciting curses as they stumbled, trapped up to their knees in the shifting earth.

The duel escalated into a frenzy. The captain lunged like a striking viper, his twin blades a whirlwind of fire and steel, each strike precise and fueled by years of battlefield dominance. Felix drew his Firesong Blade. Steel met steel in a cascade of sparks, the impact jarring up Felix's arms. His Wind Crystal surged in response, a cool rush filling his limbs, boosting his speed to a blur that matched the captain's relentless assault. But the man's fire magic was unyielding—a constant barrage that turned the air stifling, sweat beading on Felix's brow.

A fiery arc swept toward Felix's chest; he rolled aside in a desperate tumble, the heat blistering his exposed skin, leaving red welts that throbbed like embers. He countered with a focused whirlwind from the Wind Crystal, the vortex scattering the captain's flames into harmless wisps and shoving him back several paces, his armor scraping against the rough bark of a tree.

The captain snarled, his scarred lip curling in fury, and hurled a barrage of fireballs—compact orbs of compressed inferno that streaked through the dusk like falling stars, trailing comet tails of smoke. Felix reacted instinctively, raising another stone wall with the Earth Crystal, the projectiles exploding against it in showers of molten rock. But the captain was already in motion, vaulting over the crumbling barrier with acrobatic prowess, his flaming slash aimed unerringly at Felix's shoulder.

Felix twisted at the last instant, Firesong Blade deflecting the primary blow with a resonant clang, but the second sword grazed his arm—a shallow cut that parted fabric and flesh, blood welling hot and sticky through the tear. Pain lanced through him, a sharp clarion that honed his focus amid the adrenaline haze. He couldn't match the captain's pure sword mastery; the man moved like a flame incarnate, unpredictable and devouring.

But Felix had the elements as allies. Channeling Earth with gritted teeth, he cracked the ground beneath the captain's feet, a precise fissure that threw the man off balance, his armored boot slipping into the crevice. As the captain stumbled, Felix summoned a tight, razor-sharp gust from the Wind Crystal, slamming him backward into a moss-covered boulder with a dull, bone-jarring thud. The impact echoed through the clearing, dislodging leaves from overhead branches.

The captain recovered with inhuman swiftness, shaking off the blow like a hound shedding water. His eyes blazed crimson, pupils dilating as he tapped deeper into his pyromantic reserves—a forbidden surge that risked burning out his own life force. He unleashed a torrent of flame, a roaring wall of heat that advanced like a tidal wave, scorching the grass to ash and forcing Felix to leap back, his cloak smoldering at the edges. The air shimmered with intensity, the duel teetering on the edge of catastrophe, as Felix readied his next move—perhaps a fusion of crystals to turn the tide.

Felix's gaze flicked to the empty pit. The soldiers had clambered out and were fleeing into the twilight, their serpent-marked cloaks vanishing down the trail. His speed could overtake them, but the captain demanded his full attention. "Creator, guide my hand," he whispered, centering himself.

He thrust both hands forward, the Fire Crystal flaring. Divine flame surged into Firesong Blade, its firestone glowing fiercely. The captain charged, his swords a fiery whirlwind, but Felix was ready. He sidestepped, using a wind-enhanced burst of speed, and drove his blade through a gap in the captain's guard. The strike pierced armor and flesh, the captain's flames flickering out as he gasped, collapsing to his knees.

Felix stood over him, chest heaving, blood trickling down his arm. The captain's red eyes dimmed, his swords clattering to the ground. Felix knelt, searching the man's cloak, and found a scrap of parchment. Unfolding it, he read the scrawled words: *The fleet gathers in strength. Prepare for the invasion. The time is near.* His pulse quickened. A fleet? An invasion? The note offered no hint of the target, only the chilling certainty that Daegon's forces were mobilizing on a grand scale. He slipped the parchment into his cloak, its vague warning a puzzle to unravel later.

He rose, scanning the clearing. The soldiers were gone, their retreat swallowed by the night's embrace, their footsteps fading into the distant rustle of leaves. They'd carry tales of the Element Hero's power—tales that might sow doubt in Daegon's ranks, or spur them to greater vengeance. For now, the trail was clear, the camp a smoldering ruin of charred tents and scattered ashes. The distant sea breeze stirred the air, carrying the faint tang of salt and the promise of a new dawn. Felix adjusted his grip on Firesong Blade, the weight of the parchment and the looming threat it foretold heavy on his mind.

As twilight deepened into night, Felix made camp a short distance away, the stars emerging like scattered lanterns above. He sat by his own small fire, the parchment resting in his hand, its words replaying in his mind: *The fleet gathers in strength. Prepare for the invasion.* The captain's fire magic had been a fierce challenge, a testament to the power Daegon still commanded through his followers. Yet Felix had prevailed, his mastery of the crystals and his wits proving stronger.

But the parchment gnawed at him. A large fleet implied a significant strike—perhaps against Parelkaap's harbors, or another coastal stronghold. Without a location, it was a shadow looming over Pangea, a threat he could feel but not yet grasp. His resolve deepened. He would reach Parelkaap, secure the Water Crystal, and uncover the truth behind this invasion. Daegon's plans, whatever they were, would not succeed.

Felix leaned back on his bedroll, gazing at the stars stretching endlessly above, their light a testament to the Creator's vastness. Clasping his cross pendant, he whispered, "Creator, guide me to Parelkaap and unveil the truth of this invasion. Watch over Rowan and all I hold dear." The Wind, Fire, and Earth Crystals pulsed steadily at his chest, their warmth mingling with the ocean's distant murmur. With his prayer anchoring his heart, Felix closed his eyes, the promise of tomorrow's journey to Parelkaap carrying him into a deep, restful sleep.

Chapter 12: The Harbor's Hope

The first light of dawn crept over the Southern Marches, casting a golden glow across the rugged cliffs and the distant shimmer of the Cordelia Ocean. Felix Aldric stirred from his bedroll, the parchment's cryptic message still burning in his mind: *The fleet gathers in strength. Prepare for the invasion. The time is near.* His pulse quickened with urgency Parelkaap, a vital coastal city, could be Daegon's next target, and he couldn't let it suffer the same fate as Meadowbrook, reduced to ash and ruin. He sprang to his feet, the cool morning air sharp against his skin, and swiftly packed his camp. With practiced ease, he mounted his horse, its copper coat gleaming in the rising sun, and urged it into a gallop, the wind whipping through his dirty blonde hair.

The journey through the Southern Marches—a land of jagged hills and coastal cliffs—unfolded in a blur. What would typically take a full day's ride shrank to less than half as Felix pushed his steed to its limits, the rhythmic thunder of hooves echoing his racing heart. The landscape flashed by: rocky outcrops, windswept grasses, and the ever-closer shimmer of the sea. His cloak snapped behind him, the crystals at his chest—Wind, Fire, and Earth—pulsing faintly as if sharing his resolve. He whispered a prayer under his breath, "Creator, let me reach them in time," his fear for Parelkaap's fate driving him onward.

By mid-afternoon, the silhouette of Parelkaap rose on the horizon, its sturdy walls stretching to the southern shores where massive harbors opened to the Cordelia Ocean. Relief washed over Felix as he saw the city still standing, its spires and rooftops defying the ruin he'd dreaded. As he drew nearer, an orange flag caught his eye, fluttering proudly above the ramparts. It bore a white cross and a herring—a symbol of the Kaapvaarders' faith and maritime heritage. Yet signs of recent battle marred the scene: scorched patches in the surrounding fields, cracked stone along the outer defenses, and a faint tang of smoke lingering in the air. This must be the attack King Cedric had spoken of, repelled with the Kronemarkers' aid but leaving its mark.

Closer still, Felix felt the warm spring breeze off the coast, carrying the scent of salt and blooming wildflowers. Parelkaap was breathtaking despite its scars—a city of merchants and sailors, its walls embracing harbors alive with ships, their masts swaying like a forest of timber. The architecture blended sturdy stone with ornate woodwork, a testament to its wealth and resilience. His heart lifted at the sight, though the parchment's warning kept his urgency sharp.

At the northern gate, two guards in polished armor stepped forward, their hands resting on sword hilts, barring his path. "Halt! State your business," one commanded, his voice firm with a faint Dutch accent that marked the people of Parelkaap.

Felix dismounted, his boots crunching on the gravel as his cloak settled around him. "I am Felix Aldric, the Element Hero, sent by the Creator to stop Daegon's heresy," he said, his tone steady and earnest. "I ride from Oakridge, seeking to aid Parelkaap and, in return, I hope for your help in my quest."

The guards exchanged a glance, their expressions skeptical. After a brief silence, the second guard spoke, his Dutch lilt cautious. "If you are who you say you are, can you prove it?"

Felix nodded, raising his right hand to form the sacred triangle with his fingers—index and middle extended, thumb tucked beneath, ring and pinky folded down. He traced the sign of the cross: forehead, chest, left shoulder, right. As he did, the crystals at his chest glowed brightly—Wind, Fire, and Earth shimmering in unison—and a small gust of wind swirled around him, rustling the guards' cloaks and the nearby banners. Their eyes widened in shock, hands twitching toward their weapons before stilling.

"I mean you no harm," Felix assured them, his voice calm as the gust faded. "Only to help against the threat Daegon poses."

The first guard recovered, awe softening his features. "By the Creator… you speak true." He turned to his companion. "He's the Element Hero. I'll escort him to Father William—he'll want to speak with this one."

The second guard nodded, stepping aside. "Aye, pass then. Follow him."

Felix inclined his head gratefully, leading his horse as the first guard guided him through the gate. Inside, Parelkaap unfolded in vibrant splendor. Unlike Oakridge's humble warmth, this city exuded grandeur: merchant stalls lined the cobblestone streets, their colorful awnings fluttering, while sailors mended nets and traders bartered in a bustling symphony. The buildings rose higher, their stone facades adorned with maritime carvings, and the air thrummed with life. Signs of battle lingered—cracked walls, scorched banners—but they seemed days, perhaps weeks old, the city's spirit unbroken. It was clear this was a place of commerce and seafaring, its people resilient as the tides.

They approached the Great Sanctuary of Parelkaap, a towering edifice of weathered grey granite, its ancient stones hewn from the primal cliffs of Pangea's coast, their surfaces etched with swirling runes that sang of the Creator's dominion over sea and storm. Its twin spires pierced the twilight sky, their tips gilded with the fading amber of the afternoon sun, standing as sentinels of faith against the gathering shadows of Daegon's threat. Stained-glass windows, radiant with hues of sapphire, emerald, and coral, adorned the facade, each pane depicting ships braving tempestuous waves bowing beneath the Creator's radiant gaze, their colors casting a mosaic of divine light across the cobblestone courtyard. The guard beside Felix, his armor glinting faintly, knocked firmly on the heavy oak doors. The sound echoed through the courtyard, a solemn summons that stirred the air like a distant bell tolling across the harbor.

Felix's gaze swept the surroundings, the weight of his mission settling anew upon his shoulders, heavy as the Firesong Blade at his hip. The parchment's warning, tucked within his satchel, loomed large in his mind: Daegon's fleet was gathering, its dark sails poised to choke Parelkaap's harbors, the lifeblood of the city's trade and its hope for survival. The cross pendant at his chest, his father's gift, seemed to pulse with quiet resolve, an anchor to Torin's teachings: *Trust in the Creator's strength, my son, when the path grows dark.* Yet doubt gnawed at Felix's heart—could he, a wanderer marked by loss, rally this merchant city to stand against such a tide? The crystals at his chest—Wind, Fire, and Earth—warmed faintly, as if whispering courage, and he steeled himself, ready to face whatever lay beyond the doors with the hope of new allies and the Creator's guiding light.

The oak doors swung open with a deep, resonant groan, like the sigh of an ancient sea, and Father William emerged, his black robe flowing like a shadow across the stone steps, its hem embroidered with silver waves that caught the stained glass's glow. His long brown hair cascaded over his shoulders, blending into a thick beard that framed a face of solemn wisdom, etched with the quiet burdens of a shepherd guarding his flock amidst a storm. The guard straightened, his voice carrying a faint Dutch lilt, resonant of Parelkaap's maritime heritage. "Father, this is Felix Aldric, the Element Hero. He's come to aid us."

William's eyes widened, a flicker of shock giving way to a radiant joy that broke across his face like dawn over a troubled sea, his trembling smile a beacon of hope. "Praise the Creator!" he exclaimed, his voice rich with relief, its subtle lilt echoing the cadence of the city's sailors. "We have prayed for aid in this hour of peril, and here you stand—a miracle wrought by the Creator's hand, the Hero foretold to wield the Elements against the shadow." He stepped aside, gesturing warmly with a hand calloused by years of turning sacred texts. "Welcome, Felix, into our sanctuary, where the faithful of Parelkaap gather under the Creator's gaze."

Felix followed, his boots echoing on a floor of gravestones, each slab a testament to the mariners, merchants, and priests who had built this city, their names and sigils— anchors and ships—etched in fading script, a silent chorus of the faithful gone to dust. The nave stretched vast and solemn, its ceiling a marvel of medieval craftsmanship: a vaulted canopy of dark oak, hewn in ages past when the first ships sailed Pangea's seas, its beams adorned with faded paintings of the Creator calming storms and shaping the tides. The wood, ancient as the cliffs, seemed to hum with sacred history, whispering tales of those who had knelt here, their prayers woven into the grain like threads of divine will. The stained-glass windows, towering above the pews, cast vibrant beams of sapphire, coral, and gold, each pane a testament to Parelkaap's merchant wealth and unyielding devotion—ships braving maelstroms.

Felix paused, his breath catching as the sanctuary's grandeur pressed upon him, its silence a profound embrace that seemed to weigh his soul. The Firesong Blade at his hip pulsed faintly, its hidden runes echoing the carvings on the church's facade, as if blade and sanctuary were forged in the same divine fire. The cross pendant at his chest grew heavy, while the crystals warmed, their light mingling with the stained glass's glow, casting a radiant halo around him. Memories of Rowan's scars and Meadowbrook's ashes surged within, mingling with the fear that he might falter before Daegon's fleet. Yet the sanctuary's sanctity kindled a spark of resolve, a whisper of the Creator's strength that steadied his trembling heart.

William led him to a quiet corner near a side altar, where a single candle flickered, its flame a beacon in the dimness. His robe whispered against the gravestones, a soft counterpoint to the organ's distant hum, as if the sanctuary itself sang a chant of hope. "Is there anything you need, my son?" he asked gently, his eyes searching Felix's face with a priest's compassion. "Food, rest, perhaps a prayer to guide you to Thegnfast?"

Felix shook his head, his voice steady and humble. "Thank you, Father, but I'm fine. I only wish to know why you wanted to see me."

Father William's gaze softened, hope flickering in his eyes. "We have been praying for a miracle, Felix. Daegon's forces have plagued our shores, and though we've held them at bay with the Kronemarkers' help, we fear it's not enough. When I heard of your arrival, I knew you were the Creator's answer—the Element Hero sent to save our city. With you here, perhaps we can stop Daegon's darkness."

Felix nodded, his resolve firm. "I'll do all I can, Father. But I still need the Water Crystal. It lies at the heart of the ocean, and without it, I cannot face Daegon."

The priest's tone shifted slightly, a shadow of concern creeping in. "I understand, and I wish to aid you. But the recent attacks have left many of our ships damaged, and the seas are perilous. Daegon's forces raid any vessel that strays too far, and few dare sail deep into the ocean now."

Felix's chest tightened, but his voice remained steady. "I know the dangers, Father, but without the crystal, Daegon cannot be stopped. We have no choice."

Father William paused, his brow furrowing in thought. After a moment, he nodded. "You're right. We must trust in the Creator. I will take you to Captain Noah, the city's finest maritime captain. If anyone can help you reach the crystal, it's him."

Relief warmed Felix's voice. "Thank you, Father."

The priest's expression grew grave. "But know this, Felix—the Republic of Parelkaap is vulnerable. Even with your aid and the Kronemarkers, our military and mercenaries cannot hold Daegon back forever."

At that, Felix reached into his cloak and pulled out the crumpled parchment he'd found on the road. "I found this on my way here," he said, handing it to the priest. "It speaks of an attack coming soon."

Father William unfolded the note, his face paling as he read. "Creator preserve us," he whispered, horror etching his features. "Do you know where or when this will strike?"

Felix shook his head, urgency sharpening his words. "No, Father, but it's coming soon. We must be ready."

The priest's eyes hardened with determination. "Then we must go to the captain at once. He's likely at the harbor now. Come, Felix—there's no time to lose." As they turned to leave, he added, "Your horse will be cared for here at the church. You have my word."

Felix nodded, gratitude softening his tone. "Thank you, Father."

They stepped into the bustling streets, the priest leading the way toward the harbor. The city of Parelkaap sprawled before them, its vast harbor gleaming in the distance. The ocean sparkled under the sun, its massive waters stretching endlessly, dotted with ships of all kinds—merchant cogs, fishing boats, and sturdy galleons—swaying at the docks. The air buzzed with the shouts of sailors and the creak of timber, a lively pulse beneath the beauty.

At the edge of a sturdy cog ship, Father William spotted Captain Noah. The seafaring man stood tall, his broad, muscular frame weathered by years at sea. Gray-and-blonde hair, streaked like sea foam, was bound back in a rough knot, while a thick beard framed a face whose lines had been carved deep by salt and storm. His deep, resolved voice carried over the din as he directed his crew—a man who had seen much in his lifetime.

"Father William," Captain Noah called, his Dutch accent thick and gravelly. "What brings you here?"

The priest gestured to Felix. "This is Felix Aldric, the Creator's chosen Element Hero. He seeks your aid."

The captain's gaze snapped to Felix, shock flickering in his sharp eyes. "The Element Hero?" he asked, glancing at the priest. "Are you sure of this?"

Felix stepped forward, his tone earnest and humble. "I am the Creator's chosen, Captain. I humbly need your aid. I must reach the Water Crystal at the heart of the ocean. I know the seas are dangerous, but without it, Daegon cannot be stopped."

Captain Noah hesitated, his eyes searching Felix's face. He looked to Father William, who nodded solemnly. "If you're sure of this, Father, I'll aid him," the captain said, his voice gruff. "But the ocean is a treacherous place now. I cannot promise a safe trip."

Felix held his gaze. "I understand, Captain, and I thank you for your trust." He handed over the parchment. "I found this on the road. It's proof an attack is coming."

The captain read it, horror dawning in his eyes. He looked out at his men, then to the city beyond, love for his people etched in every line of his face. Closing his eyes, he murmured a soft prayer for protection. When he opened them, his voice was firm. "I'll ready my ship. We'll set sail by tomorrow morning. I'll alert the military and mercenaries, too—messengers will spread word across Pangea of this threat."

Felix bowed his head, gratitude flooding him. "Thank you, Captain."

Father William placed a hand on Felix's shoulder, his smile warm. "You'll stay at the church tonight, Felix. We'll provide food and rest for the journey ahead."

Felix nodded, the weight of the day settling over him. "Thank you, Father."

Before Felix and Father William could depart the harbor, Captain Noah cleared his throat, halting their steps. "Hold a moment, lad," he said, his weathered voice cutting through the salty air. "I know this island you're after. It's a wee speck smack in the heart of the Cordelia Ocean—not even big enough for a village to take root. The only island at the center of these waters, we call it the Heart of Cordelia."

Felix turned back, his curiosity piqued. "The Heart of Cordelia," he repeated. "Is there anything else you can tell me about it, Captain?"

Noah scratched at his grizzled beard, squinting out toward the sea. "Not much more to say, honestly. It's a small place, one no one pays much mind to these days. But it'll be a long sail, no doubt about that. I'll get you there as quick as I can, though—mark my words."

Felix offered a grateful smile. "Thank you, Captain. I'm in your debt."

With that, Felix and Father William set off toward the church, the harbor's clamor fading behind them. The streets of Parelkaap hummed with life—vendors shouting, carts rattling over cobblestones—but Felix's gaze soon caught on something unusual. In the distance, a group of soldiers stood apart from the orange-clad guards of Parelkaap. These men wore chainmail beneath black surcoats, each marked with a stark white cross and an angelic soldier soaring above it. Their demeanor was stern, their presence heavy.

Felix leaned toward Father William, keeping his voice hushed. "Father, who are those soldiers over there? They don't look like Parelkaap's men."

The priest glanced their way and nodded. "Those are the Kronemarkers, my son. Their emblem—the angelic soldier— harks back to the crusades, when they saw themselves as purifiers of Pangea, rooting out pagan raids and rituals. They no longer wage such wars, but their ties to that heritage run deep."

Felix studied them, the gleam of their armor and the sharp lines of their emblem etching into his mind. "I've read about them in my studies," he said, "but they're far more intimidating in person."

A faint smile crossed William's face. "They mean to be. It's how they showcase their strength—especially now, with Daegon's shadow creeping closer. They're a bulwark in these troubled times."

Felix frowned, a question forming. "Could the Kronemarkers invade Daegon's stronghold? With their might, maybe they could end his threat."

The priest's expression sobered. "Even the Kronemarkers aren't bold enough to try that. Daegon's magic is too dangerous— wild and ruinous. Without the Chosen Hero to stand against it, they'd risk their armies being shattered, leaving nothing to stop an invasion. They hold their ground, but they dare not strike."

The words sank into Felix like a stone, sharpening his purpose. "Then I have to get the Water Crystal quickly," he said, his voice firm with resolve.

William rested a hand on his shoulder. "You will, Felix. The Creator's hand is upon you."

They walked on in silence, the church's towering spire soon rising before them. Inside, the air was cool and thick with the scent of incense. William guided Felix to a spare room at the back, its plain walls softened by a single woven tapestry of a shepherd tending his flock.

"Rest here," William said kindly. "I'll fetch some food and drink for you."

Felix settled onto the narrow bed, his body weary but his mind alert. "Thank you, Father," he replied as William stepped out to summon the church servants.

Alone, Felix's thoughts churned: the distant Heart of Cordelia, the formidable Kronemarkers, and the ever-looming specter of Daegon. The road ahead was daunting, but his determination burned brighter than ever.

Felix sat in the small chamber of Parelkaap's sanctuary house, the weight of his mission pressing upon him like a mantle of iron, his thoughts adrift on the parchment's warning of Daegon's gathering fleet. The room, spare yet hallowed, was bathed in the soft glow of a single candle, its flame dancing upon the rough-hewn walls, casting shadows that flickered like the doubts in his heart. The Firesong Blade rested against the wall, its scabbard plain but heavy with the promise of its hidden runes. The Element Crystals hummed faintly, their glow a reminder of his calling as the Element Hero, yet the shadow of Rowan's scars and Meadowbrook's ashes stirred a fear that he might falter before his trials.

A gentle knock broke his reverie, soft as a whisper in the sacred silence. The door creaked open, and a woman stepped inside, balancing a tray of crusty bread and a clay pitcher of water, their simple scents a humble offering amidst his burdens. Her long blonde hair cascaded to her waist, shimmering like spun gold in the candlelight, each strand catching the flame's glow as if woven with starlight. Her bright blue eyes met his, their warmth startling him—a beacon of grace that pierced the weight of his thoughts. Her smile, radiant and unguarded, lit the dim chamber like a dawn breaking over Pangea's shores, and Felix found himself in awe of her beauty: a fleeting vision of hope amid the storm of his quest. He returned her smile, a reflex born of shared kindness, his heart stirring with a quiet, unspoken connection, as if the Creator had sent a spark of light to ease his path.

"Compliments of the sanctuary," she said, setting the tray on the weathered oak table, her voice gentle yet resonant, carrying a subtle lilt that echoed the tides of Parelkaap's harbors. "Can I do anything else for you, traveler?"

Felix shook his head, his voice soft, tempered by the awe her presence kindled. "Thank you, no. But may I have your name?"

"Lara," she replied, her smile broadening, a crescent of warmth that seemed to banish the chamber's shadows. "I'm so thankful to have the Creator's chosen hero among us. It's a blessing, truly, in these dark days." Her words, sincere and bright, stirred a wave of humility in Felix, and he saw in her eyes a genuine joy—like sunlight dancing on the sea—tempered by a quiet strength that spoke of trials endured.

"I'll do everything I can to help," he said sincerely, his voice steady despite the weight of her faith in him. "I hope to put a quick stop to Daegon's madness before it consumes more lives."

Lara's posture shifted, a subtle tightening of her shoulders, her expression growing serious, like a calm sea stirred by an approaching gale. She paused, her gaze drifting to the candle's flame, as if seeing memories flicker within its light. "Even we in the sanctuary fought in the last attack, just a week ago," she said, her voice steady yet tinged with the ache of memory. "The Kronemarkers came to our aid, and we won a victory, but it was hard-won, with blood and fire." In her face, Felix saw a tapestry of bold conviction and tender concern for her people—a strength forged in faith yet softened by care—and his heart ached with the shared burden of their world's peril.

He nodded, his resolve hardening like steel in a forge, the crystals at his chest glowing faintly, their warmth a divine echo of his purpose. "I hope to reach the Water Crystal quickly," he said, his voice firm, "before more attacks come to these shores." The memory of Rowan's whip-scarred form flashed in his mind, fueling his determination to shield Parelkaap from Daegon's shadow.

Relief softened Lara's features, her eyes meeting his again, their blue depths holding a quiet hope that lingered like a prayer. "Rest well, then," she said, stepping toward the door, her fingers brushing the tray's edge—a fleeting gesture that seemed to carry the weight of her trust. "You sail at first dawn, Felix." Her use of his name, spoken with gentle warmth, sent a ripple through his heart, a moment of connection that felt both fragile and profound, like a star glimpsed through storm clouds.

Felix smiled again, gratitude warming his tone. "Thank you, Lara." His voice carried a sincerity that mirrored her own, a shared spark of kindness that lingered in the air.

She closed the door quietly behind her, her silhouette fading into the corridor's shadows, leaving Felix with the bread, the water, and the echo of her presence. He ate slowly, the simple meal grounding him, its humble flavors a reminder of the sanctuary's care and Lara's quiet strength. As he lay back on the narrow bed, the candle's glow casting patterns across the ceiling, he clasped his hands, the crystals a steady warmth. He murmured a final prayer: "Creator, guide me across the ocean to the Water Crystal. Protect those I leave behind—Lara, Parelkaap, and all who hold fast against the shadow. Grant me strength for the journey ahead, that I may honor Your light and their faith." With that, he drifted into sleep, the memory of Lara's smile and the weight of his mission weaving together in his dreams, readying him for the long voyage to come.

Chapter 13: The Shadow of Invasion

The first light of dawn crept through the small window of the spare room in the church, casting a faint glow on the stone walls. Felix lay asleep, his chest rising and falling steadily, until a gentle but firm knock stirred him. Father William's voice followed, warm yet tinged with urgency.

"Felix, my son," William called softly through the door. "The day has come. Captain Noah is here and nearly ready to sail."

Felix blinked awake, the weight of his mission settling over him like a cloak. He sat up, rubbed his eyes, and swung his legs over the bed, his feet meeting the cool stone floor. Quickly, he gathered his belongings—his staff, the Firesong Blade, and a small pouch of supplies—his hands moving with practiced efficiency as he prepared for the journey ahead.

Just as he reached for the door, a lighter knock sounded. It creaked open, and Lara stepped inside, her long blonde hair catching the dawn's light, her blue eyes shimmering with hope and concern. In her hands, she held a small cloth bundle.

"Felix," she said, her voice soft and melodic. "I brought you something for the travel—salted beef. It's not much, but it should help."

Felix paused, struck once again by her beauty, the way the early light seemed to frame her like a sacred vision. He smiled warmly, accepting the bundle with a nod. "Thank you, Lara. This means more than you know."

She stepped closer, her shy smile faltering as emotion crept into her voice. "I hope to see you back soon, safe and victorious."

His expression softened, but his resolve hardened. "I will," he said firmly, meeting her gaze. "I'll protect everyone the best I can."

Relief washed over her features, and her smile widened. "May the Creator guide you," she whispered, then stepped back and slipped out of the room, leaving Felix to finish his preparations.

He tucked the salted beef into his pouch, shouldered his gear, and stepped into the church's main hall. Father William stood near the altar, his hands clasped in prayer. Seeing Felix, he offered a gentle smile.

"Are you ready, my son?" William asked.

"Yes, Father," Felix replied, his voice steady.

They walked out together into the crisp morning air, the sky a pale blue streaked with sunlight. As they approached the harbor, William stopped and turned to Felix, his expression solemn.

"Before you go," he said, "let me offer a prayer for you and the crew."

Felix bowed his head as William raised his hands. "Creator, we ask Your protection over Felix, Captain Noah, and all who sail with them. Guide their ship through the perils of the sea, and grant them strength and wisdom for the trials ahead. May they return victorious in Your name."

A warmth spread through Felix, the prayer steadying his spirit. "Thank you, Father," he said quietly.

William nodded. "Go now. The Creator is with you."

Felix continued to the harbor, where Captain Noah stood waiting. His deep, gravelly voice carried a Dutch accent as he called out, "Felix Aldric! Ready to set sail, lad?"

Felix smiled, excitement stirring within him. "Yes, Captain. Let's get to the Heart of Cordelia."

Noah gestured to the ship docked nearby—a sleek caravel named The Windward Cross, its hull gleaming under the dim light of dawn. Its lateen sails were furled tightly against the spars, and the weathered wood bore intricate carvings of a white cross entwined with a herring, a symbol of Parelkaap's seafaring pride. "Fastest ship in the fleet," Noah said, his voice brimming with pride, his broad frame casting a shadow across the deck. "We're taking a skeleton crew with only essential supplies—keeps us light and swift. The rest stay to hold Thegnfast's walls. If the winds favor us and trouble stays clear, we'll reach the Heart of Cordelia in four days."

Felix murmured a quiet prayer under his breath, "Creator, guide our path and keep us swift," as he followed Noah aboard, his boots thudding against the polished deck. The ship stirred to life, its timbers creaking like a living beast roused from slumber. Seven seasoned sailors greeted Felix with curt, respectful nods, their hands busy with ropes and gear, eyes sharp with the focus of men who knew the sea's whims.

At the helm stood Dirk, Noah's first mate, a wiry figure with a salt-streaked beard and eyes like chipped flint, glinting with a mix of cunning and unyielding loyalty. His lean frame belied a wiry strength, honed by years wrestling sails in gales and hauling nets through icy waters. "All hands ready, Captain," Dirk called, his voice sharp and clear, cutting through the morning mist. He shot Felix a quick, appraising glance, as if weighing the mage's resolve, before turning to bark orders, his movements precise as he guided The Windward Cross away from the dock and toward the open waters of the Cordelia Ocean.

Below deck, Felix found a small cabin and stowed his belongings near a narrow bunk. Returning to the top deck, he paused at the rail, watching Parelkaap's spires fade into the distance as the ship pulled away. The sight tugged at his heart, but he turned resolutely toward the bridge, where Noah stood at the helm.

Noah glanced at him, curiosity in his eyes. "Tell me, lad— how are you with a sword?"

Felix hesitated, then smiled ruefully. "I had some militia training back in Eldenwold. My father taught me the basics— strike swift, guard low. I miss them sometimes, but I've leaned on my crystals more lately."

190

Noah chuckled, a deep, rumbling sound. "Well, we've got a few days ahead. How about we spar? I've been at this longer than I care to admit—mastered a few tricks. Could teach you something."

Felix's eyes lit up, eagerness replacing his earlier melancholy. "I'd like that, Captain. I want to be ready for Daegon. No crystals, though—I'll hone my natural skills."

Noah grinned, approving. "Good lad. Let's see what you've got."

They moved to the deck's center, the weathered planks of The Windward Cross creaking underfoot, worn smooth by years of salt spray and the relentless tread of sailors who had braved Pangea's treacherous currents. Noah drew a sturdy, well-worn arming sword from its scabbard, its blade nicked from countless skirmishes against pirates, its hilt wrapped in leather darkened by the grip of a man who had sailed Pangea's wild waters for decades. Felix unsheathed the Firesong Blade, its firestone-inlaid steel glinting with a radiant warmth of the Creator's light, mined from the Ashen Crags, pulsing faintly as if singing a hymn of divine resolve. The captain's stance was fluid, a dance honed by age and experience, his beard framing a grin that belied the steel in his eyes, his strength and speed a testament to a life where survival demanded both cunning and might.

As their blades clashed for the first time, a resonant clang echoing across the deck like a forge hammer's strike, the crew gathered in a loose circle, their weathered faces alight with interest. Felix felt the first spark of growth ignite within him, a burgeoning flame on this journey to come—a path that would temper him like iron in the Crags' forges, forging bonds and honing skills against the looming shadow of Daegon's heresy.

The deck of The Windward Cross thrummed with tension, the fading sunlight casting elongated shadows that danced like specters across the timbers, the air thick with the tang of lake water and the faint, acrid scent of distant volcanic vents. Felix and Captain Noah circled each other, their sparring match a whirlwind of steel and strategy, blades flashing in the golden light like comets streaking through dusk. The crew watched in awe, their cheers punctuating the rhythmic clash of steel—a chorus of "Aye, Cap'n!" and "Show 'im, lad!" that swelled with each exchange. Felix darted forward, his Firesong Blade slicing through the air in a precise arc. The firestones embedded in its hilt flared brighter, their golden radiance a beacon of the Creator's will, the blade's edge humming faintly as it sought Noah's guard.

Noah parried with a flick of his wrist, his movements fluid and precise, the parry redirecting Felix's strike with the ease of a man who had turned back foes alike. For a moment, Felix gained ground, his speed pressing the captain back, and he landed a glancing blow on Noah's arm—a shallow nick that drew a thin line of blood, the fabric of the captain's sleeve singed by the blade's radiant heat. Gasps rippled through the onlookers, the crew leaning forward, their eyes wide with the thrill of witnessing a worthy challenge to their leader's prowess. Yet Noah's experience shone through like a lighthouse in fog; with a deft twist, he countered, his sword weaving a defensive web that forced Felix to retreat. The captain's strikes grew sharper, each one a calculated test of Felix's limits, probing for weaknesses in footwork and form, his grizzled features set in focused determination.

The fight stretched on, the sun dipping lower to paint the lake in hues of crimson and gold, sweat dripping from Felix's brow and stinging his eyes as he matched Noah's relentless pace. His breaths came in ragged bursts, the Elemental Crystals pulsing warmly against his chest, their energy a quiet reservoir he held in reserve, focusing instead on the pure clash of steel and skill. Noah's blade whistled through the air, a series of feints and thrusts that kept Felix on the defensive, the captain's age-granted wisdom turning each move into a lesson etched in muscle and mind. Finally, with a swift maneuver born of countless battles, Noah hooked Felix's blade with his own, the metal grinding in a shower of sparks. With a powerful yank, he sent the Firesong Blade spinning from Felix's grasp, the sword clattering across the deck to rest against a coiled rope. In the same fluid motion, Noah pressed forward, pinning Felix with the flat of his sword against his chest, the cool steel a firm but unyielding reminder of the captain's mastery.

The crew erupted in applause, their pride in their captain palpable, a thunderous roar that shook the rigging, fists pumping the air as they swarmed forward to clap Noah on the back. Yet in their eyes gleamed respect for Felix too, the young Element Hero who had held his own against a legend of the waves. Noah lowered his sword, a broad grin cracking his weathered face as he extended a hand to help Felix up. "You've got fire in you, lad," he rumbled, his voice carrying the melodic lilt of coastal folk. "But the sea teaches patience—and so will I, if you'll learn."

Felix, humbled yet eager, bowed his head slightly. "Thank you, Captain. I'd be honored to learn from you."

Noah clapped him on the shoulder. "Good. Let's make the most of it."

The crew's admiration was evident in their murmurs—impressed by Felix's tenacity and awestruck by Noah's mastery. "Never seen the captain pushed like that!" one sailor exclaimed, while another nodded, "We're proud to serve under him, and that lad's no slouch either!"

For the next hour, they sparred again, Noah guiding Felix through stances and strikes, the deck alive with the sound of their efforts. As the sun sank below the horizon, they called it quits for the day. Felix wiped his brow, exhilarated. "Thank you, Captain. I'm looking forward to tomorrow."

Noah nodded, his eyes glinting with respect. "Rest up, lad. We've got work ahead."

Later, as the ship rocked gently on the waves, Felix approached Noah near the helm. "Captain," he began, his tone curious, "what made you agree to help me? I was just a stranger when I arrived."

Noah leaned against the railing, gazing out at the sea. "I place much trust in Father William," he said simply. "He's looked after me and half the city's people at one time or another. Years ago, I came back from a voyage half-dead—pirates had ambushed us, left me wounded and broken. William was there every day, tending my wounds, praying for me. He's as wise as he is kind, and if he vouches for you, that's enough for me."

Felix saw the sincerity in Noah's eyes and nodded. "I understand. He offered me a place to stay without hesitation. It's not something you see every day."

Noah chuckled softly. "That's William for ya—always eager to help."

Felix's gaze drifted to the horizon, worry creeping into his voice. "I hope they'll be okay while we're gone. Daegon's forces…"

Noah turned to him, his expression firm. "Don't you worry, Felix. Once you've got that Water Crystal, we'll put an end to Daegon's tyranny. You're the key to this, and I believe in you."

Determination surged in Felix's chest. "I won't let them down," he vowed.

"Good," Noah said, clapping him on the back. "Now, get some rest. We'll train again tomorrow."

Felix descended to his quarters, the small space lit by a flickering lantern. He sat on the bunk, letting the day's events wash over him, then whispered a prayer: "Creator, guide me. Keep them safe." His fingers brushed the cross pendant at his chest, grounding him.

Reaching into his pack, he pulled out the salted beef Lara had given him. Her beautiful smile flashed in his mind as he unwrapped it, the rich, smoky scent filling the air. He took a bite—salted and dried, yet flavorful, a taste of home amidst the sea's vastness. Lying back on the bed, he reflected on his journey: the battles, the losses, the moments of hope. Each step had led him here, to this ship, this mission.

Hours slipped by as the ship's gentle sway lulled him. With the taste of beef lingering, he drifted into sleep, ready for the next day's challenges.

The second day of the voyage greeted Felix Aldric with another stunning sunrise over the Cordelia Ocean. He awoke in his quarters, the faint creak of the ship stirring him from sleep. Rising, he pulled on his boots and made his way to the deck, the wooden planks cool beneath his feet. As he stepped into the open air, the vast emptiness of the ocean unfurled before him. The waters sparkled clear and bright, catching the first rays of the sun as it painted the sky in hues of orange and pink—a breathtaking sight that filled him with quiet awe.

At the helm stood Captain Noah, his weathered hands steady on the wheel, his gaze fixed on the horizon. Felix approached, the soft tap of his steps announcing his presence. Noah turned with a nod, a faint smile tugging at his lips.

"Morning, lad," Noah said, his voice steady as the sea itself. "We're doing well so far. No sign of Daegon's forces yet, and I hope it stays that way."

Felix exhaled, a wave of relief washing over him, tinged with gratitude. "I feel blessed, Captain. Let's pray this calm holds for an easy trip to the Island."

Noah's eyes crinkled as he glanced at the sails billowing above. "Aye, the winds are generous today. They're pushing us right along the path we need."

He shifted his stance, his tone taking on a familiar edge of challenge. "Ready to begin training?"

Felix's face lit up with eagerness. "I'm ready, Captain."

They moved to the center of the deck, the crew pausing their tasks to watch. Noah drew his sword, its blade catching the morning light, while Felix unsheathed the Firesong Blade, its firestone pulsing faintly. For the next couple of hours, they sparred—first with drills, then a full duel. Felix's movements were swift and precise, his confidence growing with each clash of steel. The crew murmured in approval as the session stretched on, blades ringing in a steady rhythm.

In their final duel, Felix parried a swift strike and countered with a deft maneuver, locking their swords in a stalemate. Breathing hard, they stepped back, the match ending in a draw. The crew erupted in stunned applause, one sailor shouting, "He's matched the captain!"

Noah sheathed his sword, a broad smile breaking across his face. "You're a quick learner, Felix. If only I could keep you on my crew permanently."

Felix wiped sweat from his brow, returning the smile with respect. "I've learned much from a great veteran and swordsman like you, Captain."

Noah laughed, a warm, hearty sound. "Glad even I can teach the Chosen Hero a thing or two."

Felix joined in the laughter, his voice light. "Even heroes can always learn and improve."

"Ain't that the truth," Noah agreed, clapping him on the shoulder.

They sheathed their swords, calling it quits for the day. Noah's gaze drifted to the horizon, his expression turning thoughtful. "Halfway there with no incidents—unheard of in these waters lately. Makes me wonder what's going on."

Felix's mind flickered to the parchment's warning of a fleet invasion. "Do you think it's tied to the invasion?"

Noah's face grew grim but firm, his jaw set. "Aye, I do. Feels uneasy, like something's brewing. We need to get that crystal and back quickly."

He paused, then softened. "But I won't worry over it now. All we can do is sail and complete our task. Learned a long time ago there's no wisdom in fretting over what you can't control—just do what you can with what you have and let the Creator guide you along the way."

Felix absorbed the words, feeling their weight settle in his chest. "You're right, Captain. I'll keep that in mind."

198

They stood together, staring out at the open ocean, its surface empty and serene yet heavy with unspoken possibilities. Felix's thoughts drifted to Eldenwold—to Rowan, his brother, and Kirkhaven. He wondered how Rowan's recovery was faring, hoped Kirkhaven remained safe. A flicker of fear stirred, but he recalled Noah's advice and shook it off.

Later, in his quarters, Felix lay on his bunk, the ship's gentle rocking soothing his mind. He whispered a prayer for peace—for Rowan, for Kirkhaven, for their mission—and let the words carry his worries away as he drifted into sleep, ready for whatever the next days might bring.

Felix awoke on the third day of the voyage, the gentle rocking of The Windward Cross pulling him from restless dreams. He climbed to the deck, where he found Captain Noah standing at the helm, gazing out at the sunset painting the horizon in hues of gold and crimson. Felix joined him, the two of them staring eastward in companionable silence.

"Not much farther now," Noah said, his voice steady. "By tomorrow, we should be there."

Felix's heart quickened at the thought of finally reaching the Heart of Cordelia. "Good," he replied, his eagerness barely contained. "I'm ready to get that crystal."

Noah nodded, his eyes scanning the horizon. "Still no sign of Daegon's forces. But there's no doubt in my mind something big is coming."

Felix's thoughts drifted to the parchment he'd found days earlier, its cryptic message hinting at a plot he was desperate to unravel. Before he could dwell on it, Noah straightened up, turning to him. "This is it, Felix—the last day before we reach the island. Are you ready to get that crystal?"

Felix met his gaze, his voice firm with resolve. "Yes. I've come too far to turn back now."

Noah chuckled, a rare lightness in his tone. "Good. I'd hate for you to back out after all this."

Felix smiled, the tension in his chest easing for a moment. "Not a chance."

"I'll man the helm for now," Noah said, clapping him on the shoulder. "Take this day to rest. You'll need your strength tomorrow."

Felix nodded, lingering by the ship's railing as Noah returned to the wheel. The sea stretched endlessly before him, and with a final glance at the horizon, he descended to his quarters for some rest.

Hours later, a cacophony of shouts from above jolted Felix awake, ripping him from a fitful dream of firestone-lit altars and coiling serpent runes. His heart pounded like a war drum, the Crystals at his chest pulsing faintly as he scrambled from his hammock in the dim confines of The Windward Cross's lower deck. The air was thick with the briny tang of sea water and the faint acrid scent of distant volcanic vents. He bounded up the narrow ladder, his boots thudding against the worn timbers, and emerged onto the deck, where the crew had gathered along the eastern rail, their silhouettes stark against the fading twilight. Their eyes fixed on the horizon. Felix followed their gaze and froze, a chill slithering down his spine like a cold current from the Azure Falls.

A massive fleet loomed in the distance, its dark sails slicing through the twilight like the wings of giant ravens, their crimson edges emblazoned with Daegon's serpent. The ships—hulking galleys of blackened timber, their prows carved with snarling serpent heads—stretched across the ocean's expanse. The sheer scale of the armada, dozens of vessels moving in disciplined formation, was a testament to Daegon's unyielding ambition, a shadow of war descending westward. Lanterns hung from their masts, their corrupted glow casting an eerie, blood-red haze across the water, tainting the twilight with an aura of menace. Felix's grip tightened on the rail, his knuckles whitening, as the weight of the threat settled over him like a storm cloud, the Element Crystals at his chest humming with a restless energy that mirrored his own.

Felix found Noah at the helm, his broad silhouette steady against the ship's weathered wheel, his beard catching the last glimmers of twilight. The captain's face was stoic. "Is that Daegon's invasion fleet?" he asked, his voice tight, the words catching in his throat like a stone.

"Aye," Noah replied, his voice calm as the deep waters. "It is."

Felix watched helplessly as the fleet moved steadily westward, its dark sails slicing through the twilight like blades of obsidian. The sheer scale of the armada—dozens of hulking galleys—sent a chill through his bones, colder than the ocean's depths. "What do we do?" Felix asked, his mind racing, thoughts tumbling like waves in a storm.

Noah's gaze remained steady, his hands firm on the wheel. "There's nothing we can do but press forward," he said, his tone unyielding yet measured. "They won't risk delaying their invasion to chase a lone ship like ours. Those heavy vessels, laden with troops and siege gear, can't match The Windward Cross's speed, even if they tried." His words were grounded in the pragmatism of a man who had outrun tempests and pirate fleets, but they carried a weight that steadied Felix's racing heart.

Felix's chest tightened with conflict, torn between the urge to turn back and the mission ahead. "They're heading west," Noah added, his eyes narrowing as he tracked the fleet's path. "They've passed Parelkaap—it's not their target. Must be somewhere farther westward, deeper into Pangea's heart."

Felix's thoughts turned to home and to Thegnfast, perched on the rugged edge of Lake Gildermere. The fortress city was the bastion of western Pangea, its blue banners a symbol of Witsgar's unyielding faith. If Daegon's forces reached it, the fall of Thegnfast would be a death knell for the west. Fear gripped Felix, a cold weight that threatened to smother the spark of hope within him. But Noah's voice cut through the haze, firm as an anchor. "There's still time, lad. That fleet's slow—crawling like a wounded beast. It'll take days to reach shore. We'll get the Water Crystal from the Heart of Cordelia and be back before they can strike."

The words steadied Felix, his fear giving way to an ember of determination. He nodded, whispering a prayer under his breath: "Creator, grant me strength to protect those I love." As if in answer, he looked up to see Titania, the golden eagle, soaring high above the sunset, her wings catching the last rays of light in a blaze of gold. Her presence was a sign, a reminder that the Creator's light shone even in the shadow of Daegon's ambition, guiding Felix to save Pangea.

Noah glanced over, his weathered face softening, though his tone remained firm. "Remember what I told you yesterday—focus on what you can control."

"I will," Felix said, his resolve hardening like iron in a forge, the Wind Crystal's hum a quiet reassurance against his chest.

As the sun dipped below the horizon, painting the sky in hues of crimson and indigo, the fleet's sails faded into the distance, their path diverging from The Windward Cross as it sailed toward the Heart of Cordelia. The promise of the Water Crystal, said to rest in a sacred grove where the lake's currents converged, drew them onward, its power a beacon of hope against the looming war. Felix lingered on the deck, the sea breeze cool against his skin, carrying the faint song of the waves. He watched until the last trace of the fleet vanished, swallowed by the twilight's embrace. With a final prayer for Witsgar, for his family, and for all of Pangea, he turned and headed below, steeling himself for the challenges of the next day, the weight of his vow to protect Pangea burning brighter than any firestone.

Chapter 14: The Tides of Faith

Felix Aldric awoke on the fourth day of the voyage aboard The Windward Cross, his heart thrumming with a potent mix of eagerness and urgency. The restless night had been haunted by the image of Daegon's vast fleet, its dark sails slicing westward across the Cordelia Ocean under yesterday's twilight sky. That chilling sight had seared itself into his mind—a looming threat to all he held dear—driving him toward the final piece of his quest: the Water Crystal. Rising swiftly from his narrow bunk, he dressed in his weathered tunic and cloak, the familiar weight of his staff and Firesong Blade steadying his resolve. The gentle rocking of the ship urged him upward, and he climbed to the deck, the salty breeze greeting him as dawn painted the horizon in soft golds and pinks.

Captain Noah stood at the helm, his weathered hands firm on the wheel, gray-and-blonde hair tied back against the wind. As Felix approached, Noah turned, a warm smile crinkling the corners of his eyes. "Morning, lad," he said, his Dutch-accented voice carrying over the creak of the ship. "The island's in sight."

Felix's pulse quickened. He hurried to the bow, gripping the railing as he peered south. There, rising from the shimmering sea, lay a small tropical island lush with greenery, its sandy shores kissed by gentle waves. The Heart of Cordelia, sacred refuge of the Water Crystal, lay before him at last. Relief flooded through him, washing away days of tension. He had finally reached the island where the final crystal awaited—the key to confronting Daegon and saving Pangea.

Noah joined him at the rail, gaze steady on the distant shore. "We can't get too close, Felix," he cautioned. "The shallows'll run us aground. You'll need to take the shore boat from here."

Felix nodded. "I'll be back as soon as I can," he promised, voice firm with determination.

The crew sprang into action, seasoned hands lowering the small boat with practiced ease. Felix climbed aboard, settled onto the bench, and gripped the oars. With a final nod to Noah and the crew, he began to row, the rhythmic splash cutting through the quiet sea. As he drew closer, anticipation built within him—a tingling energy coursing through his veins. Each stroke brought him nearer to the shore and the crystal that could turn the tide against Daegon's heresy.

The boat glided into the shallows. Felix leapt out, pulled it onto the white sand with a soft crunch, then straightened, boots sinking slightly into the warm earth. He took a deep breath of the humid, flower-scented air. Stepping away from the boat, he walked up the shoreline where the jungle's edge loomed—palm trees swaying, leaves whispering secrets of the ancient power pulsing within this sacred place. With a glance back at *The Windward Cross* bobbing in the distance, Felix steeled himself and ventured forward, ready to face the trials ahead.

Felix pushed through the dense mangroves of the Heart of Cordelia, humid air thick with salt and the distant crash of waves. His boots sank into damp earth, roots twisting beneath him, but a stone marker etched with "The Lord is my shepherd" guided his path. The tide ebbed and flowed, testing his footing, yet faith kept him steady. Beyond the tangled trees lay the island's core—a sacred pool aglow with bioluminescent light, its calm waters framed by vibrant foliage. Nearby, a stone basin held holy water, surface shimmering in filtered sunlight.

Drawn to the basin, Felix peered into its depths. The water, dark and still, seemed to hum with a pulse older than the stones that cradled it. A vision rippled across the surface: his younger self, helpless as Rowan vanished into strange lights, guilt etched deep. A whisper hissed, raw and cold: "You failed him." Felix's chest tightened, but he knelt, tracing the sign of the cross with trembling fingers. The water quivered; the image dissolved. Yet a faint tremor stirred beneath, as if the basin itself breathed. Shadows coiled in its depths—fleeting, vast—and a low, resonant hum filled the air, like the distant call of the sea.

Felix rose, resolve firming though his heart pounded with the weight of unseen eyes. The air grew heavy, charged with presence that pressed against his skin. Then, from the sacred pool, Neriel, the Leviathan, emerged with majesty that stilled the world. His colossal, serpentine form unfurled endlessly—a living current of muscle and scale weaving through the depths and beyond mortal sight. His body, vast and sinuous, coiled with fluid grace, as though the ocean had taken shape to guard its own heart. Each scale shimmered with iridescent brilliance, reflecting deep sapphire, emerald green, and the soft silver of moonlit waves—colors dancing and shifting like the sea under a restless sky. Light played across them, rendering him almost translucent at times—a creature not wholly bound to the material world but woven from water's essence.

His eyes gleamed like twin pools of molten silver, aglow with ancient, otherworldly light hinting at the wisdom of countless tides. They flickered subtly—calm and tranquil one moment, stormy and piercing the next—yet always carrying depth that spoke of divine purpose. When they settled on Felix, it was as if the Leviathan peered into his very soul, weighing it against the currents of eternity.

A faint mist clung to Neriel's form, rising in delicate, swirling tendrils that shimmered with spectral glow. It lent him an aura of enigma, as though he existed between realms—a bridge from earthly to divine. With every subtle shift of his massive frame, the pool rippled outward, small waves lapping the shore in reverence. The air hummed faintly, charged with his energy, a testament to dominion over the tides.

When Neriel spoke, his voice rolled forth like the ocean's own song—deep and resonant, a thunderous echo of waves crashing against cliffs, yet capable of softening to the gentle murmur of tide caressing sand. It reverberated through the clearing, a sound Felix felt in his bones—both commanding and comforting, as though the Creator Himself spoke through the Leviathan's ancient throat.

Despite overwhelming might, Neriel exuded serene wisdom, a quiet strength enveloping Felix in awe and reassurance. Towering yet gentle, fierce yet compassionate, he was a paradox of power and peace—a guardian whose existence proclaimed the majesty of the Creator's design.

"Welcome, Element Hero," Neriel intoned, voice a deep current thrumming through him. "I am Neriel, Keeper of the Tides, servant of the Creator. To claim the Water Crystal, prove your soul's purity. Answer this: What is the source of true strength?"

Felix considered his journey—the battles endured, fears confronted, quiet assurances of faith. "True strength comes from the Lord," he replied, voice unwavering. "His grace upholds me when I falter, and through faith, His power shines."

Neriel's gaze warmed; his head dipped slightly. "Well said. Faith is the root of strength. One trial remains—purification. Enter these waters and let them cleanse you of the old self."

Felix shed cloak and staff, stepping into the pool. Warm water wrapped around him, a comforting embrace easing tired muscles. He inhaled deeply and submerged, the world fading to soft murmur of bubbles and glowing light.

Beneath the surface, memories rushed in like a flood: Rowan's laughter by the Cragbeck, sparring under the mead-hall's eaves, the night he was lost to the Cragspire Hills. Guilt swelled: *I should have gone after him.* Then Eldenwold's flames, wraiths' shrieks, the burden of his calling. *Am I enough?* Doubts pressed down, heavy as the water above.

But scripture surfaced—teachings of baptism, being buried with the Savior and rising anew. This was no mere washing; it was baptism into his destiny as Element Hero. In silence, he yearned for a cleansed spirit, restored and ready.

The water stirred, answering his plea, swirling and lifting away silt of shame and regret. A vision shimmered: Pangea renewed, rivers pure, people unshackled—a land lifted from Daegon's darkness. Felix felt the old self slip away, spirit reborn not by his will but by the Creator's mercy.

He broke the surface, gasping, water streaming from his shoulders. Lightness filled him; burdens of the past truly washed away. The pool's glow intensified, then softened into tranquil sheen. Neriel towered above, presence solemn. "You are purified," he proclaimed, voice echoing. "The Water Crystal is yours."

The crystal drifted to Felix, merging with Wind, Fire, and Earth at his chest. A teardrop pendant formed in his palm, blue light pulsing warmly. "Wield this power with faith, Element Hero," Neriel said, form sinking back into the pool, leaving only ripples.

Felix stood at the water's edge, island's wild splendor surrounding him. Baptism had scoured away doubts, leaving clarity that steadied his soul. With the Water Crystal's power—

soothing waves, mending wounds—and the Creator's light within, he was prepared to face Daegon's fleet and reclaim Rowan.

Felix stood at the edge of the sacred pool, water streaming from hair and tunic, breath steadying as cool air brushed his skin. The teardrop pendant hung against his chest, soft blue glow pulsing faintly—a tangible sign of purification. He felt reborn, cleansed of doubt and fear, faith now a steady flame within. Yet the vision of Daegon's dark fleet lingered, a shadow he could not ignore.

Neriel rose partially from the pool, serpentine form shimmering with iridescent scales catching dim light. Molten-silver eyes locked onto Felix, ancient and piercing, radiating quiet authority. The air thrummed with divine presence; Felix straightened, meeting the gaze.

"You have passed through the waters, Element Hero," Neriel said, voice deep and resonant like rolling distant waves. "The Creator's grace has washed you clean; your spirit shines with newfound strength. You are ready for the trials ahead."

Felix's hand brushed his chest, feeling the four crystals— Wind, Fire, Earth, and now Water—humming in unison. "I feel it," he replied, voice firm yet tinged with awe. "The Creator's light. But Daegon's fleet... I saw it yesterday, ships stretching across the horizon, sailing west. I need to know their target."

Neriel's eyes flickered, light shifting like tide's ebb and flow. "Daegon's shadow falls upon Thegnfast, the western heart of Pangea and capital of Witsgar," he intoned, voice heavy with warning. "There, where rivers meet the sea and the Creator's faithful stand resolute, he seeks to shatter the seat of power second only to Kroneburg. Its spires of strength and beauty are his prize, for its fall would break your people's spirit and open Pangea's west to his heresy. You must hasten, Felix Aldric, for time slips like water through your fingers."

Felix's breath caught, heart lurching at the name. Thegnfast—the Witsgarian people's proud capital, grand cathedrals, bustling markets, towering stone halls—a beacon of faith and resilience. He had visited as a boy, clinging to Torin's hand, awestruck by its grand church and blue banners bearing the white cross and raven in flight. Eldenwold lay under Thegnfast's protection, its militia sworn to the capital's lords. If Thegnfast fell, the Kingdom of Witsgar—his family, his kin—would face ruin. Rowan's vision, bound in fiery mountains, intertwined with the threat. "Thegnfast," he whispered, the weight grounding his resolve. "I won't let Daegon take it."

Neriel's massive head tilted, scales shimmering in cascade of sapphire and silver. "You ask for knowledge, and the Creator grants it through His servant. Trust in His guidance and in the power He has placed within you. The crystals—Wind, Fire, Earth, and Water—are bound by your faith. Wield them boldly, but know this: true strength lies in the faith that commands them."

Felix absorbed the words, thoughts racing to Eldenwold's quiet streets, Torin and Elara's steadfast love, Witsgar's banners snapping over Thegnfast's walls. The uncertain boy had no place here. He was the Element Hero, chosen to save his people.

"Thank you, Neriel," he said, bowing his head in reverence. "I'll protect Thegnfast and all of Pangea. For the Creator, for my kin."

Neriel's form sank back into the pool, voice softening to a whisper on the wind. "Go now, Element Hero. The sea awaits, and with it, your destiny."

Felix trudged northward through the mangroves, thick mud sucking at his boots with every step. Air hummed with the drone of insects and the gentle lap of water against twisted roots. Mind buzzing with success and looming threat, he pushed aside damp branches to reach the shore. There, the small boat bobbed in the shallows.

With a steadying breath, he shoved the boat into the water, cool waves splashing his knees. Climbing in, he gripped the oars and rowed with purpose—rhythmic creak of wood and splash marking his path back to *The Windward Cross*. The ship loomed larger with each stroke, a beacon against endless blue.

A flash of gold caught his eye as Titania, the majestic eagle, soared down from the sky, wings cutting the air with grace. She perched on the boat's bow, piercing gaze locking onto Felix's.

"Felix Aldric," her voice rang in his mind, warm and resonant. "You have completed your quest. The Water Crystal is yours—well done. I will remain your guide until Daegon is defeated."

Felix's chest swelled with gratitude. "I'm honored to have you by my side, Titania. Your wisdom has carried me this far."

She tilted her head, feathers glinting in sunlight. "As you go to rescue your people from Daegon's wrath, have faith. Do not let fear or revenge consume you. Remember your fight with Valthor—how you prevailed."

Felix's jaw tightened as memory surfaced: Valthor's snarling fury, temptation to give in to rage. "I won't let that happen again," he vowed, voice firm. "I'll save them with a clear heart."

Titania's eyes softened. "Then you are ready."

The boat bumped against *The Windward Cross*. The crew tossed down a rope ladder; rough hands hauled him aboard. Captain Noah stepped forward, weathered face alight with awe.

"Felix!" Noah's voice boomed, Dutch accent curling around the words. "We all saw it—a huge beast rising from the island! Never seen anything like it. Was that an Elemental Beast?"

Felix nodded, catching his breath. "Yes, Captain. Neriel, the Leviathan. Guardian of the Water Crystal."

The crew erupted in hushed murmurs, eyes wide with wonder. "Incredible..." one muttered, while another craned his neck as if the beast might still be visible.

Noah's gaze dropped to the crystal glowing faintly at Felix's chest. "Were you successful, lad?"

Felix managed a brief smile. "I was." But the smile faded as urgency gripped him. "Captain, Daegon's fleet is heading for Thegnfast. My people are in danger."

214

Noah's brow furrowed, picking up the strain. "Thegnfast? You must be of Witsgar."

Felix nodded. "I am."

Noah rubbed his chin, then met Felix's eyes with resolve. "We don't have enough supplies to reach Thegnfast from here, but I vow this: as soon as we're back in Pavelkaap, we'll get you there as fast as we can."

Felix's urgency softened into gratitude, though time's weight pressed on. "Thank you, Captain. You've already done so much. I pray we make it back swiftly."

Noah clapped him on the shoulder, then turned to the crew. "All hands! Ready the sails—full speed to Pavelkaap!"

The deck burst into motion, sails unfurling with sharp snap as the ship groaned and swung toward home. Felix stood at the rail, eyes on the horizon, Titania circling above. The Kingdom of Witsgar needed him—and he would not fail them.

The sun dipped toward the horizon, painting the deck of The Windward Cross in hues of gold and amber. Felix paced near the railing, Water Crystal glowing faintly against his chest, its rhythm syncing with his quickening pulse. Thegnfast—the city of his ancestors, heart of the Witsgarian people—was in peril, and every moment deliberating felt like a risk he couldn't afford.

Captain Noah stood at the helm, steady hands guiding the ship as he pored over a weathered map of Pangea—parchment bearing creased edges, faded ink, and annotations in Noah's precise hand. He looked up as Felix approached, weathered face calm but expectant.

"Captain," Felix said, voice taut, "Neriel's warning was clear: Daegon's fleet is sailing for Thegnfast. He's coming from the west, around Pangea's edge, where his forces haven't struck before. It's a surprise attack—they won't see it coming."

Noah's brow furrowed as he traced a finger along the western coastline. "Clever devil. Western Pangea's been quiet—too quiet. He's betting on catching Thegnfast off guard, hitting them before they can muster a proper defense."

Felix nodded. "If Thegnfast falls, the Witsgarians lose everything. We need to get to Pavelkaap first—it's our only chance to resupply and figure out what's next."

Noah tilted his head, sharp eyes meeting Felix's. "Pavelkaap's the smart move. We're low on provisions, and the crew's been pushed hard. But what's your plan once we're there? Resupply and sail on, or something bigger?"

Felix took a deep breath, mind racing. "Burhgard's the key. It sits between the sea and Lake Gildermere. Daegon will have to breach it to reach Thegnfast. That buys us time—but not much."

Noah tapped the map where Burhgard's jagged outline marked the southwestern coast. "Burhgard's a fortress, alright. Walls like iron, and a navy that could make any fleet think twice. If they hold the line, it'll slow Daegon down. But they'll need warning—and fast."

"Exactly," Felix said, voice gaining strength. "We dock at Pavelkaap, resupply, and send word to Burhgard to brace for attack. But I'm thinking bigger—convince the Kronemarkers to march west. An army from Kroneburg could turn the tide."

Noah let out a low whistle, folding his arms. "Ambitious, lad. Kroneburg's got its hands full in the east—Daegon's been hammering them there. You'd need a hell of a pitch to get them to send troops across Pangea."

Felix's hand brushed the Water Crystal, its warmth steadying him. "What if I'm the pitch? The Chosen Hero, with all four crystals. That's not just a warrior—that's a sign from the Creator. They'd have to listen."

Noah's lips curved into a faint, approving smile. "Aye, that might do it. The Kronemarkers are practical, but they're devout. Show up with that crystal glowing and a story of divine purpose, and you could sway them. Still, it's a gamble—overland from Kroneburg to Thegnfast is a week, maybe more."

Felix's jaw tightened. "A week's too long if Daegon's already moving. But if Burhgard holds him off, it could work. We resupply at Pavelkaap, rally what support we can there, and send a messenger to Kroneburg. Even a small force from Pavelkaap could reach Burhgard in time to bolster their defenses."

Noah studied him a moment, then nodded. "It's a plan with teeth. Pavelkaap's our first stop either way—supplies are non-negotiable. From there, we split the load: you work the

Kronemarkers, I'll get word to Burhgard. We'll make it tight, but we'll make it work."

Felix exhaled, relief and resolve settling over him. "Then that's what we do. Pavelkaap first—everything hinges on it."

Noah clapped him on the shoulder, grip firm. "You're starting to sound like a leader, Felix. Let's hope and pray we make it in time."

As the ship cut through the waves, Felix turned his gaze westward, where Daegon's unseen fleet lurked beyond the horizon. The fight was coming—and he'd be ready.

The second day dawned with restless energy aboard The Windward Cross. The sky hung heavy with clouds; the sea churned beneath the ship, mirroring Felix's unease. He emerged from his quarters, Water Crystal pulsing steadily against his chest. His hands still fumbled with its power, but the urgency of Thegnfast's fate pressed him forward—he had to master this, and soon.

At the stern, away from the crew's morning tasks, Felix faced the water. He raised trembling palms and focused. The sea stirred; small ripples spread beneath his touch. A thin stream rose, wobbling unsteadily before collapsing with a splash. Felix gritted his teeth, ignoring the ache in his arms.

A few sailors paused, eyes flickering with curiosity. "Hero's still learning, eh?" a burly man with salt-crusted hair chuckled, scrubbing the deck.

Felix's cheeks burned, but he pressed on. He coaxed the water into a shaky arc. It wavered, then steadied, holding for a fleeting moment. The crew's murmurs shifted—less mockery, more interest.

"Look at that," a younger sailor whispered, nudging his companion. "He's getting it."

Releasing the arc into fine mist, Felix caught his breath. It wasn't much, but it was a start. Satisfaction flickered within him—fragile but real.

By afternoon, clouds parted; sunlight glinted off the waves. Felix joined Captain Noah at the helm, the older man squinting into the horizon. "Saw you back there," Noah said, voice gruff but warm. "Not bad for a beginner. Water's tricky—got a will of its own. Move with it, not against it."

Felix nodded, wiping sweat from his brow. "It's less... solid than the other crystals. Takes more focus."

"Aye, but you'll get it," Noah replied. "You've got the grit."

As evening fell, Felix practiced again, summoning a small whirlpool that spun for nearly a minute before unraveling. The crew's glances turned from skeptical to impressed; whispers carried a new tone. "He's the real deal," one muttered, coiling rope. "Chosen by the Creator." Felix overheard, and his resolve hardened—for Thegnfast, for Pangea, for them all.

The third day broke with clear sky and brisk wind, The Windward Cross cutting swiftly through the waves. The crew worked with renewed energy, sensing Pavelkaap drawing near. Felix felt it too—his bond with the Water Crystal growing stronger, more instinctive.

At midday, he stood at the ship's edge, sun blazing overhead. The crew, now anticipating his sessions, gathered quietly as he extended his hands. The water answered eagerly—a thick column rising at his call. Felix shaped it into a helix, surface shimmering as it twisted through the air.

Gasps rippled through the sailors. "Creator's mercy," one breathed, clutching his cap. "He's taming the sea."

Felix pushed further, splitting the helix into two streams that danced around each other before merging again. The crew burst into cheers, awe spilling over. "Do it again, sir!" a young deckhand shouted, grinning ear to ear.

Obliging, Felix drew the water into a shimmering orb, holding it steady above the waves. The crystal's power thrummed through him—alive, vibrant. He let the orb burst into mist, a gentle veil settling over the deck. Sailors laughed, shaking their heads in disbelief.

Captain Noah approached, rare smile creasing his weathered face. "That was something, Felix. You've come far in a day."

Felix ducked his head. "Thanks, Captain. Couldn't have done it without your advice."

"Nonsense," Noah said, waving a hand. "It's the Creator's gift. You're ready for what's ahead."

As dusk painted the sky in hues of orange, Felix lingered at the stern, gazing at the horizon. The crew's faith bolstered him, but the true challenge awaited in Pavelkaap. Tomorrow, they'd arrive—and the fight for Thegnfast would begin in earnest.

First light of dawn crept over the horizon as *The Windward Cross* sliced through the waves, Pavelkaap's spires now visible in the distance. The crew bustled with activity, preparing for arrival, but Felix and Noah stood together at the helm, gazes fixed on the approaching city.

Noah broke the silence. "We'll dock within the hour. Once ashore, I'll arrange the fastest messenger to ride to Burhgard. You'll need to speak with Father William and the city's leaders—convince them to lend whatever aid they can spare."

Felix nodded, jaw set with determination. "I'll make sure they understand what's at stake. Thegnfast isn't just a city—it's the heart of my people. If it falls, Daegon's heresy will spread like wildfire."

Noah clapped him on the shoulder, grip firm and reassuring. "You've got the fire of a true leader in you, Felix. Pavelkaap will rally to your cause, and with the Creator's blessing, so will Kroneburg."

Felix managed a small smile, though the weight pressed heavily on his shoulders. "I won't let them down. For Thegnfast, for my family, for all of Pangea."

The ship sailed steadily toward Pavelkaap, rising sun bathing the city in golden light. Felix stood at the bow, cloak billowing in the wind, eyes locked on the horizon. Above, Titania soared, golden wings catching the dawn's rays—a symbol of hope and guidance.

Noah joined him, voice steady. "We'll get your army, lad. I'd stake my ship on it."

Felix nodded, resolve unshakable. "And I'll lead them to victory."

With the city drawing nearer and Titania's cry echoing in the sky, Felix knew a grand battle was close at hand. He was ready.

Chapter 15: The Gathering of Allies

The Windward Cross sliced into Pavelkaap's harbor, its sails taut against the morning breeze. Felix Aldric stood at the bow, the Crystals pulsing softly beneath his tunic, his gaze fixed on the city's spires piercing the golden dawn. Pavelkaap thrummed with life—vendors shouting, ships creaking, the air sharp with salt—but Felix's heart was with Thegnfast, Witsgar's capital, now a target of Daegon's advancing fleet. As the ship docked, he turned to Captain Noah, his voice urgent.

"Captain, send a rider to Oakridge," Felix said, gripping his staff. "If we can't save Thegnfast in time, they need to be warned Daegon's forces could sweep through the west."

Noah nodded, his weathered face grim. "Wise move, lad. Oakridge'll get word."

"Thank you," Felix replied, stepping onto the pier, his boots striking wood with resolve. The streets of Pavelkaap buzzed with life—merchants bartering, gulls crying overhead, the tang of salt heavy in the air. Felix moved with urgency, his cloak trailing behind him as he approached the towering stone church. Its doors stood open, a sanctuary amidst the chaos. Inside, the air was cool and thick with incense, and there, near the altar, stood Father William, his robes a quiet symbol of authority.

"Father," Felix said, urgency sharpening his words, "Daegon's fleet is closing on Thegnfast. If Burhgard falls, the capital has no protection from the sea. I need help."

William's expression tightened. "A grave threat. The Holy Order of Saint Baldwin from Kroneburg is here, and my priesthood works closely with them in Pavelkaap. I can get you to their leader in Parelkaap, Marshall Konrad von Stein."

Relief flickered in Felix's chest. "Can we meet him now? Time's short."

"Of course," William said, his eyes resolute. "Konrad's faith is iron, but his trust is hard-earned. Come."

As they stepped into the sunlight, a soft voice halted Felix. "Felix?"

Lara approached through the morning mist that clung to Pavelkaap's cobblestone streets, her blonde hair shimmering like spun gold in the sun's first rays, her blue eyes bright with relief and a quiet, unspoken warmth that stirred Felix's heart. She held a small cloth bundle, a loaf of fresh bread, its warm, yeasty scent rising like a promise of hearth and home. "I heard you'd returned," she said, her voice gentle as the breeze that rustled the linden trees lining the square. "For your journey, Felix." Her words carried the weight of their shared past—nights spent poring over tales of old heroes in the village hall, her laughter a light in darker days.

Felix's tension, knotted from days of travel and battle, softened under her gaze. A fleeting smile broke through, like sunlight piercing a clouded sky. "Thank you, Lara," he said, his voice low, the weight of her kindness settling deep within him. His fingers brushed the rough cloth of the bundle.

Her gaze lingered, a quiet intensity in her smile that held him fast, as if she saw beyond the dust of the road to the heart he shielded. "Stay safe," she murmured, her fingers grazing his arm, a fleeting touch that sent a warmth through him, like the first spark of a kindled fire. She stepped back, her silhouette framed by the golden light, and Felix felt the moment cling to him, a fragile thread of hope amidst the gathering storm.

Father William laid a gentle hand on Felix's shoulder, his touch steady as an anchorite's prayer. "Come, my son," he said, his voice a low, resonant cadence. "The Order awaits." Felix nodded, tucking the bread into his satchel, his fingers lingering on the cloth as if to hold onto Lara's warmth. He followed William through Pavelkaap's cobblestone streets, their path leading to a stern stone hall that loomed like a sentinel at the city's heart. Its facade, carved with angular runes of devotion, stood unyielding as the faith it enshrined. Black banners hung from the walls, each bearing the Holy Order's white cross and an angelic soldier soaring above it, wings spread wide as if to guard the faithful, their edges frayed yet proud, testaments to battles fought in the Creator's name.

Inside, the air was thick with the scent of frankincense, curling from bronze censers that glowed faintly in the dim light, and the weight of disciplined silence pressed upon Felix like a sacred vow. Relics of past crusades stood enshrined along the walls: a notched sword, its blade etched with prayers; a dented shield, its surface scarred by blows struck for the Light; a tattered flag, its faded threads woven with the blood and faith of martyrs. These were the revered symbols of the Order's storied devotion, each a beacon of the Creator's enduring will, and Felix felt their weight settle upon him, a call to rise above the fleeting warmth of Lara's touch and face the trials ahead.

Knights stood in perfect formation, their black surcoats stark against the gray stone, the white crosses emblazoned on their chests glowing like beacons of faith. The dark fabric, heavy and unadorned, spoke of their stoic resilience, a refusal to bend under trial or temptation. Their faces were stern, eyes fixed ahead, their posture a living testament to the Order's militaristic rigor. At the hall's front, Marshall Konrad von Stein commanded the space, his broad frame draped in a cloak adorned with the Order's emblem—the angelic soldier in mid-flight, its wings spread over the cross. His gray hair was cropped close, and his piercing eyes seemed to pierce Felix's soul, weighing his worth in an instant.

The silence was a palpable force as Felix entered, the knights' scrutiny a heavy mantle upon him. Yet he stood tall, the warmth of the Elemental Crystals against his chest fueling his resolve. William stepped forward, his voice steady. "Marshall, this is Felix Aldric, the Creator's Element Hero. He seeks your aid against a dire threat."

Konrad's voice cut through the stillness of the stone hall, a low rumble with a faint German accent, resonant as a bell tolled in a distant cloister, summoning the faithful from shadowed vales.

"You claim to be the Creator's chosen, Junge. What proof do you bring?"

Felix met his gaze unflinching, the weight of the Elemental Crystals warm against his chest, like ancient embers kindled anew in the forge of destiny. "I carry the Crystals, gifts from the Creator through His Elemental Beasts—guardians of wind, fire, water, and earth, woven into the very tapestry of Pangea's creation. With them, I've fought Daegon's lieutenants, those shadow-wreathed fiends, and shielded the faithful from their blades of despair."

Konrad's eyes narrowed, his tone sharp as honed steel forged in the fires of decades of battle. "Words are wind, scattering like leaves before the storm. Show me."

Felix's gaze flicked to a simple clay goblet on a nearby table, its water glinting faintly in the hall's dim light, a humble vessel of life amidst the sacred relics. He raised a hand, the Water Crystal flaring to life with a soft, azure glow, like moonlight caught in a mountain spring that bubbled from the roots of the world. The water in the goblet trembled, then rose in a shimmering stream, drawn forth by the Crystal's will, and formed a radiant orb above Felix's palm, hovering steadily. Its surface rippled, reflecting the hall's censer-glow in a dance of liquid starlight, as if echoing the Creator's own breath upon the primordial seas. The knights stirred, their stoic faces breaking into faint murmurs, as if the divine power glimmering before them stirred memories of ancient miracles scribed in illuminated tomes, tales of heroes who tamed the elements to safeguard the realms of men.

Konrad stepped closer, his indigo cloak sweeping the stone floor. His gaze locked on the orb, searching for deceit, but a flicker of awe softened his stern features, reminiscent of a pilgrim beholding a sacred relic unearthed from forgotten catacombs. "Impressive," he conceded, though skepticism lingered like a shadow at dusk. "But faith is not proven by tricks alone, no more than a blade is forged by spark without hammer. Tell me, what drives you? What makes you worthy of the Creator's favor?"

Felix lowered his hand, the orb dissolving back into the goblet with a gentle splash, the water settling as if returning to its sacred repose. A faint mist curled upward, drifting through the hall toward the rafters, where ancient beams hewn from sacred oaks bore carvings of elemental beasts entwined in eternal vigilance. "I am driven by love for my family, my people, and all of Pangea," he said, his voice steady, though the memory of Meadowbrook's ashes tightened his throat like a noose of sorrow. "I seek to protect them from Daegon's heresy, that foul blight which twists the Creator's harmony into discord. I am but a vessel for the Creator's will, a humble thread in the grand weave of fate."

Konrad studied him, his weathered face unreadable, then nodded slowly, as if weighing a soul's worth against the scales of legend. "You speak with conviction, Junge, and your eyes hold the fire of truth. Perhaps you are the one foretold, the Elemental Hero of old prophecies, who shall harness the Crystals to mend the fractured world and stand against the encroaching void." He turned to his knights, his voice rising with the authority of a marshal forged in crusade, echoing off the walls like a warhorn calling across mist-shrouded hills. "Brothers, we face a choice. Daegon's fleet threatens Thegnfast, and with it, the stability of western Pangea, that verdant cradle of our kin. If we do not act, his heresy will spread unchecked, a blight upon the Creator's works, devouring the light like nightfall that never ends."

A grizzled knight, his surcoat marked with faint scars like the lines of a sacred text etched by trials endured, spoke up. "Marshall, our forces are stretched thin, like bowstrings taut against the endless foe. Kroneburg itself faces raids, shadows nipping at our borders."

Konrad raised a hand, silencing the murmur that rippled through the hall like wind through ancient leaves. "Ja, I know. Yet if Thegnfast falls, Daegon's path to Kroneburg opens wide, a floodgate unleashing darkness upon our lands. We must weigh the greater good, as protectors of the Creator's realm." He turned back to Felix, his cloak settling like a mantle of judgment, his stern gaze softening with a glint of resolve, as if beholding a long-awaited dawn. "We cannot spare an army with raids on our flanks, but I will give you a vanguard, our finest knights, sworn to the cross and the blade, to hold Burhgard and buy time for Thegnfast to prepare its walls and hearts."

Felix bowed his head, gratitude surging within him like a tide swelling in a hidden cove. "Thank you, Marshall. Your support means everything, a beacon in these shadowed times."

Konrad's stern features softened further, a rare glint of respect in his eyes, like sunlight piercing a canopy. "Go with the Creator's blessing, Felix Aldric. Prove yourself worthy of the title 'Element Hero,' as the legends whisper of one who bears the Crystals not for glory, but for the sacred duty to shield the innocent, uphold the faith, and restore the harmony shattered by ancient strife." He paused, then raised a hand, his voice taking on a solemn timbre that filled the hall like a chant rising from a cloistered abbey. "Kneel, Junge, and receive the consecration of our Order, that you may carry forth the weight of knightly responsibility: to defend the weak, honor the Creator's will, and stand unyielding against the tide of heresy."

Felix obeyed, dropping to one knee on the cold stone, the weight of the moment settling over him like a sacred mantle woven from threads of prophecy and oath. The knights closed ranks, their black surcoats forming a circle of faith, their faces stern yet reverent, as if standing before a holy relic unearthed from the annals of time, eyes alight with the trust that this youth might indeed fulfill the age-old tales of the Elemental Hero, the hero who would awaken the Beasts and turn back the darkness. Konrad drew a small vial from beneath his cloak, its contents shimmering with holy oil, catching the light like liquid starfire distilled from the heavens. He stepped forward, his boots echoing in the hushed hall like the measured tread of fate itself, and anointed Felix's forehead with a cross, the oil cool and fragrant with myrrh, seeping into his skin as a seal of divine trust. "By the Creator's light, we consecrate this mission," he intoned, his voice resonant as a cathedral's bell tolling across the vales. "May your path be true, Felix Aldric, bearer of the Crystals, sworn to the Light, guardian of Pangea's fragile peace, exemplar of knightly valor, and fulfillment of the prophecies that have sustained our Order through centuries of vigil." The knights responded in unison, their voices rising in a low, powerful chant: "Für den Schöpfer, für den Glauben." For the Creator, for the Faith. The words wove through the air, mingling with the frankincense that curled from censers like the breath of ancient guardians, a vow etched into the very stones of the hall, binding Felix to a legacy of heroes who had borne similar burdens in eras long faded into legend.

Felix rose, the oil a cool weight against his skin, the chant's echo stirring his soul like a call to destiny, filling him with the profound gravity of his role—not merely a wanderer with Crystals, but a knightly vessel entrusted with the hopes of a world teetering on the brink. He felt the Crystals pulse faintly at his chest, as if affirming the blessing, their warmth a reminder of the Creator's trust and the immense responsibility now upon his shoulders: to lead with wisdom, fight with honor, and inspire the faithful as the Elemental Hero of lore. Konrad met his gaze, his hand resting briefly on Felix's shoulder, a gesture heavy with unspoken faith, as if passing the torch of an unbroken line. "Thegnfast awaits, Junge. Sway their council, rally the vanguard, and hold fast against the shadow, for the fate of kingdoms rests in your steadfast hands."

As Felix turned to leave the Great Sanctuary, its oaken doors closing behind him with a solemn thud, Father William stepped to his side, his indigo robe flowing like a shadow cast by the Creator's light. His eyes, kind yet resolute, gleamed like a sage guiding a prophesied heir through the mists of uncertainty. "Come, my son," he said softly, his voice a gentle anchor amidst the ritual's afterglow, its faint Dutch lilt echoing the tides of Pavelkaap's harbors. "The council must be gathered, and swiftly. I'll summon the Republic's leaders to hear your plea for Thegnfast." He clasped Felix's shoulder, his touch steady as a ship's helm, a silent blessing that lingered as he turned toward the cobblestone streets. Felix nodded, the weight of the knighting oil still cool on his forehead, the Firesong Blade at his hip pulsing faintly, its hidden runes a quiet vow of duty. The knights' chant— Für den Schöpfer, für den Glauben—faded behind him, a solemn promise weaving his path into the grand saga of Pangea, like a thread in the Creator's tapestry. Hope burned brighter in his chest, tempered by the legend's mantle and the challenge ahead, yet a shadow of doubt lingered—could he rally Thegnfast's council before Daegon's fleet struck? With a final glance at William's retreating figure, his robe fluttering like a sail caught in the evening breeze, Felix stepped into Pavelkaap's bustling streets, each cobblestone worn smooth by centuries of mariners and pilgrims, leading him toward the harbor where his fate awaited.

The harbor of Pavelkaap hummed with life, a symphony of creaking rigging, shouting sailors, and the rhythmic slap of waves against weathered piers. Ships of oak and iron lined the docks, their masts rising like a forest of ancient trees. The salty breeze tugged at Felix's cloak, carrying the scent of tar and brine, a reminder of the sea's vast, untamed power, as old as Pangea's primal shores. Felix's mind raced—Daegon's fleet gathering, its dark sails poised to choke Thegnfast's harbors. Every moment counted, and the weight of Pangea's future pressed upon him, a burden as vast as the sea itself. Yet the memory of Lara's smile, radiant in the sanctuary's chamber, kindled a spark of hope, a beacon to guide him through the gathering storm.

As Felix approached the pier where The Windward Cross was docked, its prow adorned with a carved cross entwined with waves, a figure caught his eye amidst the flurry of crewmen securing ropes and crates. Captain Noah stood near the gangplank, his weathered face framed by a salt-streaked beard, his eyes sharp as a gull's scanning the horizon. Spotting Felix, he raised a hand in greeting, his boots thudding against the wooden planks.

"Felix," Noah called, his voice carrying over the creak of ships and the cries of seagulls. "I've got news for you."

Felix met him halfway, his expression expectant. "The riders?"

Noah nodded, a faint smile creasing his weathered face. "They're on their way to Oakridge, just as you asked. If we can't reach Thegnfast in time, at least the west will be warned."

A flicker of relief crossed Felix's face. "Thank you, Noah. That's one less burden." He paused, then added, "There's more. The Holy Order has agreed to send a vanguard. Marshall Konrad himself pledged their support."

Noah's eyes widened, and he let out a low whistle. "That's a coup, lad! With the Order behind us, the council won't dare turn a blind eye." He rubbed his chin thoughtfully. "I've got ties with the merchants here—old friends who owe me favors. If we play this right, we might get more than just ships. Supplies, maybe even a few extra hands."

Felix's jaw tightened with determination. "That's what I'm counting on. We need everything we can muster to reach Thegnfast before Daegon's fleet."

Noah clapped him on the shoulder, his grip firm. "We'll make it happen. You focus on the council, I'll rally the merchants to our side."

Felix nodded, gratitude swelling in his chest. "I'll do my best."

As Felix turned to leave, a soft voice called his name. "Felix?"

He glanced over his shoulder to see Lara standing nearby, her blonde hair catching the sunlight, her blue eyes filled with concern. She stepped closer, her hands clasped in front of her, a small smile playing on her lips.

"I heard about the council meeting," she said, her voice gentle but edged with worry. "Are you nervous?"

Felix hesitated, then gave a small shrug. "A little," he admitted, his gaze softening as he met her eyes. "But I know what's at stake. I have to convince them."

Lara's smile widened, though her brow remained furrowed. "You will. You've already come so far." She reached out, her fingers brushing his arm in a fleeting touch. "Just remember, you're not alone in this."

The warmth of her words settled over him like a balm, easing the tension in his shoulders. "Thank you, Lara," he murmured, his voice thick with emotion. "That means more than you know."

For a moment, they stood in silence, the bustling harbor fading into the background. Then, with a reluctant sigh, Felix stepped back. "I should go. The meeting…"

Lara nodded, her eyes lingering on him. "Creator be with you, Felix."

He offered her a quick, reassuring smile before turning away, his heart a little lighter despite the weight of his task.

Two hours later, as the sun climbed higher in the sky, Felix stood outside the grand council hall, its stone facade looming over the square. The doors creaked open, and Father William emerged, his face calm but expectant.

"Felix," William said, his tone steady. "The council is ready. It's time."

Felix took a deep breath, squaring his shoulders. He glanced back toward the harbor, where Noah was already speaking with a group of merchants, his gestures animated. Lara stood near the church steps, watching him with quiet encouragement.

With a final nod to William, Felix stepped forward, his boots echoing against the cobblestones. The fate of Thegnfast—and all of Pangea—rested on what happened next.

The council chamber of Pavelkaap gleamed with the pride of a maritime republic. Vaulted ceilings loomed overhead, etched with carvings of crashing waves and towering ships. A long table, carved to resemble a galleon's hull, stretched across the room, surrounded by councilors in vibrant robes of orange and blue. Maps of Pangea's jagged coastlines hung on the walls, dotted with tiny ship models marking trade routes. The air smelled faintly of salt and wax, a reminder of the sea that sustained this city.

Felix stood at the threshold, his cloak still damp from the harbor winds. To his left, Father William adjusted his holy vestments; to his right, Captain Noah stood tall, his weathered face a map of a life at sea. The councilors' murmurs fell silent as William raised a hand.

"Esteemed councilors," William began, his voice resonant, "I present Felix Aldric, the Element Hero, chosen by the Creator and anointed by the Holy Order. He comes with dire news and a humble request."

Felix stepped forward, meeting a dozen pairs of eyes—some curious, some skeptical. "Daegon's forces march on Thegnfast," he said, his voice steady despite the knot in his chest. "If it falls, his shadow will stretch across Pangea. Pavelkaap's trade, its ships, its very freedom will be next. The Holy Order has pledged a vanguard, but we need your ships and men to reach Thegnfast in time."

A ripple of whispers spread through the room. A naval officer stroked his beard, considering, while a merchant tapped a jeweled finger on the table. Then, a sharp voice sliced through the murmur.

"A bold tale," said Councilor Brandt, a wiry man with a merchant's cunning and a hawk-like stare. "But who's to say you're not one of Daegon's own, sent to strip us bare? A spy, luring our fleet away so he can sack Pavelkaap unopposed!"

Gasps erupted, followed by a chorus of disbelief. "Ridiculous!" barked a burly naval captain. "A spy wouldn't dare walk in here so brazenly," scoffed a merchant woman with silver braids. Yet a few councilors hesitated, their gazes flickering to Felix with fresh doubt.

Felix's fists clenched, but he forced his voice calm. "I've faced Daegon's lieutenants—felled them with the Elemental Crystals granted by the Creator." The Water Crystal began to shine, blue glow pulsing. With a flick of his wrist, a ribbon of water spiraled into the air, glittering in the candlelight before dissolving into mist. "Does this look like Daegon's work?"

Brandt snorted. "A conjurer's trick. Daegon's sorcerers could do the same."

Before Felix could retort, Noah slammed a fist on the table, his voice a thunderclap. "Enough, Brandt! I sailed with Felix to the Heart of Cordelia. I watched him receive the Water Crystal from the Leviathan. He's no spy—he's the real thing. And if Thegnfast falls, your precious trade routes go with it."

William nodded gravely. "The Holy Marshall Konrad trusts Felix, as does the Creator. This is no deception, but a call to stand against heresy."

The room stilled. The silver-braided merchant leaned forward. "Even so, our fleet's spread thin. Daegon's raids have hit us hard. What can we spare?"

Felix seized the opening. "I don't need your whole navy—just enough ships to carry the vanguard and a handful of your sailors. Thegnfast guards the west. Save it, and you save your own harbors."

Brandt crossed his arms. "And if we say no? What's to stop Daegon from sailing here first?"

"Then I'll fight with what I have," Felix said, his eyes blazing. "But if Thegnfast holds, Daegon's plans crumble. Help me now, and I'll stand for Pavelkaap if he ever dares come."

A heavy silence fell. The councilors exchanged glances, weighing duty against risk. At last, the head councilor—a stately man with a voice like tempered steel—stood. "Pavelkaap will grant four ships, provisioned, with a company of volunteers. It's not an armada, but it will carry your vanguard."

Felix bowed, relief warring with the weight of what lay ahead. "Thank you. We'll make it count."

As the council dispersed, Brandt shot Felix a lingering glare, but the others offered nods of cautious respect. Noah grinned, clapping Felix's shoulder. "Four ships'll do, lad. Now let's get 'em ready."

The aid was secured—barely. Felix knew it was only the first step in a war that would test them all. But for now, he had ships, men, and a chance to save Thegnfast.

The council chamber's heavy doors swung shut behind them, sealing away the tension of the meeting. Felix, William, and Noah stepped into the cool evening air of Pavelkaap, the distant hum of the harbor a reminder of the urgency still ahead. As they walked, Noah turned to Felix, a satisfied grin breaking across his weathered face.

"Got some good news for you, lad," Noah said, his voice low but triumphant. "A couple of the merchants came through— lent us two extra ships and a small band of mercenaries. They're not keen on seeing Daegon's fleet choke the trade routes."

Felix's shoulders relaxed, a wave of relief washing over him. "That's more than I hoped for. Thank you, Noah. Your efforts paid off."

Noah waved a hand dismissively, though his eyes gleamed with pride. "Rest up now. We'll be ready to sail west toward Burhgard at dawn—hoping to get there in time."

Felix nodded, the weight of the day settling into his bones. "I will. See you at first light."

As Noah strode back toward the harbor, Felix and William made their way to the church, its stone spire a quiet beacon against the darkening sky. The streets were quieter now, the city's bustle giving way to the soft glow of lanterns. Inside the church, the air was still and sacred, the scent of incense lingering from the day's prayers.

William paused at the sanctuary door, his expression solemn but kind. "I'll be leading a sermon soon, Felix. I'll pray for your journey and for the safety of all who sail with you."

Felix bowed his head in gratitude. "Thank you, Father. That means a lot."

With a final nod, William retreated into the sanctuary, leaving Felix to make his way to the small room at the back of the church. He had barely settled onto the narrow bed when a soft knock sounded at the door.

"Come in," Felix called, sitting up.

The door creaked open, and Lara stepped inside, balancing a tray with eggs, fresh bread, a cluster of grapes, and a jug of water. Her smile was warm, though her eyes carried a trace of worry.

"Thought you might need this," she said, setting the tray on the small table beside the bed.

Felix's stomach growled in response, and he chuckled softly. "You're right about that. Thank you, Lara."

She lingered as he began to eat, her fingers fidgeting with the hem of her apron. After a moment, she spoke, her voice hesitant but curious. "My mother was from Thegnfast, you know.

She met my father when he was on a voyage from Pavelkaap. His ship needed repairs, and he was stuck there for a while. In that short time, they fell in love, and she gave up everything to come here with him."

Felix paused, a piece of bread halfway to his mouth, then set it down. "I'm from Eldenwold, a small village north of Thegnfast. It's not much, but it's home."

Lara's eyes brightened, and she sat on the edge of the bed. "I've never seen Thegnfast—my mother's homeland. I've always wanted to, though."

Felix's heart ached at the longing in her voice. "When this is over—when Daegon is defeated—I'll come back. I'll take you to Thegnfast to see your kin."

Lara smiled, hope flickering in her eyes. "You'd do that?"

"I promise," Felix said, his voice firm with conviction.

For the next hour, they talked—sharing stories of their families and dreams for the future. Lara laughed at Felix's tales of village life, and he listened intently as she spoke of her life in Pavelkaap. The weight of the world lifted briefly, replaced by the simple joy of connection.

As the night deepened, Lara stood, smoothing her apron. "You should sleep, Felix. Tomorrow's a big day."

He nodded, rising to his feet. "You're right. But before you go—can we pray together?"

Her smile softened, and she nodded. They knelt side by side, their voices soft as they whispered a prayer for strength and safety. When they finished, Lara squeezed his hand briefly. "Goodnight, Felix."

"Goodnight, Lara," he replied, watching as she slipped out the door.

Alone in the quiet room, Felix lay back on the bed, his mind swirling with thoughts of the voyage ahead. He clasped his hands and whispered one last prayer: "Grant me the strength to protect my people and keep my promise to Lara."

With that, he closed his eyes, letting the gentle hum of the church lull him into sleep, ready for the dawn and the battle to come.

Chapter 16: The Race to Burhgard

The first light of dawn crept through the narrow window of the small room at the back of Pavelkaap's church, casting a soft golden glow over Felix Aldric as he stirred from sleep. His eyes snapped open, heart already racing with fierce eagerness to begin the voyage to Burhgard. Today was the day he would set sail to bolster the fortress city's defenses against Daegon's advancing fleet—a desperate race to save not just Burhgard, but Thegnfast and all of western Pangea from the fallen sorcerer's wrath. There was no time to linger.

Felix sat up swiftly, mind sharp and resolute. He dressed in his weathered tunic and cloak, the familiar weight of his staff and Firesong Blade grounding him as he moved. The Elemental Crystals—Wind, Fire, Earth, and Water—rested against his chest, their faint hum a constant reminder of the power he wielded and the responsibility he bore. With a quick, practiced motion, he gathered his equipment—staff in hand, blade sheathed at his side—and stepped toward the door, boots tapping softly against the stone floor.

As he reached for the handle, a murmur of voices from the sanctuary caught his ear. He paused, then turned back, drawn toward the front of the church. There, bathed in the gentle morning light streaming through stained-glass windows, Father William and Lara were preparing for the morning service. William arranged candles on the altar with steady hands, while Lara folded linens with her usual grace, blonde hair catching the dawn's glow. They looked up as Felix approached, faces brightening with warmth.

"Felix," William said, stepping forward, voice rich with kindness but tinged with solemnity. "You're up early. Ready for the journey ahead?"

Felix nodded, jaw set with determination. "I am, Father. I can't afford to waste a moment."

Lara approached, clutching a small bundle wrapped in cloth. "We wanted to see you off properly," she said, voice soft yet steady, blue eyes shimmering with quiet intensity. "We'll be praying for your success and your safety."

William placed a firm, reassuring hand on Felix's shoulder. "May the Creator guide your path and grant you strength, Felix. You carry the hopes of many."

Felix bowed his head, gratitude swelling in his chest. "Thank you, Father. Your prayers mean more than I can say."

Lara stepped closer, offering the bundle. "It's salted beef," she said, a faint smile tugging at her lips. "For the journey. I hope it helps, even just a little."

Felix accepted it, fingers brushing hers briefly as he took the offering. "Thank you, Lara. This will keep me going." He paused, gaze locking with hers, her beautiful blue eyes holding him a moment longer than necessary. The morning light framed her face, and a surge of resolve steadied him. "I'll come back," he promised, voice low but unwavering. "I'll see you again soon."

Lara's smile deepened, though her eyes glistened with unspoken emotion. "I'll hold you to that, Felix."

For a heartbeat, they stood in silence, the weight of the moment binding them. Then, with a final nod to William, Felix turned and strode out of the church, the bundle tucked securely under his arm, his promise to Lara echoing in his mind.

The streets of Pavelkaap were just beginning to stir as Felix made his way toward the harbor. Merchants unfurled their stalls, the clatter of crates and murmur of early risers filling the cool morning air. The sun climbed steadily in the east, its golden rays painting the cobblestones in hues of amber and casting long shadows behind him. As he reached the docks, the harbor was already a hive of activity—sailors shouting orders, ropes creaking, the sharp scent of salt and tar hanging thick. The sun's light reflected off the calm waters to his left, illuminating the bustling scene with a radiant glow.

Captain Noah stood near the gangplank of The Windward Cross, sharp eyes overseeing the final preparations. When he spotted Felix, he raised a hand in greeting and strode over, boots thudding against the wooden pier.

"Morning, lad," Noah said, Dutch-accented voice cutting through the harbor's din. "Everything's in order. The Holy Order's Vanguard is boarding now, and the mercenaries are settling in."

Felix's gaze swept over the ships, taking in the disciplined knights of the Holy Order moving with precision, their black surcoats emblazoned with white crosses stark against the morning light. Nearby, the mercenaries—a rougher, livelier bunch—loaded supplies and weapons, their chatter rising above the creak of the docks. Seven vessels lined the harbor, including The Windward Cross, sails furled and ready.

"Seven ships in total," Noah continued, gesturing to the fleet. "Four from the council, two from the merchants and mercenaries, and The Windward Cross. It's not a grand armada, but it's what we've got."

Felix studied the small fleet, brow furrowing slightly. "It's not much," he admitted, "but it will have to be enough. With this, the Thegnfast, and whatever Burhgard can muster, we might just stop Daegon's forces from destroying Witsgar."

Noah turned to him, eyes crinkling with a confident smile. "Aye, lad. With this fleet, your people's strength, and you as the Element Hero, we've got a solid chance at victory. The Creator's favor is with us—don't doubt that."

Felix returned the smile, warmed by Noah's trust. "Thank you, Captain. For everything. I couldn't have come this far without you. I just hope we all make it back safely."

Noah waved a hand dismissively, though his grin widened. "Ah, don't go getting all sentimental now. I've been sailing these seas longer than you've been alive, and I haven't been killed yet. Doubt today's the day that changes."

Felix chuckled, tension in his chest easing as a light laugh escaped him. "I hope it stays that way for you, Noah."

"Same to you, Felix," Noah replied, tone light but sincere. He gestured toward the ship. "Now, come aboard. We'll be casting off soon."

Together, they walked up the gangplank, the deck of The Windward Cross solid beneath their feet. The crew moved with practiced efficiency, finalizing preparations as the sun rose higher, its light glinting off the waves. Felix paused to glance back at the harbor, the city of Pavelkaap aglow in the dawn. He thought of Lara's hopeful smile, William's steady prayers, and felt a renewed surge of determination. He would return—he had promised.

As the last of the crew boarded and the sails unfurled with a sharp snap, The Windward Cross pulled away from the dock, leading the small fleet westward. The wind caught the sails, and the ship surged forward, cutting through the waves with purpose. Felix stood at the bow, cloak billowing behind him, eyes fixed on the horizon. Above, Titania soared, golden wings catching the sunlight—a constant reminder of the Creator's presence.

The voyage to Burhgard had begun, the first leg of a desperate journey to confront Daegon's forces and protect Thegnfast. Felix whispered a quiet prayer, heart steady with resolve. Whatever lay ahead, he would face it with faith and courage—for his people, for his family, and for all of Pangea.

The fleet carved a steady path westward along the coast of Southern Pangea, dark waters of the Cordelia Ocean lapping against the hulls. The Windward Cross led the charge, sails taut with the wind, guiding the other ships like a beacon through the calm sea. Rugged cliffs and thick forests of the southern shore loomed in the distance—a silent promise of the trials to come. Felix Aldric stood on the deck, eyes tracing the horizon, when Captain Noah approached, stride confident despite the rolling of the ship.

"Felix," Noah said, voice carrying over the wind, "it'll take us about two and a half days to reach Burhgard at this rate. These ships are faster than Daegon's fleet—lumbering beasts, those are. Hopefully, Burhgard's still holding their ground."

Felix nodded, gaze unwavering. "We'll get there in time. We have to."

Noah flashed a reassuring grin, eyes glinting with mischief under the midday sun. "That's the spirit, Felix. How about we shake off that tension? Another day of sparring, maybe? Last match ended in a draw—you owe me a proper challenge."

Felix's lips curved into a reluctant smile, the knot in his chest loosening at the prospect of a friendly duel. Noah's easy confidence was infectious, and the idea of proving himself with a blade felt like a lifeline. "I'm in," he said, voice steadier than he felt.

They moved to the center of the ship's deck, boots thudding on weathered wood as the crew scrambled to clear a space. Barrels were shoved aside, ropes coiled hastily, and the air buzzed with anticipation. The crew's eyes were alight with excitement, murmurs, a mix of bets and banter. Felix caught snippets—some still doubted his skill, others curious if he could hold his own against their captain. He gripped his sword hilt tighter, leather wrapping creaking under calloused fingers.

Noah drew his blade with a flourish, steel catching the sunlight in a silver arc. Felix mirrored him, the metallic ring of their swords harmonizing as they squared off. The deck seemed to shrink, the world narrowing to the space between them—ten paces of salt-stained planks, the creak of the ship, the tang of sea air sharp in Felix's lungs.

"Ready?" Noah asked, stance loose but gaze sharp, like a hawk sizing up its prey.

Felix nodded, heart pounding. "Let's do it."

The first clash came fast—Noah's blade slicing toward Felix's shoulder. Felix parried, the impact jarring his arm, but he held firm, pivoting to counter with a low slash. Noah sidestepped effortlessly, laugh ringing out over the clatter of steel. "Not bad, but you're still thinking too much!"

For the next hour, they sparred with fierce intensity, blades flashing in a blur of silver and sparks. The crew's cheers faded to a dull roar in Felix's ears as he focused, sweat beading on his brow. Noah was a storm—relentless, unpredictable, strikes precise yet playful. But Felix was no longer the hesitant novice. Noah's guidance had sharpened his instincts, teaching him to read the subtle shifts in his opponent's balance, the flicker of intent in his eyes.

Felix ducked a high swing, feeling the air whistle above his head, and lunged forward, aiming for Noah's side. Noah parried, but Felix anticipated it, twisting his wrist to redirect the blow. Their swords locked, hilts grinding, and Felix pushed, muscles straining as he forced Noah back a step. The crew gasped, sensing the shift. Noah's grin widened, a spark of pride in his eyes.

"You're learning," Noah grunted, breaking the lock with a deft spin. He feinted left, then struck right, testing Felix's reflexes. Felix barely blocked in time, the clash vibrating through his bones. But he didn't falter. He pressed forward, movements smoother now, each strike carrying newfound confidence. He wasn't just reacting anymore—he was dictating the fight.

The rhythm of the duel shifted, Felix's blade a silver blur as he drove Noah across the deck. The crew's shouts grew louder, skepticism giving way to awe. Felix's heart thundered, not with fear but with exhilaration. He saw an opening—Noah's guard dipped, just for a fraction of a second. Felix seized it. With a swift twist of his wrist, he hooked Noah's blade and sent it spinning from his hand. The sword clattered to the deck, skidding to a stop against a coil of rope.

Silence gripped the ship for a heartbeat, broken only by the creak of the mast and the distant cry of a gull. Then the crew erupted into gasps and cheers, some clapping Felix on the back, others staring wide-eyed at their captain's defeat. Noah stood there, hands on hips, sweat-dampened hair falling into his eyes. He let out a low chuckle, brushing a hand through the mess with theatrical flair. "Well, I'll be damned, Felix. You didn't just win—you owned that. I'm impressed."

Felix sheathed his sword, chest heaving, a grin breaking across his face. The victory felt like more than a sparring match—it was proof, to the crew and to himself, that he was growing into the fighter he needed to be. Noah clapped him on the shoulder, grip firm but warm. "Keep that fire, mate. You're gonna need it."

As the crew dispersed, still buzzing with excitement, Felix caught Noah's eye, smiling modestly. "I've learned a lot from you in a short time, Noah. Couldn't have done it without you."

Noah's grin widened. "Just happy to play my role in helping the hero along. You're coming into your own."

They took a moment to rest, settling against the ship's railing as the sea breeze cooled their skin. After a beat, Felix's tone grew serious. "What's the plan to help Burhgard?"

Noah's expression sobered. "If Burhgard's still under siege when we arrive, we'll sail to shore fast and rush in to aid the city. Every sword counts."

Felix frowned, considering the worst. "And if Daegon's forces have already reached Thegnfast?"

Noah paused, eyes narrowing as he weighed the odds. "Then we'll have to rush in ourselves, hit them from behind—hopefully flank them with a surprise attack."

Felix leaned forward, determination sparking in his chest. "I'll use my abilities the best I can—wind and water, whatever it takes to disrupt their lines and sink Daegon's ships."

Noah's grin returned, bold and approving. "That'd be a great help, lad. With you wielding those crystals, we might just turn the tide."

A few hours later, as the sun dipped below the horizon, Felix descended to his cabin. The weight of the days ahead pressed on him, but a small comfort awaited. He opened the bag of salted beef Lara had given him, the savory scent stirring memories of her beauty, her warm smile, her steady presence. He ate a few pieces, the taste grounding him, then lay back on his bunk. The gentle sway of the ship eased him into sleep, resolve firm for the challenges of the next day.

Felix awoke to the familiar sway of The Windward Cross, the ship's gentle motion a quiet reminder of the journey that had brought him this far. He lingered in bed for a moment, mind tracing the winding path of his adventure. It began at the Sky Altar, where Titania, the majestic golden eagle, had descended with a voice that resonated in his soul, naming him the Creator's chosen. He remembered the weight of the Wind Crystal as it fused with his chest—a moment that changed everything. Then came the painful farewell to his family in Eldenwold, his parents' proud tears, their prayers a shield around him. Finding Rowan, his brother, alive yet marked by Daegon's shadow, had been both joy and burden. The faces of Kirkhaven and Oakridge followed: William's unshakable faith, the warmth of the villagers, and

Lara—her blue eyes and steady presence haunting him even now. He wished she were here, her strength beside him, but he pushed the thought aside. There was no time to linger on what could not be.

Rising from his bunk, Felix stepped onto the deck, morning air sharp with salt and promise. Noah stood at the helm, hands firm on the wheel, gaze steady on the horizon. Felix approached, wooden planks creaking beneath his boots.

"How's the journey going, Noah?" he asked, voice carrying quiet hope.

Noah turned, a faint smile tugging at his weathered face. "The winds are moving us quickly, lad. It's a sign of the Creator's will, pushing us to aid the Witsgarians."

A wave of relief washed over Felix, easing the tension that had settled in his chest. The signs of a promising voyage bolstered his spirit. "That's good to hear."

"Aye," Noah replied, tone calm but firm. "We should rest well today. We'll reach Burhgard by noon tomorrow."

Felix nodded, eyes drifting eastward. The faint memory of Pavelkaap lingered there, a distant place now far behind him. He turned westward, toward Burhgard and Thegnfast, feeling the weight of the moment he'd been waiting for drawing near.

"Don't worry, Felix," Noah said, voice cutting through the silence. "We can only control what we can. No sense fretting over the rest."

Felix paused, the words striking a familiar chord. Noah had said something like this before, on their last voyage, and it had steadied him then as it did now. He looked at the captain, gratitude warming his voice. "You're a good man, Noah. Wise and strong."

Noah chuckled, a deep, hearty sound. "I don't know about wise, but I do my best."

Felix smiled, hope flickering brighter within him. He lingered for a moment, gazing at the ocean's endless expanse, its beauty a quiet balm to his restless heart. Then, with a final glance at Noah, he returned to his cabin.

Back in his bunk, Felix sank to his knees, clasping his hands in prayer. He poured out his fears, his hopes, and his trust in the Creator, seeking strength to face what lay ahead. Hours slipped by in deep reflection, the ship's rhythm a steady companion to his thoughts. As the day waned, he lay down to rest, resolved to wait for morning. Burhgard loomed on the horizon, and with it, the next step of his destiny.

Felix awoke with a jolt, urgency of the day pulling him from sleep. The dim light of dawn filtered into his cabin aboard The Windward Cross, and he wasted no time. Eager to begin, he leapt from his bunk and grabbed his equipment: the Firesong sword, its blade shimmering faintly as he sheathed it at his side, and his staff, its familiar weight a comfort in his hand. With gear secured, he strode quickly to the deck, boots thudding against the wooden planks.

The morning air greeted him with a sharp bite of salt as he emerged topside. Captain Noah stood at the helm, steady hands guiding the ship through the waves, eyes fixed on the horizon. Felix approached, voice taut with anticipation. "How much further, Noah?"

"Only a few hours," Noah replied, tone calm yet firm. "We're closing in."

Felix nodded, chest tight with determination. He turned his gaze westward, the vast expanse of sea stretching before him, waiting for the southwestern edge of Pangea to rise into view. The waiting gnawed at him, but he stood resolute, resolve unwavering.

Time passed, marked only by the creak of the ship and the rhythmic crash of waves. At last, the rugged outline of Pangea's southwestern corner emerged on the horizon. *The Windward Cross* began its turn north toward Burhgard, the fortress city perched where Lake Gildermere met the sea. But as they drew closer, a dark tendril of smoke curled into the sky, staining the morning light. Felix's heart sank, a surge of urgency propelling him to the front of the ship.

"Faster," he muttered under his breath, though he knew the sails were already straining.

As the ship sailed toward the western entrance of Lake Gildermere, the scene grew grim—a shadow cast over Pangea's ancient heart. Ship debris littered the sea: splintered masts jutting like broken bones, shredded sails drifting aimlessly—the wreckage of Burhgard's once-mighty navy, timbers scarred by Daegon's forces. Ahead, Burhgard itself smoldered, proud walls reduced to ash and ruin, breached ramparts crumbling into jagged stumps that pierced the heavens like a cry of defiance silenced. Spiral Serpent banners fluttered amidst the devastation, red coils writhing in the wind—a taunting emblem of Daegon's victory, mocking the faith of the Witsgarian people who had held this fortress as a bastion of the Creator's light for centuries.

Felix stood at the ship's prow, hands clenched into fists, knuckles whitening as anger and sorrow surged within him—a tempest threatening to drown his heart. The air carried the bitter tang of ash and the faint, anguished cries of the lost, a mournful dirge weaving through the lake's stillness like a requiem for the fallen. His eyes traced the ruins, now silenced, their lives snuffed out by Daegon's heresy. The memory of Rowan, his brother, bound and dragged to the Crags' lava caves, flashed in his mind, mingling with the weight of his failure: *I wasn't fast enough to save them.* The Element Crystals at his chest pulsed faintly, azure and crimson glow dimming as if sharing his grief. "Creator, forgive me," he whispered, voice breaking, raw with the ache of a wound unhealed. "I didn't make it in time to shield Your people."

He bowed his head, a silent prayer forming: *Grant me strength to honor their memory, to carry Your light against this darkness.* Felix's resolve stirred, a spark kindled amidst the ashes of his guilt, as he vowed to save Thegnfast from a similar fate—to wield the Crystals and Firesong Blade in the name of those lost to Burhgard's fall.

Captain Noah stepped to his side, weathered face etched with regret, salt-streaked beard catching the twilight's glow. His eyes, sharp as a gull's scanning the horizon, held sorrow tempered by the resolve of a mariner who had faced countless storms. "I'm sorry for your loss, Felix," he said, voice steady, a deep rumble like the sea's eternal song. "Burhgard was a beacon of Witsgar, its walls a testament to their faith and resilience. But we can't linger here in grief. There's still time to sail into Lake Gildermere, to reach Thegnfast before Daegon's shadow falls. If it still stands, we can rally to its defense and hold the line."

Felix nodded, throat tight, the Crystals warming faintly as if affirming Noah's words. He unclenched his fists, hands trembling as he touched the hilt of the Firesong Blade, its leather grip a reminder of the Fyrclad Kin's trust and his duty as the Element Hero. "For Burhgard," he said softly, voice resolute, "and for Thegnfast."

Felix's anger softened, tempered by a fragile flicker of hope, though doubt gnawed at him. *What if we're too late again?* The ship turned northeast, cutting through the dark waters toward the lake, leaving Burhgard's ruins to fade into the haze. As they entered Gildermere, the atmosphere aboard grew heavy. The crew fell silent, hands gripping ropes or weapons, eyes darting to the horizon. Felix felt their unspoken fears pressing against him—*Can the Element Hero save us?*—and his own pulse quickened, the Crystals humming with restless energy.

The lake stretched before them, surface deceptively calm, reflecting the smoke-stained sky in muted grays. Felix scanned the distance, searching for any sign of Thegnfast.

As the ship pressed deeper into the lake, shapes emerged—dark, ominous silhouettes against the haze. Felix's breath caught as Daegon's fleet materialized to the northwest, black sails blotting out the horizon like a storm cloud. The ships loomed, vast and menacing, oars slicing the water with relentless precision, blockading the route to Thegnfast. On the encircling shores, movement stirred—Daegon's armies landing, red-coiled banners snapping in the wind, a tide of steel and malice closing in on the capital.

Thegnfast loomed through the roiling haze, ancient gray walls rising like a titan's bulwark, defiant against the tide of chaos that sought to swallow it. Smoke curled skyward, thick and acrid, weaving a shroud over the city's spires, while distant cries of battle carried on the wind. Along the ramparts, archers stood resolute, silhouettes etched against the flickering glow of firelight, loosing volleys into the shadowed masses below. Arrows arced through the dusk, glinting briefly before finding their marks in the writhing ranks of Daegon's siege. The enemy pressed forward, undeterred, war machines groaning as they hurled jagged stones that shattered against Thegnfast's unyielding stone.

The mighty harbor burned, a cauldron of flame and ruin. Daegon's fleet—sleek and merciless—choked the waters with black-hulled ships, sails emblazoned with the crimson sigil of a coiled serpent. Fire licked at the docks, consuming the proud vessels of Witsgar's navy, blue banners sinking into the inferno. The defenders fought with desperate fury, hurling spears and boiling oil from the harbor's towers, but the tide of Daegon's forces seemed endless—their assault a relentless hymn to destruction.

Felix stood at the bow of his ship, salt-stung wind whipping his cloak as Thegnfast's plight seared itself into his soul. The gray walls, though scarred, stood unbroken, but they were surrounded on all sides—a lone bastion in a sea of foes. The blue banners of Witsgar fluttered faintly, mere specks against the encroaching darkness, colors dulled by the haze of battle. His anger flared anew, a molten fire in his chest. *I won't let them take it.* His hand tightened on his staff, the Crystals embedded in its length pulsing with otherworldly light—a silent vow to act.

Noah's voice cut through the mounting tension, sharp and steady as a blade. "They've only just begun their siege. There's still time to save Thegnfast!" His eyes, keen as a hawk's, scanned the horizon, reading the battlefield with a warrior's instinct.

Felix's gaze locked on the distant walls, where faint glimmers flickered—torchlight catching on steel, proof his people still fought. But the sight of Daegon's forces, vast and unrelenting, stirred a surge of dread. *We're outnumbered. Outmatched.* He crushed the thought, resolve hardening to iron. *I have the Crystals. I have to make that enough.* The Wind Crystal on his chest pulsed faintly, and a gust swirled around him, unbidden, tugging at his cloak and stirring the air across the deck. The ship surged closer to the shore, every crest of the waves a race against the tightening noose around Thegnfast.

The dark tide of Daegon's army pressed closer, banners like wounds against the twilight sky. Felix's anger forged itself into determination, the Crystals flaring brighter, light casting faint shadows that danced like spirits across the deck. The air hummed with power, winds now howling, as if the very elements rallied to his will.

Noah signaled the fleet with a sharp gesture, voice rising above the gale. "Land quickly on the eastern shore—we'll flank them from the south!" The ships obeyed, hulls slicing through the churning waters, spray glinting like scattered stars. Felix stood unmoving, eyes fixed on Daegon's forces, winds intensifying into a tempest around him.

Thegnfast stood as a beacon of defiance, walls a testament to the unyielding spirit of Witsgar. Yet the flames in the harbor roared higher, and the enemy's shadow grew ever darker. Felix's heart thundered—not with fear, but with mythic resolve, as if the Creator himself watched from the heavens. He would wield the Crystals' might, summon the winds, and unleash the fire within. Thegnfast would not fall—not while he drew breath.

Chapter 17: The Siege of Thegnfast

The waters of Lake Gildermere shimmered under a sky choked with smoke as Felix Aldric stood at the prow of The Windward Cross. Ahead, the fortress city of Thegnfast loomed, its gray stone walls battered yet unbowed. Daegon's forces swarmed around it like ants besieging a hill, their black banners emblazoned with the spiral serpent snapping in the wind. The air thrummed with the twang of bowstrings as defenders along the battlements loosed volleys of arrows, cutting down attackers who dared approach the walls. Ladders rose and fell, splintered by boulders hurled from above, while the deep bellow of war horns echoed across the lake.

Within the ancient, weathered walls of Thegnfast, the Witsgarians waged a desperate stand, their resolve as unyielding as the granite battlements that had guarded their valley for seven generations. The fortress, hewn from the bones of the Ashen Crags, stood as a bastion of hope amidst the rugged highlands, its towers crowned with firestone lanterns that cast a defiant glow against the encroaching dusk. Archers in blue tunics, their woolen garb dyed with woad from the river meadows, leaned over the parapets, their longbows singing as arrows streaked through the smoky air. Each shaft, fletched with raven feathers, pierced shields of blackened oak and found flesh, eliciting sharp cries from Daegon's soldiers below. Along the ramparts, men and women, their faces etched with the stoic grit of a people born to hardship, heaved cauldrons of boiling oil, the viscous liquid hissing as it splashed over the enemy ranks. Scalding screams rose like a chorus of the damned, the oil searing through leather and cloth, leaving chaos in its wake. The southern wall bore the brunt of the assault, where Daegon's army massed in a disciplined phalanx, their shields, emblazoned with the charred serpent rune, locked tight, their boots churning the earth as they readied for a relentless charge.

Felix stood atop the deck of the ship. He clenched his oaken staff, the four Elemental Crystals humming warmly against his chest. Their energy thrummed through him, a symphony of elemental voices, but each invocation drained his vitality, a toll he paid willingly for Thegnfast, the heart of his people, a sanctuary of faith, beauty, and knowledge that would not fall while he drew breath. He glanced back at Noah, whose face framed a grim nod. Noah's eyes, sharp as flint, gleamed with unspoken trust. Felix took a deep breath, tasting the acrid tang of smoke and the metallic bite of steel on the wind. It was time.

With a cry that echoed like a thane's battle-horn, Felix vaulted over the ship's railing, his cloak billowing like a storm cloud. As he plummeted toward the lake's glassy surface, he thrust his staff forward, the Wind Crystal flaring with a pulse that roared through his veins like a gale born of the heavens. A whirlwind erupted around him, its currents spiraling with ferocious intent, lifting him just above the water. Waves rippled outward in concentric rings as he glided forward, his cloak snapping like a banner in the wind's embrace. The howl of his vortex drowned out the distant clamor of battle, screams, clashing steel, and the thunder of siege ladders against stone. Felix was a storm given form, a living tempest hurtling toward Daegon's fleet with the wrath of the Creator in his wake.

The enemy ships loomed ahead, hulking galleys of blackened timber, their prows carved with snarling serpent heads, bristling with soldiers in iron helms and crimson cloaks. Oars sliced through the lake's surface in rhythmic cadence, propelling the vessels toward Thegnfast to reinforce the siege. Felix raised his staff, its glyphs blazing, and the air itself bent to his will. Tornadoes erupted from the lake, their spiraling columns rising like the wrathful spirits of drowned mariners. The whirlwinds slammed into the ships with devastating force, tearing sails to ribbons and snapping masts like brittle kindling. Soldiers shouted in panic, their voices swallowed by the roaring winds as the vortices flung them overboard, their heavy armor dragging them into the lake's churning depths. Felix followed with the Fire Crystal, its heat surging through him like molten iron. Blazing orbs conjured from its glow streaked through the air, each fireball a comet of divine fury. They struck the wooden decks, igniting rigging and planks in a voracious blaze. Flames roared skyward, devouring the fleet in a chaos of burning wrecks, the lake glittering with reflections of sinking ships and flailing men—a testament to Felix's unrelenting power.

As the last tornado dissipated, its winds scattering embers across the water, Felix turned his whirlwind toward the eastern shore. On the muddy banks, slick with silt and tangled with river reeds, Noah's crew disembarked from the ship. They were joined by the Holy Order's Vanguard, and a ragtag band of mercenaries, their mismatched armor clinking as they moved.

The Holy Order's Vanguard stepped ashore with solemn purpose, chainmail in black surcoats emblazoned with white crosses. Their armor clinked softly as they formed up under their Commander, his stern face framed by a neatly trimmed beard, his eyes alight with unwavering faith.

Before the charge, their commander raised his sword, its blade etched with a silver cross, and turned to his knights. "Brothers and sisters of the Order," he intoned, his German accent thick with reverence, "we stand in the Creator's light. Let us call upon His strength to shield us and smite our foes."

The knights knelt as one, their heads bowed in prayer.

The commander rose, his voice steady. "We are the Creator's sword. We shall hold the line and break their ranks. For the Creator!"

"For the Creator!" the Vanguard echoed, their voices a unified chorus. They formed a phalanx, shields interlocking, spears leveled—a wall of faith and steel ready to meet Daegon's forces head-on. Their discipline was palpable, a stark contrast to the chaos of battle, and Felix felt a surge of admiration for their unyielding conviction.

Nearby, the mercenaries gathered under their grizzled leader, Liam, a man whose patchwork leather and chainmail bore the scars of countless battles. His face, etched with lines of experience, gleamed with a cunning that belied her rough exterior.

"Alright, you lot," Liam growled, his voice gravelly and commanding. "We're not here for glory, we're here for coin and survival. But that doesn't mean we can't fight smart."

He gestured toward Daegon's forces, massed at Thegnfast's southern wall. "They're bunched up tight, like sheep waiting for the slaughter. We'll hit 'em quick and dirty. Archers, loose your arrows high, aim for their officers.

A chorus of grunts and nods followed. The mercenaries spread out, forming lines behind the knights. Their archers took position on a nearby rise, nocking arrows with practiced ease. Liam caught Felix's eye and gave him a curt nod. "You do your magic, lad. We'll make sure they regret turning their backs."

Felix smiled faintly, appreciating their pragmatic ruthlessness—a perfect complement to the Holy Order's steadfast defense.

Captain Noah stood at the helm of *The Windward Cross*, his weathered hands gripping the wheel. His crew, tough sailors hardened by years at sea, moved with purpose across the deck, their eyes fixed on the smoke-wreathed shore. Felix's elemental onslaught had just torn through Daegon's fleet, leaving burning wrecks and scattered soldiers in its wake. The chaos provided the perfect opening, and Noah intended to seize it.

Noah turned to his first mate, Dirk. "Take a skeleton crew—ten of our finest hands—and hold the ship fast. Keep her primed to fend off Daegon's raiders or sail at my signal. The rest of you, arm yourselves to the teeth. We're storming the shore with the mercenaries."

"Aye, Captain!" Dirk's voice cracked like a whip, his salute crisp as he turned to the crew. With the ease of a man born to the sea, he gave orders, dividing the sailors with ruthless precision. Those chosen to guard the ships hefted crossbows and arming swords, their weathered faces set as they took posts along the rails, eyes scanning the burning harbor for Daegon's black-sailed vessels. The others, bound for the fight, slung shields across their backs and buckled on swords, their crossbows clattering with bolts ready to sing.

Noah led his shore-bound sailors toward Lake Gildermere's edge, their boots churning the shallow, reed-choked waters that lapped at Thegnfast's eastern shore. Ahead, the mercenaries waited, hardened men and women clad in mismatched armor, their blades glinting like shards of starlight. They eyed Noah's crew with a mix of wary curiosity and grudging respect, their hands never straying far from their weapons.

Liam strode forward, his hand resting on the hilt of her blade. "Sailors on dry ground, eh? You sure you won't trip over your own feet without a deck to sway under you?"

Noah flashed a grin, his Dutch accent coloring his words. "We've danced with storms fiercer than this rabble. My crew's quick and mean—perfect for tearing into their flanks."

He smirked, sizing them up. "Fair enough. We're hitting fast and hard, disrupting their lines, cutting off their commanders. Can your sailors keep pace?"

"Keep pace?" Noah chuckled, hefting a cutlass. "We'll carve 'em a new path. Watch."

His crew fanned out, their movements fluid despite the unfamiliar terrain. These weren't disciplined soldiers like the Vanguard, but they were scrappy, resourceful, and fearless— qualities that paired well with the mercenaries' brutal efficiency.

Liam nodded, impressed despite himself. "Alright, Captain. Let's make this quick and bloody. Move!"

The Knights of the Holy Order surged forward, their gleaming armor a beacon of resolve amidst the chaos. They marched in a disciplined phalanx, shields hoisted high and interlocked, forming an impregnable wall of steel. Arrows streaked from the southern flank of Daegon's forces, their fire-tipped points whistling through the smoke-choked air, but the knights' shields held firm, each projectile clanging harmlessly against the tempered surface. Their boots pounded the earth in unison, a rhythmic thunder that echoed the unyielding purpose of their faith, each step a prayer made manifest against the heresy of Daegon's charred serpent rune.

Behind this armored vanguard, Liam's mercenaries took their positions, their movements as precise as a predator's stalk. Grizzled and unflinching, they drew longbows of yew and horn, arrows nocked with the ease of men who'd hunted both game and foes across the lands. At Liam's crisp command—a barked syllable that cut through the din—a volley erupted, the arrows soaring southward in a deadly arc. The shafts, fletched with goose feathers and tipped with barbed iron, sought the exposed ranks of Daegon's soldiers, piercing leather and flesh with lethal intent. Cries of pain mingled with the clatter of falling shields, the enemy's southern flank reeling under the sudden onslaught.

From the north, atop Thegnfast's towering southern wall, a relentless barrage descended like a storm unleashed. The Witsgarian archers, their blue tunics vivid against the granite parapets, loosed a torrent of arrows, each shaft a whisper of death raining down upon Daegon's troops. The dual assault—mercenaries from the south and Thegnfast's archers from the north—wove a merciless pincer, ensnaring the enemy in a web of feathered doom. The air thrummed with the whistle of arrows, their paths crisscrossing the twilight sky like threads of fate, each strike eroding the Iron Legion's discipline.

As the knights closed within striking distance, their shields still raised against the dwindling arrow fire, Felix stepped forward, his staff gripped tightly in his hands, worn raw by battle. The four Element Crystals pulsed warmly against his chest. With a focused breath, he channeled the Earth Crystal, its deep, resonant thrum grounding him like the roots of the ancient cedars that fringed the lake. Just before the knights reached the enemy's line, the ground beneath Daegon's soldiers erupted into a violent tremor. A guttural rumble surged through the earth, the soil fracturing in jagged fissures that swallowed boots and toppled spears. The enemy's spearwall buckled, soldiers staggering as their once-tight formation shattered, their discipline dissolving into chaos as they fought to steady themselves on the quaking terrain.

The knights seized their chance, their shields absorbing the last erratic arrows with a chorus of metallic clangs, each impact a testament to their unshakable resolve. They charged into the broken formation with unrelenting force, swords flashing like shards of starlight through the disorganized ranks. Steel bit through leather and bone with little resistance, blood spraying across the churned earth as the southern flank collapsed under the weight of their assault. Daegon's troops, already battered by the ceaseless volleys from above and below, stood no chance against the knights' precision, their blades carving a path through the chaos like a scythe through ripe wheat.

In the midst of this carnage, Felix's elemental wrath blazed unchecked. He raised his staff, the Fire Crystal flaring with a heat that scorched his veins, and conjured fireballs that arced through the twilight like comets of divine fury. The blazing orbs struck the remnants of Daegon's siege engines—catapults and battering rams cobbled from blackened timber—igniting them in a voracious blaze. Flames roared skyward, devouring ropes and wooden frames, the acrid smoke curling like a funeral shroud over the battlefield. With a flick of his wrist, Felix summoned the Wind Crystal, its cool surge weaving gusts that scattered the enemy's last arrows, their fire-tipped points winking out like dying stars. The knights' bravery, the mercenaries' cunning, and the defenders' desperation melded into a symphony of triumph, the air alive with the clash of steel, the crackle of fire, and the cries of the fallen.

The southern flank began to buckle under the relentless assault, Daegon's soldiers falling back step by bloody step. Felix pressed forward, his staff a blur as he wove wind and fire into his attacks, when something caught his eye, a figure gliding across the lake from the west. The man moved with unnatural grace, a faint shimmer of elemental power trailing behind him, mirroring Felix's own wind-borne flight.

Clad in flowing robes of deepest crimson and shadowed black, the figure cut an imposing silhouette against the flickering firelight, the fabric rippling like liquid night as it caught the wind. Across his chest, a meticulously embroidered serpent coiled in a spiral, its scales glinting with threads of silver and obsidian, as though alive with malevolent intent. His bald pate shone like polished marble under the flame's glow, unadorned save for the intricate play of light and shadow that danced across its surface. A beard, thick and gnarled, cascaded from his chin, its hue a striking blend of ash-grey interwoven with strands of dark brown, like the twilight melding with the earth's deep roots. His stern face, carved as if from weathered stone, bore the weight of unyielding resolve, and his brown eyes burned with a cold, unquenchable intensity, like embers smoldering in a frost-rimed hearth. In his right hand, he clutched a staff of ebon wood, its surface smooth yet seeming to pulse with an inner darkness. At its crown, a gem of midnight red gleamed with an otherworldly light, its facets catching the fire's glow and casting fractured beams of scarlet across the ground. Coiled about the staff's length was a serpent wrought of blackened metal, its sinuous form gleaming faintly, its ruby-red eyes glinting with a predatory malice that seemed to watch all who drew near.

As he approached the shore, his tread heavy with purpose, he raised his left hand with a gesture both deliberate and disdainful. From his palm erupted a fireball, a roiling orb of searing flame that tore through the air, its heat warping the very atmosphere in its wake. Felix, with instincts honed by desperation, flung himself aside, the fireball's scorching breath grazing his cloak, singeing its edge to a charred crisp that smoked faintly in the damp air. He rolled to his feet, his own staff gripped tightly, its familiar weight a steady anchor against the chaos. The figure touched down upon the blood-soaked ground with a grace that belied his foreboding presence, his robes settling about him like a storm cloud come to rest, the serpent-wound staff held aloft as if it were an extension of his indomitable will.

"So," the stranger said, his voice smooth and dripping with arrogance, "you must be the Element Hero. I've heard whispers of your meddling."

Felix tightened his grip, his heart pounding. "And I assume you're the one leading this army."

The man threw back his head and laughed, a sharp, mirthless sound that cut through the din of battle. "Not only am I leading this army, boy, but I am the one who will soon sit upon the throne of Thegnfast." He spread his arms, as if claiming the chaos around him. "I am Daegon."

Felix's breath caught, his eyes widening in shock. Here, at last, was the face of the man who had brought ruin to Pangea, the fallen sorcerer whose ambition had shattered lives and set this war ablaze. Anger surged through him, tempered by a fierce resolve. He squared his shoulders, meeting Daegon's gaze without flinching.

"Then this ends here," Felix said, his voice steady despite the storm raging within.

The battlefield was a cacophony of chaos, the air heavy with the scent of charred earth and the cries of clashing steel. Felix Aldric, the Element Hero, stood firm amidst the turmoil, his chest heaving as he faced Daegon, the dark sorcerer whose ambition threatened all of Pangea. The fate of Thegnfast teetered on the edge, and Felix's resolve burned brighter than ever.

Daegon's mocking laughter sliced through the din, cold and biting. "Look at you, Felix Aldric, just a boy pretending to be a hero," he taunted, his brown eyes glinting with malice. "A carpenter's son with no true power of his own. You cling to those pitiful crystals like a child to a blanket. Me? I need no such crutches to command the elements." He said proudly. "I was trained on the Isle of the Gifted, where only those born with magic's spark are deemed worthy. My skill surpasses anything a naive whelp like you could ever hope to achieve."

Felix's grip tightened on his staff, the Element Crystals pulsing faintly against his chest. "Your pride blinds you, Daegon," he shot back, his voice steady despite the storm of emotions within. "I fight for something greater than myself."

272

Daegon's sneer deepened. "Oh, you've been a thorn in my side, I'll grant you that," he said, his tone dripping with anger. "But now, at least, I'll have the pleasure of crushing you before I take my rightful throne."

Without warning, Daegon thrust his hand forward, unleashing a burst of flaming fire that roared toward Felix. Instinct kicked in, and Felix dove to the side, the searing heat grazing his cloak as the flames scorched the ground where he'd stood. But Daegon was relentless, his speed matched Felix's, and in an instant, he was behind him. With a flick of his wrist, Daegon summoned a tornado that seized Felix, hurling him skyward. The world spun wildly before Felix crashed back to earth, the impact rattling his bones.

Groaning, Felix clawed his way up from the blood-slick earth, his muscles screaming as he forced himself upright. Daegon charged forward, his black boots churning the mud, one aimed in a vicious arc toward Felix's ribs. With a desperate twist, Felix rolled aside, the boot whistling past his ear, spraying dirt across his face. He sprang to his feet, resolve igniting like a spark in dry tinder. His hand flew to Firesong's hilt, and as he drew the blade in one fluid motion, he willed the crystal's power. The steel erupted into flame, a roaring cascade of orange and gold that licked along the edge, casting jagged shadows across the churned ground. The air crackled with heat, the scent of scorched metal sharp in his nostrils.

Felix lunged, Firesong slashing in a swift, blazing arc, the flames trailing like a comet's tail. Daegon, with a serpent's grace, sidestepped the strike, his crimson-and-black robes swirling as if stirred by an unseen wind. His laughter, cold and mocking, cut through the night. "A sword? How quaint," he sneered, his voice dripping with disdain, the midnight-red gem atop his serpent-wound staff pulsing like a heartbeat. "Did your father teach you that trick, carpenter's son?"

Fueled by resolve, Felix rushed forward again, swinging Firesong with all his might. Daegon countered by raising an earthwall, the ground rumbling as stone and soil erupted to block the strike. The blade clanged uselessly against it, the shock reverberating up Felix's arm. Before he could react, Daegon darted around the barrier, a fireblast crackling from his hand. Felix ducked, the flames singeing his hair, and retaliated with a low swipe at Daegon's legs. The sorcerer stumbled, crashing to the ground with a grunt.

Seizing the moment, Felix lunged, aiming to drive Firesong into Daegon, but the sorcerer blasted him back with a gust of wind. Felix tumbled through the air, landing hard in the dirt, the breath knocked from his lungs. Daegon rose, his expression dark with fury. "Enough of this!" he snarled. He stomped the ground, triggering a violent quake that split the earth beneath Felix's feet. Three flaming tornadoes spiraled into existence, their fiery maws shrieking as they hurtled toward him.

Desperation surged through Felix. He sprinted westward toward the lake, summoning the Water Crystal's power. A massive wave erupted from the water's depths, crashing into the tornadoes and snuffing them out in a cloud of hissing steam. But

Daegon charged through the mist, his fist wreathed in flames, and drove it into Felix's stomach. The blow sent Felix flying, skidding across the muddy shoreline until he lay gasping at the water's edge.

Panting heavily, Daegon loomed over him, his robes singed and his face twisted with grudging respect. "You're stronger than I assumed, boy," he admitted, his voice low. "But it won't be enough."

Felix wiped blood from his lip and forced himself up, his muscles screaming. "I don't need to outmatch you, Daegon. I just need to stop you." With a roar, he charged, Firesong raised high. Daegon sidestepped, but Felix pivoted, slashing at his flank. The sorcerer twisted away, the blade missing by inches.

Felix's strength ebbed like a tide receding from a battered shore, each swing of Firesong heavier than the last, its crystal enchanted flames flickering fitfully, as though mirroring his waning resolve. The Element Crystals pulsed with a feeble glow, their once-vibrant energy dimming as he parried another of Daegon's searing assaults, the fireball hissing past to scorch the earth in a burst of acrid smoke. Around him, the battlefield churned in a maelstrom of chaos, clashing steel rang like a discordant hymn, punctuated by the desperate cries of Noah's crew as they fought tooth and nail, their blades flashing in the firelight. The Holy Order's Vanguard, clad in gleaming chainmail marred by blood and soot, strained to hold the southern flank against the relentless tide of Daegon's forces. Without Felix's rallying presence at the fore, his attention ensnared by Daegon's taunts and fiery sorcery, the enemy's overwhelming numbers began to reclaim the field. Daegon's army, a swarm of grim-faced soldiers wielding serrated blades and shields, surged forward with renewed ferocity, their boots trampling the fallen as they pressed the southern flank, driving the Vanguard back in a grinding, bloody retreat. Hope bled away like the life from the corpses strewn across the mire, and Felix's mind raced, a single thought hammering in his skull: *We're running out of time.*

Then, a faint tremor shuddered through the earth, a low, resonant rumble that sliced through the cacophony of battle like a blade through silk. Felix's head snapped up, his sweat-streaked face turning toward the eastern horizon, where the Vineland Vale stretched into a haze of smoke and shadow. At first, his eyes caught nothing but the roiling gloom. But the sound swelled—a steady, rhythmic thudding, like the heartbeat of some ancient beast stirring from a primordial slumber. Dust rose in the distance, a thin veil that thickened with each passing moment, swirling into a tawny shroud that blotted the stars. Felix's breath caught in his throat, a spark of desperate hope kindling in his chest. Reinforcements? The thought teetered on the edge of doubt, fragile as a candle in a gale.

Daegon, too, sensed the shift, his serpent-wound staff— its midnight-red gem pulsing with malevolent light—lowering slightly as he turned his piercing gaze eastward. A flicker of unease rippled across his stern features, the ash-grey and dark-brown strands of his beard catching the firelight as his lips tightened. For the first time, the sorcerer's unshakable confidence wavered, his eyes narrowing as the distant thunder grew louder, heralding an unknown force that threatened to reshape the tide of battle.

The dust parted like a veil torn asunder, revealing a sight that stole the breath from Felix's lungs: rank upon rank of soldiers emerging from the haze in unyielding formation, their polished armor catching the dim, overcast light with a gleam like distant stars. Green banners snapped fiercely in the gusting wind, each emblazoned with a stark white cross entwined with the gnarled silhouette of an oak tree, the proud sigil of Derwgor. At their forefront rode Arthur, astride a towering warhorse whose sable coat glistened with sweat, its hooves churning the earth with thunderous intent. Arthur's chainmail shimmered beneath a surcoat of verdant green, the oak-and-cross emblem wrought in silver thread across his chest, glowing as if kissed by some divine light. In his gauntleted grip rested his longsword, its blade honed to a razor's edge, its surface whispered of ancient retribution. His face, framed by a helm adorned with a crest of white feathers, was a mask of unyielding resolve, his eyes blazing with a fire that promised no quarter.

A surge of relief flooded Felix, warm and fierce, like a tide washing away despair. Across the scarred battlefield, the sight rippled through friend and foe alike. Noah's crew, their faces gaunt with exhaustion, loosed ragged cheers that tore from their throats, their faltering spirits kindled anew as they brandished their notched blades with fresh vigor. The mercenaries, grim and weathered, tightened their grips on swords and axes, their eyes narrowing as they sensed the tide's shift. Daegon's soldiers, their disciplined lines once as unyielding as iron, faltered—boots scuffing the bloodied earth, shields dipping as fear wormed into their ranks. Even Daegon, his serpent-wound staff clutched tight, its midnight-red gem pulsing like a baleful heart, betrayed a flicker of unease; his sneer twitched, and his voice, low and venomous, hissed through the air: "This means nothing."

But it did. Arthur thrust his sword skyward, its tip piercing the leaden clouds like a spear of light. "For the Creator! For Pangea!" he roared, his voice a thunderclap that rolled across the Vale, shaking the very earth. His army answered with a bellow that rent the heavens a unified cry of defiance and fury, raw and primal, that seemed to draw strength from the Creator himself. Then, they charged.

The ground quaked beneath the weight of their advance, a tremor that pulsed through the blood-soaked soil like the heartbeat of a wakened giant. The cavalry surged forward, a rolling tide of steel and sinew, their lances gleaming like slivers of starlight as they leveled at Daegon's eastern flank, hooves drumming a relentless cadence that drowned the clash of steel. High on the rise, archers of the Derwgorians nocked their longbows, their movements swift and precise, unleashing a storm of arrows that hissed through the air like a swarm of vengeful hornets. The shafts arced high, their fletched tails whistling a deadly song before plunging into the enemy ranks, felling soldiers in sprays of crimson. Behind the cavalry, the infantry advanced, their shields locked into a gleaming wall of steel, each step deliberate, their war-cries rising in a crescendo that matched the fury of the charge. The assault was a symphony of raw power—

coordinated, relentless, and awe-inspiring—as if the very spirit of Pangea had risen to smite its foes.

Felix seized the opening. Channeling the Wind Crystal, he unleashed a gust that staggered Daegon, breaking the sorcerer's focus. With a shout, Felix pressed forward. Around him, his allies rallied—Noah's crew and the Vanguard surged into the fray, their blades carving through Daegon's disoriented ranks. Arthur's forces slammed into the enemy lines, shattering their formation and driving them back in a chaotic retreat.

Daegon's roar of frustration echoed over the battlefield, but it was drowned out by the clash of steel and the triumphant cries. The tide had turned.

The battlefield before Thegnfast was a scarred tableau, strewn with the wreckage of war, shattered swords glinting like broken teeth in the fading light, tattered banners fluttering like the last gasps of the fallen, and the faint hum of fading magic lingering in the air like a dying echo. Daegon stood at the heart of the chaos, his crimson cloak billowing, the charred serpent rune on his breastplate pulsing with a malevolent glow. His face, a map of fury, contorted with rage as he surveyed the crumbling remnants of his Legion. "No!" he bellowed, his voice a thunderclap that shook the ash-choked air. "This isn't over!" But the tide had turned. From the east, Arthur's army, clad in steel and tartan, their war cries a hymn of defiance, carved into Daegon's flank, their longswords and axes flashing through enemy ranks with relentless precision. From the south, Noah's crew from *The Windward Cross*, wiry and battle-hardened, fought alongside the Holy Order's Vanguard, their polished armor gleaming with the cross, and Liam's mercenaries, whose brutal efficiency left blood-soaked trails in their wake. Together, they shattered Daegon's spearwall, scattering his forces like leaves before a storm.

Daegon's eyes, burning with the crimson fire of his heretical magic, locked onto Felix Aldric, who stood resolute amidst the fray, his staff gripped tightly. "You've won this day, boy," Daegon spat, each word a dagger aimed at Felix's heart. "But I'll return to crush you and your precious Pangea! Along with those crystals!" In a final act of defiance, he thrust his hands skyward, his own mastery of the elements surging forth. A massive gust of wind erupted, a howling vortex laced with the acrid tang of his corrupted power. The gale struck Felix like a hammer, hurling him backward into the cold embrace of Thegnfast's lake. The cold water swallowed him, its depths a shock that stole his breath, but the Water Crystal at his chest flared to life, its azure glow pulsing like a heartbeat. The waves parted around him, a shimmering corridor of liquid held at bay by the crystal's will, and Felix strode back to shore, dripping and unbowed, his cloak heavy with water but his eyes alight with determination. He scanned the battlefield, only to find Daegon gone—vanished into the twilight like a wraith, leaving only the fading echo of his wind.

Frustration gnawed at Felix's core, a bitter ache that rivaled the throbbing pain of his wounds. He'd been so close to ending the war, to severing the serpent's head and sparing Pangea further torment, yet Daegon had slipped through his grasp like smoke. The battlefield was a graveyard of fallen foes, their crimson cloaks pooling with blood, their charred serpent runes dimming as life fled their bodies. The remnants of Daegon's army fled in disarray, northern troops scrambling to rowboats that bobbed frantically toward their retreating ships, while the western fleet's galleys, their serpent prows barely visible, melted into the horizon's haze. Felix turned his fury on the stragglers, his staff a blur as he channeled the Wind Crystal from his chest. Gusts roared forth, toppling those too slow to escape, their screams swallowed by the wind as he refused to let them regroup. The Fire Crystal flared next, its heat a molten tide in his veins, sending fireballs arcing to ignite fleeing boats, their timbers crackling as flames devoured them. Each strike was a vow: Daegon's forces would find no respite while Felix drew breath.

As the last enemy fell or vanished into the dusk, a triumphant cheer erupted from the allied forces, a thunderous cry that rolled across the battlefield like a wave breaking on the shore. "Victory!" they roared, their voices weaving a tapestry of defiance and relief. The blue banners of Witsgar, woven with woad-dyed threads and emblazoned with the iron cross, still flew high above Thegnfast's granite walls, a symbol of their unyielding resilience. The fortress stood tall in the distance, its firestone lanterns casting a warm glow against the smoke-filled sky, a beacon of hope amidst the carnage. Yet Felix's heart remained heavy, the weight of Daegon's escape a shadow on his soul. Standing amidst the celebration, knights raising their swords, sailors clapping each other's backs, and mercenaries counting their coin, he vowed to hunt the sorcerer down. For his family, for his people, for the

Creator's light that burned in his chest, he would pursue Daegon across Pangea, no matter the cost.

"Felix!" Noah's voice rang out, sharp and warm, cutting through the haze. The grizzled captain strode toward him, his boots crunching on the trampled earth, his eyes wide with amazement. Felix turned, meeting Noah halfway as they closed the distance between them.

"By the Creator, lad," Noah said, his voice thick with awe, "the way you fought with those elements—fire dancing at your fingertips, wind tearing through the enemy, earth rising to your call, water bending to your will—it was like nothing I've ever seen. And to face Daegon himself? I've sailed every corner of Pangea, but that... that was something else."

Felix offered a weary smile, his gaze flickering to the horizon where Daegon had vanished. "Yes, but he escaped, Noah. The war's far from over."

Noah's excitement dimmed only slightly, his grin softening as he clapped Felix on the shoulder. "Aye, that's true enough. But look around you, Felix. Thegnfast still stands because of us. That's no small victory."

Felix let Noah's words settle into him, his eyes tracing the city's walls, scarred but unbroken. Thegnfast, the heart of Witsgar, had been saved. A quiet gratitude began to bloom in his chest, easing the sting of Daegon's retreat. He turned to Noah, his voice steady and sincere. "Thank you, Noah. For everything."

Noah laughed, a hearty sound that cut through the somber air. "Don't thank me, lad. If it weren't for you, Daegon would've ripped us all apart. You're the one who held the line."

Above them, a golden flash streaked across the sky as Titania soared, her wings catching the sunlight. Felix's smile deepened, and he tilted his head back, whispering a silent prayer to the Creator for this victory and for the safety of his people.

The moment was interrupted by the thunder of hooves. Felix and Noah turned to see Arthur riding up, his green surcoat emblazoned with the Derwgor's crest billowing behind him. He dismounted with a knight's grace, his face breaking into a warm smile. "Felix, my friend! It's been a while."

Felix stepped forward, clasping Arthur's arm in greeting. "Arthur, I'm so glad you're here. Thank you for coming to my people's aid."

Arthur's expression softened, though his eyes carried the weight of the fight. "We got word from Pavelkaap that Daegon was marching on Thegnfast. The King rallied every soldier we could muster and sent us to stand with you. Pangea can only defeat Daegon if we fight together. His Majesty knows that. He's indebted to you for saving Oakridge, so it's only fair Derwgor help save your people's city."

Felix felt a warmth spread through him, touched by the loyalty of Derwgor's people. "Your support means more than I can say, Arthur."

Noah grinned, stepping closer. "Aye, we were glad to see your banners crest the hill. A welcome sight, that was."

Arthur inclined his head, his tone chivalric and firm. "It was my honor to fight beside you both. The Creator's will shines through our unity."

A new figure approached, his presence commanding despite the quiet of his steps. Clad in the black surcoat of the Holy Order, a white cross stark against the fabric, he stood tall and broad-shouldered. "Commander Lars," he introduced himself, his voice stern and carrying a faint German accent. "It was an honor to fight alongside you all—especially you, Chosen Hero. Marshal Konrad was right to send us with you."

Felix nodded, extending a hand. "Thank you, Commander Lars. Your aid was invaluable today."

Arthur glanced toward Thegnfast's Eastern gates, now creaking open to welcome the victors. "We should head into the city and speak with the King. He'll want to hear of this victory."

Felix met Noah's gaze, and the captain shrugged with a chuckle. "I'll stay with the crew and help them secure the ships. I'm not much for formalities, lad. You go on."

Commander Lars stepped forward, his tone resolute. "I will join you. The Holy Order should be present for this."

"Agreed," Felix said, his mind already shifting to the road ahead. As they turned toward the city, the cheers of the allied forces echoed around them, a testament to their hard-fought triumph. Thegnfast was safe for now, and with allies like these, Felix dared to hope they could face whatever came next.

Chapter 18: The Heart of Thegnfast

Felix Aldric stepped through the Eastern Gate of Thegnfast, his boots striking the worn cobblestones with a steady rhythm. Flanking him were Arthur and Commander Lars, their presence a quiet testament to the victory they'd won. As they passed, the guards lining the gate snapped to attention, but their discipline faltered. Their eyes locked onto Felix, wide with reverence. Whispers buzzed among them tales of his stand against Daegon, of storms summoned from clear skies, of fire raining down like judgment. "A carpenter's son," one muttered, "wielding power like that…" Felix caught the words, and a tangle of emotions twisted within him: gratitude for their awe, relief that his home capital still stood, yet sorrow for the scars it bore from the siege.

Thegnfast stretched out before them, the second greatest and most beautiful city in all of Pangea. Its pale stone towers gleamed in the fading light. Fortified walls, stout as the burhs of old, encircled the city, their stones etched with crosses, standing defiant amidst the wreckage of war, cracked ramparts and charred timbers bearing the scars of Daegon's assault. Yet within those walls, Thegnfast thrummed with life, its narrow, cobbled streets crooked as the lanes of a medieval market bustling with the resilient spirit of the Witsgarian people. Timber-framed buildings, their wattle-and-daub facades leaning like weary warriors, lined the thoroughfares, where artisans hauled oaken beams to shore up homes, merchants bartered bread and cloth, and healers bandaged the wounded with careworn hands, their labor a testament to a faith unbroken by heresy.

Arthur's voice cut through his reverie. "The Witsgarians are a loyal and strong people," he said, his gaze sweeping the bustling streets. "It reminds me of my own back in Oakridge."

Felix turned to him, a faint smile tugging at his lips. "It's our faith that unites us," he replied. "It teaches us to be strong, to look out for one another. That's what holds us together in times like these."

Arthur's stern features softened, a rare smile breaking through. "Indeed," he agreed. "Faith and strength, Pangea's truest blades."

As they pressed deeper into the city, Felix's eyes lifted to the Grand Cathedral, its spires soaring untouched above the chaos. Beside it stood the Legendary Library, its carved stone facade a monument to knowledge. Both had weathered the battle unscathed, and a thrill coursed through him at the sight. He'd always found the cathedral magnificent, its arches a symphony of craftsmanship, and the library a masterful haven of study. *If only I had more time to lose myself in those shelves,* he mused, a pang of longing threading through his awe.

The inner castle loomed ahead, its gates flanked by knights in polished armor. One stepped forward, helm under his arm, his weathered face stern yet kind. "I am Knight-Captain Eadgar," he said, his voice carrying the weight of command. "On behalf of Thegnfast, I offer our deepest gratitude for your aid."

Felix met his gaze, stepping forward. "I'm Felix Aldric, from Eldenwold," he said firmly. "I couldn't let my people down."

Eadgar's eyes widened, a spark of shock igniting within them. "Eldenwold? The Chosen is one of our own?" His voice lifted with sudden excitement. "The king will be overjoyed to hear this!"

He turned to Arthur, a grin breaking his formality. "And Sir Arthur, welcome back. It's been too long."

Arthur bowed his head, his tone warm yet tinged with regret. "I'm happy to be here, Eadgar, though I wish it were under better circumstances."

"Aye," Eadgar replied, his smile fading. "As do I."

Commander Lars spoke then, his voice steady and clipped. "I am Commander Lars of the Order of the Holy Sword, the Holy Order. We request an audience with the king."

Eadgar nodded sharply. "Granted. Follow me."

They were led through the castle's grand corridors, stone walls draped with tapestries of Witsgarian valor, woven tales of triumph and sacrifice. At last, they stepped into the throne room, a vision of breathtaking beauty. Dark oak beams arched overhead, carved with swirling knotwork. Tapestries adorned the walls, their rich hues depicting ancient battles and revered kings. The throne itself rose from a dais, a towering seat of polished wood sculpted like a great tree, its roots sprawling across the floor. Iron sconces held flickering candles, bathing the room in a golden glow that danced across the intricate carvings. Tapestries adorned the stone walls, their rich hues depicting the storied history of the Witsgarians battles won, kings crowned, and the ever-present raven soaring through stormy skies. At the far end, upon a dais of polished wood, stood the throne, a majestic seat carved to resemble a great tree, its roots sprawling across the floor like ancient veins, symbolizing the deep roots of the Witsgarian lineage.

Seated upon the throne was King Leofric, of House Oswin, a young man in his late twenties, his presence commanding despite his youth. He wore a suit of gleaming chainmail, over which a surcoat of deep blue bore the emblem of Witsgar: a white cross with a raven in flight, its wings spread wide as if guarding the realm. His dirty blonde hair fell to his shoulders, framing a face marked by a thick beard and eyes that spoke of both strength and wisdom beyond his years, traits inherited from his father, King Alaric, who had passed two years prior, leaving the throne to his son. Beside him stood Queen Mildrith, her long golden hair braided elegantly, her blue silk dress a serene contrast to the martial attire of her husband. She was a vision of grace, her presence a quiet pillar of support in the hall.

Felix, Arthur, and Lars approached the throne and knelt, their heads bowed in respect. King Leofric's voice, warm yet tinged with the weight of recent events, broke the silence. "Rise, brave defenders of Thegnfast."

The three stood, and the king's gaze settled on Felix. "I would know the name of the Chosen Hero who has brought us this victory."

Felix stepped forward, his heart steady. "I am Felix Aldric, from Eldenwold, Your Majesty."

A flicker of surprise crossed the king's face, quickly giving way to a smile that reached his eyes. "Eldenwold? Then the Creator has blessed us with a hero from our own kin. This is joyous news indeed."

Felix smiled, his voice earnest. "It is an honor to be chosen by the Creator, sire, and to arrive in time to save Thegnfast. Sadly, I could not reach Burhgard in time."

The king's body language shifted, his posture becoming stoic yet shadowed with sadness. "Burhgard's fall is a sorrow we all bear," he said, his tone measured and grave. "It was more than a city, an economic power that fueled our trade and a military defense that shielded our borders. Its loss weakens Witsgar." He paused, then lifted his chin, his voice firming. "But there will be time to mourn Burhgard. For now, we must rebuild and prepare for what may come next."

King Leofric's eyes then turned to Arthur, softening with recognition. "Sir Arthur, it is good to see you again."

Arthur inclined his head, a warm smile on his lips. "And I, Your Majesty. You've become a fine king, much like your father was."

Leofric's gaze softened with humility, a faint smile tugging at his beard. "I strive to be as good as my father, though his legacy is a high mark to reach."

The king's attention shifted to Lars, who stood with the quiet dignity of his order, his black surcoat stark against the hall's warmth. "And you, sir, your name and purpose?"

"I am Commander Lars of the Order of the Holy Sword," Lars replied, his voice steady and formal, carrying a faint German accent. "The Holy Order wishes to aid Thegnfast in these dark times and pledges myself and my knights to your command, Your Majesty, until we are summoned back to Kroneburg."

King Leofric nodded, his expression one of graceful acceptance. "Your offer is most welcome, Commander. We shall need every ally to face the trials ahead."

The throne room fell silent for a moment, the weight of their words settling over them. Yet amidst the somber air, a thread of hope lingered, a promise that, together, they could rise from the ashes of loss and stand strong against the gathering storm.

King Leofric stood tall in the throne room, his regal presence tempered by the weariness of battle. His eyes, sharp yet kind, settled on Felix. "The Kingdom of Witsgar and its people are shattered in numbers from this invasion attempt," he said, his voice carrying the weight of loss, "but I will use all I can to aid you in your quest to crush Daegon once and for all." He paused, a flicker of awe crossing his face. "The battle you fought against him… it was almost beyond belief. You've shown courage and power few could dream of."

Felix bowed his head, feeling the king's words settle into his bones. "Thank you, Your Majesty. I did it all for my people and most of all, for the Creator."

Leofric's expression softened, a faint smile breaking through. "The Creator has truly blessed us all here. But you and your companions must be tired. The city is still repairing, still healing, yet I will offer everything I can to help you all find rest."

Arthur stepped forward, his green surcoat stained with the dust of war. "Thank you, Your Majesty," he said, his tone grateful but firm. "But I must leave at first light tomorrow. Oakridge is vulnerable without its army."

Leofric nodded, understanding in his gaze. "Of course. I wish you a safe journey home. Your men will receive all the medical attention they need until you depart."

Arthur bowed deeply. "Thank you, sire. I'll go speak to my men now." With a final nod, he turned and strode from the throne room, his figure disappearing through the arched doorway.

Leofric's attention shifted to Commander Lars, who stood with the quiet strength of the Holy Order. "The same offer extends to the Holy Order and all who aided us," the king said.

Lars inclined his head respectfully. "We are grateful, Your Majesty." He, too, departed, leaving Felix alone with the king.

Leofric's gaze returned to Felix, warm and resolute. "You, however, must stay here with us tonight. It is the Creator's will that all of Witsgar serve the Chosen Hero. I will have a healer tend to you and escort you to a room where you can sleep."

Felix's heart swelled with gratitude. "Thank you, Your Majesty. I gratefully accept."

Felix bowed his head in gratitude. "Thank you, Your Majesty."

To his surprise, the king bowed his head in return. "You are the Creator's chosen, Felix. It is we who should bow our heads to you in gratitude for your courage and sacrifice."

Felix felt a wave of humility wash over him at the king's words. He was just a carpenter's son from Eldenwold, and yet here he was, being honored by the king himself. It was almost too much to comprehend. "I… I am honored, Your Majesty," he managed to say, his voice thick with emotion.

The king smiled kindly. "Rest now, Felix. You have earned it."

A servant stepped forward and gestured for Felix to follow. They walked through the castle's stone corridors to a modest chamber. A fire flickered in the hearth, casting dancing shadows across the walls, and a narrow balcony overlooked Thegnfast, its lights twinkling like stars against the night.

Shortly after, the healer arrived, her hands skilled and swift as she bound Felix's wounds with care. When she finished, she gave him a nod and left quietly.

Felix stepped onto the balcony, the warm spring air brushing his face. He touched his chest to feel the Elemental Crystals, their soft glows pulsing in his hands. They felt alive, humming with power and purpose. He closed his eyes, letting his mind drift over the journey that had brought him here.

From a carpenter's son in Eldenwold to the Element Hero, he thought. The battles, the clash of steel, the roar of fire flashed through his memory. Allies like Arthur, Noah, Bryn, and the Holy Order had stood by him. Losses, villages burned, stung like fresh wounds. And then there was Rowan, taken by Daegon's forces, and Lara, waiting for him back in Pavelkaap. *I'll see you again, Rowan,* he vowed silently. *And I'll return to you, Lara.*

The crystals pulsed brighter, and Felix opened his eyes. The city below was scarred but unbroken, its people resilient. He had fought for them, for Pangea, and he would keep fighting. A sudden chill ran through him, not from the wind, but from within. A shadow flickered in his mind: a dark fortress, Daegon's voice whispering promises of ruin. Felix gripped the pendant around his neck tight. *He's still out there. And I'll be ready.*

He lifted his gaze to the sky, where stars glittered above the smoke and chaos. His mother's prayer echoed in his heart: *"Creator, renew my heart."* Peace settled over him, a quiet strength that drowned out the ache in his body. He wasn't alone the Creator, his friends, his purpose they were with him.

A knock sounded at the door, and Noah poked his head in, his grin as irrepressible as ever. "Not bad for a carpenter, huh? You've got kings bowing to you now."

Felix laughed, the sound easing the tension in his chest. "I couldn't have done it without you, Noah."

Noah shrugged, stepping inside. "Sure, you could've. But I'm glad I got a front-row seat. Tomorrow's another fight, Felix, but we'll face it together."

"Together," Felix echoed, meeting his friend's gaze.

Noah clapped him on the shoulder and slipped out, leaving Felix alone once more. He turned back to the balcony, watching as the first hints of dawn crept over the horizon. The light was faint but growing, a promise of new beginnings. Whatever Daegon had planned, whatever trials lay ahead, Felix would meet them with faith and fire. For now, though, he let himself rest, the Elemental Crystals warm on his chest, their glow a beacon in the fading night.

Call to Action

Thank you for reading my book! If you enjoyed it, please consider leaving a review. Your feedback means the world to me and helps other readers discover my work. Just a few words about your experience can make a big difference! Join My Reader Community for Exclusive Updates! Go to virgilawalkerbooks.com

About the Author

Virgil A. Walker is an Anglican lay theologian and self-taught scholar whose deep faith shapes his writing and life. Without formal training, Virgil has devoted himself to studying church history, theology, and preserving historical Christian texts through careful editing. His first published work, *How the Jesuits Influenced Dispensationalism*, reflects his passion for uncovering the threads of Christian thought that have shaped the church's story.

In addition to his scholarly pursuits, Virgil weaves Christian themes into the fantasy genre, seeking to share the hope and redemption of his faith through imaginative storytelling. His debut novel, *Pangea's Chosen: Rise of the Element Hero*, introduces a vibrant world where faith and elemental power intertwine, inviting readers to explore the triumph of God's light in a fantastical setting. This work marks the start of a series born from his desire to bring the truths of Christianity to a genre he loves.